RED RIVIERA

RED RIVIERA

A Daria Vinci Investigation

DAVID DOWNIE

Alan Squire Publishing
Bethesda, Maryland

Alan Squire Publishing

Red Riviera is published by Alan Squire Publishing, Bethesda, MD, an imprint of the Santa Fe Writers Project.

This is a work of fiction. Names, characters, businesses, places, events, locales, and incidents are either the products of the author's imagination or used in a fictitious manner. Any resemblance to actual persons, living or dead, or actual events is purely coincidental.

Printed in the United States of America.
ISBN (print): 978-1-942892-26-7
ISBN (epub): 978-1-942892-27-4
Library of Congress Control Number: 2020952002

Jacket design and cover art by Randy Stanard, Dewitt Designs, www.dewittdesigns.com.
Author photo by Alison Harris, www.alisonharris.com.
Copy editing and interior design by Nita Congress.
Printing consultant: Steven Waxman.
Printed by Carter Printing Company.

First Edition
Ordo Vagorum

Un'altra Parigi

The Irreverent Guide to Amsterdam

Enchanted Liguria

La Tour de l'Immonde (fiction)

Cooking the Roman Way

Paris City of Night (fiction)

Food Wine Rome

Food Wine Genoa & the Italian Riviera

Food Wine Burgundy

Quiet Corners of Rome

Paris, Paris: Journey into the City of Light

Paris to the Pyrenees

A Passion for Paris

A Taste of Paris

The Gardener of Eden (fiction)

Red Riviera is one of the most high-spirited, well-informed, and exuberantly written thrillers I've read in a long time. It's also funny as all get out. With his unsparing eye for detail, Downie takes the reader on an informative and unforgettable whirlwind tour of Genoa, its history, architecture, politics, manners, and mores. A gem. —Harriet Welty Rochefort, author of *French Toast* and *Joie de Vivre*

Red Riviera is so well plotted, so sensitive to present and past Italian history, so deep in characterization, that I want to see more of Daria Vinci. What a cast. A grand, unputdownable read until the lights go out. Marvelous! —Ronald C. Rosbottom, author of *When Paris Went Dark: The City of Light Under German Occupation*

To Jan, in absentia, and Bianca, with love.

"One does see so much evil in a village."

—Agatha Christie, *A Body in the Library*

ACKNOWLEDGMENTS

Warmest thanks to my agent Alice Martell and editors Rose Solari and James J. Patterson, who took a flyer as the world shrank; to retired carabiniere F., who wisely does not wish his identity to be revealed; and to Alison Harris, Jo Stobbs, and Angela Scipioni for their diamond-tipped eyes and helpful remarks.

One

Joseph Gary peered at the shiny surface of the speedboat, mesmerized by the mahogany varnish and the mirrored reflection of his trim, sun-bronzed torso. Gary's body gleamed the same oiled tone as the vintage wooden boat, a perfectly preserved Riva Aquarama, built in 1962. That was the year Gary had turned thirty-seven years old.

The percolating growl of the Riva's twin inboard diesels and the nutty smell of the exhaust filled Gary with pleasure. Grinning, then smiling, his perfectly preserved, bleached white teeth sparkled in the morning sunlight.

Certainly, Gary thought, deeply pleased, he must be the luckiest, happiest, most perfectly preserved ninety-two-year-old in God's creation.

Every wondrous, winterless, globally warmed day for the last two years, Gary had awakened to the spectacle of dawn on the Italian Riviera, that crescent of coast with Tuscany balanced on one end and the Côte d'Azur teetering on the other, in France.

Revving the boat's engines, Gary felt amazingly virile. Virginity and virtue had few rewards, he reminded himself.

Virility was better. The only slight regret he experienced now as he motored away from Rapallo's yacht club marina was that he'd waited so long to come back. Why had he?

Simple, Gary told himself, talking aloud as he passed the breakwater into the open sea. I could not return because not all of them were dead. Because people live so damn long on the Riviera, the paradise of centenarians and refuge of rascals. Besides, he had been too busy enjoying life elsewhere, in the Bahamas, Palm Beach, or Carmel, California, et cetera, et cetera, et cetera.

Joe Gary loved the sound of that last *et cetera*. Series of three were often divine, he reminded himself. That's what his mother and the priest had told him when he was a choirboy, a reluctant choirboy singing in a thatch-roofed chapel grafted onto a crumbling medieval church smelling of hay, rat piss, and horse manure. He was free of them now, free of the ghosts, free to do as he liked anywhere, even in the blasted, dead village where he'd been born, the place he and his family had fled over seventy years ago.

Tomorrow, he said to himself, tomorrow afternoon I will grab Morgana and the dogs, drive up in the Maserati, and hike in for a look. It will be a fast drive down memory lane to the end of the paved road. A roots celebration. Hell, I could buy back the whole fucking hillside. Put the sheep back to grazing. Dress Morgana up like a shepherdess.

The vision of his platinum bimbo Morgana Stella playing Marie Antoinette in the Ligurian outback gave Gary an erection. He clutched his parts, crossed himself, and laughed out loud. Throttling up, Gary watched the nose of the arrow-shaped hull. The Riva leaped, slapping down into the troughs before slicing upwards again. The rhythmic bucking, pounding, and splashing, and the sound of the growling then roaring engines, felt to him like sex, like penetration and dominance, ejaculation and climax. It overpowered the droning of the helicopters and water bombers spinning and circling overhead.

Glancing up, the man who called himself Joseph Gary cursed. The copters and planes had been out since sunrise, he muttered, a whole fleet of strange-looking aircraft, fighting the wildfires that seemed never to burn out or even die down. Why spend all that money dumping salt water and good flame-killing chemicals on useless, barren hills? Let them burn, let everything burn, then start again, that was his motto.

The sea breeze caressed his nut-brown, sweat-dampened forehead and crewcut scalp. It bristled with stiff, dyed orange-yellow hair. He couldn't wait to get into the water. Accelerating, Gary remembered how, when a boy cooped up in that stinking boulder-built village in the hills, he had rarely had the opportunity to swim, and never in spring. The locals didn't know how to swim. They were too busy working the land. Back then even the visiting pale-skinned vacationers only swam in June, July, and August. It was unheard of, unprecedented, to take a dip in April, and he loved that, too.

Bring on the greenhouse effect, assholes, he chuckled, then shouted, raising an open hand in the salute of his youth. Bring on global warming, the fires, and the end of time and fuck you all very much, hippies, lefties, commies, and queers!

Checking his waterproof Rolex, Gary crinkled his thin lips, squinting and peering through wraparound sunglasses reprising the boat's Dolce Vita windshield. If the Rolex says it's 9:53 a.m., then 9:53 a.m. it must be, he congratulated himself.

As always, Gary was on time, perfectly on time. Punctuality was his sole virtue, he cackled, a virtue to the point of being a vice. That made it okay.

Slowing then gliding then drifting silently to a standstill, with expert ease he reached out with a gaffer hook and snagged the buoy. It floated one-quarter mile off the rocky point marking the western edge of his second-favorite seaside resort, Santa Margherita, a point precisely one nautical mile from the horseshoe-shaped bay of Portofino—Billionaire's Bay, he called it, the most magical spot on earth.

Effortlessly tying up, forming the knots he had learned in the U.S. Navy, Gary glanced at the rocky shoreline and the towering

Castello di Paraggi, hoping his great friend, the former prime minister of Italy and fellow plutocrat, was in residence, down for the long holiday weekend. But the windows of Silvio Berlusconi's faux castle were shuttered and the police escort absent.

Gary thought gleefully about the divine conjunction of wealth and political power, glancing from the castle to the mirrored reflection of his golden trinity, the gold Rolex, the gold chain around his neck with the glinting Saint Christopher medal, and the thick gold U.S. Navy signet ring on his gnarled finger. He was particularly proud of the ring. The trinity never left his wrist, neck, and finger, in that order. Never.

Plucking off his sunglasses and leaving them on the dashboard, Gary slid out of his handmade leather boat shoes, lifted and carried a pair of yellow-and-black rubber flippers to the stern of the boat, slipped them on, and lowered himself lovingly into the delicious, clear, cool water.

Lying on his back and kicking gently, watching the helicopters and wide-winged, red-and-yellow Canadair water bombers circling and dipping then diving and scooping up silvery mouthfuls of water, Joseph Gary rotated his head right then left, east to west, scanning and counting the fires on the amphitheater of Apennine hills. Though his ears were partly submerged, he could still hear the droning of the aircraft. Closing his eyes and feeling the sunshine, he imagined giant bumblebees, mud wasps, and dragonflies, and he smiled beatifically.

As he flipped onto his stomach and swam farther out, Joseph Gary's last glimpse of the bright, cloudless blue sky was darkened by a swift, sudden shadow. The open jaws of an amphibious water bomber skimmed toward him, barely touching the wave-rumpled surface as it filled its bay. Opening wider, the jaws swallowed the lone swimmer legs intact and one arm flailing, a single rawboned fist banging uselessly against the outside of the stainless-steel fuselage.

Heaving and thrusting, its belly filled, the seaplane broke free. It flew east by southeast over the harbor at Chiavari, then climbed steeply south toward a pinpoint of flames burning red and cobalt blue on a ridge one in from the sea. Tilting its wings, the plane passed over the umbrella-spangled beaches and the swarming hiking trails of the Cinque Terre, a thousand necks craning to look up and a thousand fingers tapping screens.

Slowing and dipping low over the blaze, the plane's jaws popped open again, dumping seawater and chemical flame retardant into the air. The red rain squirmed with sparkling anchovies, a crumpled, one-armed body, and what looked like a pair of mangled rubber swim fins. The plane's engines thundered. The fire spluttered. Then all was silent, save for the fiddling, slivered song of the cicadas.

Two

"**P**inky?"

Willem Bremach called over his shoulder, swiveling in his wheelchair and swiping with a handkerchief at his glistening brow. "Pinky, be a dear and bring me the other set of Kraut binoculars. You know, the ones in the leather case, in my study, on the shelf, by the propeller." Bremach paused until he was sure Priscilla had heard him. Sometimes she pretended not to. "Oh, and Pinky darling, my morning *elixir*, please." He spoke histrionically, as if adding an afterthought, his strong, reassuring baritone voice wavering piteously for effect.

Checking the aviator's watch strapped to his left wrist, Willem Bremach was surprised to see the hour, minute, and second hands converging on ten o'clock. The heat was appalling for April. The summer sound of cicadas, helicopters, and water bombers vibrated from all sides. "Not a puff of air," he said to himself philosophically, "nor a drop of liquor to slake my thirst."

Hearing Priscilla rummaging under the Spitfire propeller in his studio, Bremach swiveled the wheelchair around, studying the 180-degree view from the villa's wide verandah. He loved that

7

view. The ancient olive trees and blackish-green flame cypresses planted by his grandfather on the terraces below would need pruning soon, he muttered to himself. Otherwise their branches and floppy tips would become a visual impediment.

Lifting the heavy high-tech Zeiss binoculars to his eyes again, he repeated the words "visual impediment" and reprimanded himself for thinking in Italian and translating in his head into stilted English. Neither Italian nor English was his native language, though he had heard and spoken and read both earlier than he had Dutch. He had also used them more frequently than Dutch, except when carrying out his official duties as consul, ambassador, or military attaché in the Netherlands embassies and consulates around the globe, duties that had occupied forty precious years of his life. They had been happy years, he thought with a sigh, but, in retrospect, the best years of all were the ones when he'd strapped himself into a cockpit, with four-hundred horsepower and several machine guns at his fingertips.

"Here you are, Signor Ambassador," Priscilla said briskly, coming up from behind her husband's broad shoulders. She dangled the old leather case in front of him like bait on a hook and appeared to enjoy teasing him. Fully fleshed, suspiciously blonde, and disconcertingly energetic, Priscilla Bremach née Christiansen also appeared indecently younger than Willem, more the age of a daughter or niece than a wife. "What do we say?" she asked, raising a plucked eyebrow into an accent mark.

"Thank you, dear Pinky," Willem intoned, grinning while swapping the binoculars, then raising the smaller, older set to his bulbous, pale blue eyes. They had a mischievous, satisfied, pearly gleam. "Have you taken a look?"

Priscilla sighed. "I don't need binoculars to see the fires and the water bombers and the motor yachts," she said in her pleasant, lilting accented Nordic English. "It's supposed to be springtime and they've been out there every day for a month," she added. "Is there anything left to burn, Willem? Will it ever rain again? In my day, only barbarians swam in the Mediterranean in April. Now even the Italians have caught the disease. Look at all those boats and air mattresses."

Bremach smiled toothily. "Tut-tut, Pinky," he said. "In *my* day long before *your* day we did not complain about the weather. This isn't the first hot spring on the Riviera, either, you know. But what I mean is, have you ever seen so *many* Canadair seaplanes operating *simultaneously*?" His excitement was boyish. "Count them. There are one, two, three, four, five, six." He paused. "And my whisky?"

"It's too early, Willem," Priscilla retorted with mock alarm, "please behave. Do you want to make me a widow so soon?" Something like genuine anticipatory grief transformed her handsome face.

"Soon?" Bremach laughed, wanting to float their conversation back to the sunny surface. "But Pinky, we've been married forty-six years. I should think you'd had quite enough of me by now."

"It's strange you remember the number," she quipped, piqued by his offhand tone, "since you forgot the date last week."

Willem Bremach reddened, making a sucking, clucking sound. He wiped his brow again with a large, starched, monogrammed linen handkerchief and swallowed guiltily. "Surely that's your fault, Pinky," he said, buying time, trying to think his way out of his callousness. "How can you expect my mind to function properly if you deprive me of my elixir?" Before she could object, he went on. "Now look here, you will forgive me, won't you? What was it, my darling Pinky, April 10th?"

"You know that to be the correct date of our anniversary," she said, her Norwegian intonation more pronounced than before, her shoulders lifting unawares toward the tiny glinting diamonds in each earlobe.

"The day I twisted my knee playing tennis?" Willem stammered, his arm reaching out to volley an imaginary ball. "The day your niece and nephew showed up from Trondheim or Bremen or wherever they live? How could I possibly remember something like a wedding anniversary after such a ghastly accident and an invasion by obnoxious adolescent relations?" He reached up from the wheelchair and took her hands, studying the liver spots she refused to erase with surgery or disguise with makeup. "Now, do forgive me, Pinky. If it had been forty-four or forty-five years I would have remembered," he pleaded, histrionic again. "How could I forget the summer of 1944 or the spring of '45?"

She glared at him, then relented. "I don't know, Willem, I wasn't born yet."

"Indeed, you weren't, young Pinky," he said. "As soon as I'm out of this torture contraption I'll take us to a bang-up meal."

"What about Paris? April in Paris? Singing in the rain? It must be raining and cool somewhere," she said. "I'll check the weather report."

"Yes, of course, Pinky," he muttered. "Paris..."

But Willem Bremach was no longer listening. Following the trajectory of the swooping water bombers he counted them again, taking notes in a notebook, then he spoke out loud. "It's like a ballet, or a cat's cradle. Incredible! Some of those planes are very close to shore this morning. It's an aerial circus. Just look at how they glide and dip and scoop up the water and pull up and turn and climb and climb and disappear into the interior and then—splash, a beautiful red cloud of water and spray and vapor extinguishes the flames. It really is too marvelous. Extraordinary. I could watch them all day."

"You do watch them all day," she remarked. "That will teach you for playing singles again at your age."

"My age? What do you mean, 'my age'?" Willem lowered the binoculars, his cheeks burning as if he had been slapped. "At ninety-three my mother was still exploring the Hindu Kush," he said. "She carried her own, and I see I will have to do likewise." He released the locks on the wheels of the chair and made a motion toward the wet bar in the living room, but Priscilla sighed and relented.

"Extraordinary circumstances require extraordinary rations," she said, as if reciting.

"Exactly," Willem agreed. "Mother lived to be 102," he added with pluck, "and she always had a shot or three in the morning."

"You know very well your mother was 101 when she died." Priscilla spoke crisply, stepping back onto the verandah carrying a glass.

"Not the way the Italians count," Willem quipped, accepting the whisky gratefully, blinking at her, then using the index finger of his right hand to stir the drink and ice cubes. He licked the finger and raised his eyebrows. Taking a long, slow, luxurious drink, Willem Bremach ran his tongue around his thick-lipped mouth, blinked again, and said, "I want to fly one of those buggies before I die, Pinky, and I will fly one, you'll see."

Feeling his gaze upon her, Priscilla rolled her eyes. They were ice blue. "How can you? They are not Sopwith Camels."

"I flew Spitfires, Pinky, will you never get them straight? Camels were biplanes. Lovely to fly, like kites, but they were before my day. The Sopwith was my father's plane. In the Great War."

Tossing her head, Priscilla poured herself a glass of sparkling water from an ice bucket then sat on the bench next to Willem's wheelchair, wondering if he would ever recover and be his boyish self again. "Your mother lived to be 101 before the advent of modern medicine, which means," she calculated, squeezing shut her mascaraed eyes, "you have another decade to go."

"Oh Pinky," he said, taking her hands and kissing first the right, then the left one. "How can you be so stingy? Mother had a weak constitution by Bremach standards. Nowadays she would live to be 120. That gives me a quarter century."

"Only if you behave," she said.

"I shall behave," he teased, gulping his drink, "and no one will stop me. Or is it, 'I *will* behave and no one *shall* stop me'?"

"It's too early for your language games," she pleaded, "and too damn hot."

Accustomed to her bluff manner after forty-six years of matrimony, Willem checked his watch again and raised his binoculars. "Now Pinky, here's something very interesting," he said, pointing.

"It's really very unusual. Take a look. Follow the rocks and break-water due west from Santa Margherita and look about three centimeters above that, a hair over an inch, if you prefer, and you'll see the boat."

"I don't use inches or hairs," she said, "you do."

"Prewar English public schooling," he retorted, "not my fault. Now, let us make peace and get on with it. Do you see the boat?"

"Yes," she said, relenting. "It's Joe Gary's boat. That silly toy of his that makes noise and stinks. It's there every morning from ten to noon, as you have told me many, many times for the past two years. Are you going senile, Willem Bremach?"

"But Pinky, don't you see?" Willem protested. "The boat is empty."

Priscilla scoffed. She raised the Zeiss binoculars again, focusing them on Joe Gary's shiny Riva Aquarama. She scanned back and forth along the horizon line. "That's because Joe is swimming," she said. "That's what he does. He swims from the boat into the open sea, back and forth, a quarter mile each way, the same way you bat the tennis balls back and forth with your friends at the club in Genoa, and you're never bored, until you twist your knee and wind up in a wheelchair. You and Joe are the same age and will never grow up."

"But Pinky, that's the point," Willem insisted, finishing his drink and lifting the binoculars again. "Joe is *not* swimming. He is *no longer* swimming and he is not in his boat. I saw him go out. He lowered himself in at precisely 10:00 a.m. the way he always does, and as we talked and you played your usual game of making me beg for my drink, he swam, and then you said something unpleas-ant to me about my age, so I turned my head, and when I turned it back he had disappeared."

"I suppose that too is my fault?" Priscilla frowned and began scanning the surface of the sea, sweeping with the binoculars as the helicopters and water bombers circled and dipped, and the plumes of smoke from the wildfires on the steep hills hemming the Ligurian coast rose thicker and higher into the sky, the day growing hotter by the minute. "He must be there, Willem," she said, her voice betraying doubt for the first time.

"Yes," Bremach muttered. "He must. But he isn't." He lowered the binoculars. "Be a dear and pass me the telephone, will you?"

Priscilla retrieved the cordless phone from the living room. "Who are you going to call?"

"La Davinci," he said. "Who else?"

"Why call Daria?" Priscilla objected. "Call the emergency number—112. He may be drowning as we speak."

"Too late for that," he said, a note of wicked glee stealing into his voice. He held up a finger to silence her. "Pronto? Is that Inspector Morbido?"

"Who is it?" snarled a rich male basso. "How did you get this number?"

"Bremach here."

"Oh, *ambasciatore*," Inspector Morbido exclaimed, "my apologies, *eccellenza*, I did not recognize your voice."

"Because you have not heard it in many months, my dear Morbido. But rest assured, I am not dead yet."

"Of course not, ambasciatore, you are clearly very much alive."

"Might I speak to the Americana, otherwise referred to as La Davinci?"

Morbido hesitated, covered the handset, then came back on, saying, "Commissioner Vinci is very busy, eccellenza, she asks if she might call you back later?"

"We are all busy, Lieutenant Morbido, be kind enough to tell La Davinci that this is not merely important, it is *importantissimo*, otherwise I would not be disturbing her or you."

"Sì, eccellenza, I understand. One moment, please..."

Ambassador Bremach waited, fingering the binoculars and listening to what sounded like a muffled wrestling match. Then he heard Daria Vinci breathlessly snatching the phone from Inspector Morbido's hands.

"Pronto?"

"Daria?" he asked with brio, "how are you?"

"Wrong question," said a distant, tense female voice. "What is it, Willem? Is Priscilla all right?"

"Oh, she's fine. It's you I'm worried about." He paused and counted inwardly to three. "You're about to become extremely busy, and given Italian police protocols, you will want to get over here soonest," he added, "*subito*. Finders first."

"Impossible," she snapped, choking on something. "If you only knew."

"Come visit your dear old godfather, who misses you terribly," he said, "and has something extraordinarily important to share with you, which he cannot divulge over the telephone."

"You know it's a secure line, Willem, it's encrypted, even the Carabinieri can't hear us."

"Not on my end," Bremach said dryly. "What I have to *show* you, not only *tell* you, is very time sensitive," he added. Waiting, Bremach could feel her exasperation. She was carrying on another conversation, either in person or on another line or both. "I'm sorry to add to your plate," he said, "as your American colleagues say these days. But you really must find a way. Now."

"Hold on," she ordered. Bremach could hear Commissioner Daria Vinci of the Divisione Investigazioni Generali e Operazioni Speciali covering the phone again and shouting across the DIGOS headquarters, a stony neo-Renaissance pile westward twenty miles across the gulf in downtown Genoa. "This is the worst time ever, Willem," she said, coming back on. "We have nine new fires this morning, all apparently set by arsonists, and three dead bodies, or maybe it would be more accurate to say three plastic garbage bags with parts of human bodies in them—that's off the record, of course, and no sharing. I have been out since dawn and am going back out again now and can't take the long weekend in Rome as planned to see my mother."

"Then that's perfect," he said brightly. "Drive here on the way to wherever you're going. You will thank me, Da," he added in an undertone. "Now listen carefully. Since you claim this is a secure line, I strongly suggest you have Morbido or your young Lieutenant Gambero pull everything you've got on a certain Signor Joseph Gary. That's Gary with a 'y,' alias Gary Baldi with an "i," also known as Joe Gary Baldi. No, I am not making this up. He is or was a Canadian and American dual national of Italian descent, resident for the last two years of San Michele di Pagana, municipality of Rapallo, owner of the famous Villa Glicine. Read the material in the car, Daria, on the way over. See you shortly. Pinky will make us lunch."

Bremach hung up before Daria Vinci could object. Dialing again and speaking this time in fluent Italian, Willem Bremach asked to speak to Colonel Rossi, spoke briefly and quietly to him, then hung up, and set the phone on the bench by Priscilla's thigh. "Well, well, well," he intoned, giving the thigh a gentle pinch. "Joe Gary has gone glug-glug, either that or he's taken a very high dive. What shall we give Daria for lunch, my dear? Do you think she's become vegetarian, like everyone else these days?" He paused to eye his wife, unable to suppress a wolfish grin. "And for goodness' sake," he added in a jocular tone, "tell your perpetually famished niece and nephew to take a hike. They are not invited."

Three

Commissioner Daria M. Vinci of the Genoa Investigative Division of DIGOS, an elite unit of Italy's State Police, had never been squeamish. Her premed studies, done in part at the University of Padua and later, unhappily, at Yale, at her father's insistence, had prepared her for a clinical view of the human body. Daria had analyzed, dissected, and reassembled men and women whole or in parts, including specimens in states of advanced decomposition.

Medical school had not worked out. But twenty-three years of climbing the slippery ladder at DIGOS had bolstered her innate sangfroid.

So, she was all the more surprised that the sight—and above all the smell—of this particular rotting, butchered cadaver seemed unbearably gruesome.

A blackened, festering, bloody torso and severed head, plus other body parts, some shriveled and unrecognizable, spilled from a torn heavy-duty leaf bag onto a muddy, littered patch of ground. It flanked a partially paved turnout on the two-lane highway east of Rapallo. Daria was beginning to wonder how she could get through lunch with her godfather and Pinky after this. Three bags, each containing dismembered cadavers, each found in a strategic location, in a single morning, was too much, even for her. Steeling herself, she took a deep, calming breath through her nostrils and successfully fought off the nausea.

Flies swarmed. Dogs bayed from a scabrous farmhouse beyond the pitted highway. The perimeter of the site had been cordoned off. Florescent yellow-and-red tape and red ribbons fluttered festively each time a car passed. The narrow, twisting rural road had been choked down to a single lane. A squad of heavily armed Carabinieri, usually posted five miles away on the Via Aurelia coast highway, had been summoned. They brandished submachine guns. They were not alone.

Visibly out of their depth, a carful of nervous traffic cops from Rapallo's *polizia municipale* had been drafted to help. They chased away rubberneckers and waved vehicles past using batons. Two of the Carabinieri randomly stopped every fifth or sixth car, signaling it onto the turnout. With their submachine guns swinging menacingly, they checked documents, passenger compartments, and trunks. Daria watched them impassively. Nothing unusual had been found. The morning was almost over.

Sheltering in the shade of a dry, scruffy olive grove, a three-man ambulance crew waited for the police photographer and pathologist to do the wrap-up. Only then would the Carabinieri give the medicos the green light to remove the leaf bag.

Daria heard the driver of the ambulance whistle and mutter as he moved farther upwind to light a cigarette. She lingered at the edge of the paved road and glanced from the scarred, stinking patch of mud to the luxurious, armor-plated four-door Alfa Romeo that had conveyed her to the site. She had been assigned the car that day at dawn, shortly before six. Up to now, the vehicle had been reserved for her immediate superior, the Vice Questor of the Provence of Genoa. Daria thought of the ironies of fate and wondered what other surprises the day held for her.

Seeming to fill every inch of the car's cool interior with his large, doughy body, Inspector Osvaldo Morbido spoke animatedly on his smartphone. With the stubby fingers of his meaty right hand he drummed or poked the steering wheel, the air conditioning on full blast and the windows down.

Respecting the draconian Italian police protocol giving priority to finders, the traffic cops said nothing to Daria, letting the paramilitary Carabinieri in their upswept hats and operetta uniforms take the lead. They had arrived first. The investigation was theirs. All of the Carabinieri were young, swarthy males. All wore an expression of smug superiority. Perhaps out of an inbred sense of gallantry, three of the Carabinieri fell back, saluting Daria and bowing slightly, softly speaking or mouthing her title.

Commissioner Daria M. Vinci was not only strikingly handsome in an angular, Picasso style, she also happened to be the only female mover and shaker in the local police hierarchy. As the number three official at the provincial DIGOS headquarters, she held the rank of captain. Everyone knew Daria was slated for promotion to major or lieutenant colonel. The grapevine also prognosticated she would be named Vice Questor before the year was out.

According to the arcane Italian pecking order, Daria in theory already outranked many police, Carabinieri, armed forces, and Ministry of the Interior officials in the district. Vice Questor Ruggieri, her boss, a colonel, was soon to become a lieutenant general, moving up to the post of Questor, once the current, problematic occupant of that coveted position retired. This prominence made it unusual for Daria's lean, athletic figure, or that of any other elite DIGOS operative for that matter, to be seen on a sordid crime scene such as this.

That was why the Carabinieri watched her warily and seemed to be wondering what the murder of a homeless man or group of men could have to do with terrorism, subversion, human trafficking, or politically motivated gang violence, the normal purview of DIGOS.

Stepping forward, Daria shook the outstretched, calloused hand of the senior marshal of the Carabinieri, a grizzled, mustachioed veteran she recognized as Luigi "Gigi" De Filippo. Gigi was a lifer nearing the end of the operational line, bound for a desk job in Naples or Palermo, she couldn't remember which. A lusty Southerner, not from the Riviera, his thick accent had helped create De Filippo's tough-guy persona.

But Daria knew he had a malleable, hedonistic heart and was more dangerous these days with a fork than a gun. His prodigious, nine-month belly could not hide behind the black-ribbed bulletproof vest he wore. The body armor made him and the three identically equipped Carabinieri look like armadillos in carnival costumes with red piping on the seams.

"Pretty business," De Filippo said in a surprisingly fluty voice, stroking his salt-and-pepper push-broom mustache, then pointing to the muddy ground. "Wild boar prints. Those are from a dog. I hate to think…"

It appeared, said De Filippo, that the boars and a dog or dogs had torn open the bag and scattered its rotting contents. "The coroner says there are teeth marks on the head," De Filippo added with relish. "We're not sure if they're boar or dog teeth yet. Someone pulled over this morning at 8:05 a.m. to relieve himself. He called the standard emergency number. The Rapallo station responded. They pulled us off the Aurelia. The couple living in that house came over and tentatively identified the head."

"And?" Daria asked, brushing her dark hair out of her eyes. She wondered if her expression betrayed her distaste for De Filippo.

"They say he was a bum who slept under the autostrada trestle at the bottom of the valley. They say they gave him food sometimes."

"You'll take them in for questioning?"

"Of course, signora commissario. In Rapallo. But if you would like to speak to them in Genoa that can be arranged." He spoke unctuously, pausing for effect. "We are always glad to share with DIGOS."

Daria forced a smile and thrust out her jaw, aware De Filippo's eyes were watching her with more than professional interest. "I'll let you know," she said, her words clipped.

"Any special requests?"

"If it were my case," she said, her body language betraying distrust, "I would make sure to find the dogs and boars if they can be found." She spoke in what she hoped would pass as a conciliatory tone. "I'd check everything in the garbage bag. Find out where it came from, when and where the contents originated, so forth, and if the deceased did or dealt drugs."

"Clearly," he said, "that will be done."

Pausing to avoid any hint of arrogance, she pointed to the farther edge of the turnout. "Where does that lead?"

De Filippo peered at what looked like an overgrown hiking trailhead, half hidden by weeds and mounds of litter. He glanced meaningfully at the nearest municipal policeman, a sergeant guarding the perimeter, and waved him over. "Gianni, where does that go?"

The officer, Gianni Giannini, saluted, stepping up. "To the bunker, sir," he said crisply. The sweat stood out on his forehead and trickled into his eyes. They were a soft, baby blue. Daria blinked. Gianni was thirty-five or forty, she guessed, and too good-looking and well-spoken to have wound up a traffic cop. She had seen him before, on his beat, in Rapallo. They had spoken once or twice. She wondered what misstep Gianni Giannini had made, probably when a teenager, to wind up where he had.

"Which bunker?" De Filippo snapped.

"The bunker left over from the war, sir, I don't know what the official name is. This one is small, an anti-aircraft machine gun nest. There are others higher up on that ridge." Gianni pointed at a thick plume of smoke rising from what looked like a reinforced concrete fortress half a mile away, perched above a bluff and apparently inaccessible from below.

Daria raised a carefully plucked eyebrow and spoke to De Filippo in a conspiratorial undertone. "Has anyone been up there yet?"

"What for?"

"To see if it's squatted by bums," she said, sketching in the air with one elegant, long-fingered hand. "To see if the bag was dragged from there after the victim was cut into parts. To do a thorough job," she added, "as you have such a fine reputation for doing, Gigi."

Her irony was not lost on De Filippo. He jerked his head and grimaced, his moustache pulling away from a set of large, yellow teeth. Two of the other three Carabinieri strolled over. De Filippo asked them in an offhand way to check where the path went and look around the machine gun nest, if in fact there was such a thing up there, as Sergeant Giannini claimed. "Take Giannini with you," De Filippo added, smirking. "He's a great mountaineer. See if he can get up to that big bunker on the ridge where the fire is burning."

The Carabinieri swaggered off, followed reluctantly by Sergeant Giannini. He turned to smile at Daria before saluting the marshal of the Carabinieri. As if on stage, De Filippo stepped back a pace, allowing the commissioner to walk abreast of him along the edge of the asphalt to the spot where the pathologist and photographer waited. She recognized both. Bozzo and Brignole. They were known at DIGOS as Oliver and Hardy. Emilio Bozzo, the pathologist, based in Genoa at the main mortuary, was wiry and tall. Pino Brignole was short and stocky and could have been Osvaldo Morbido's brother. Both looked tired, hot, badly shaven, and pale. The stench here, closer to the ruptured bag, was revolting.

"Off the record," Bozzo said to Daria, "my guess is the subject has been dead at least a week." He shook Daria's hand. It was firm and dry. His was limp and damp. "I'd also guess he was dead long before anyone cut him up," Bozzo added, pausing to gauge the effect of his words. "But I may be wrong. I may also find that one of the sectioned limbs comes from another body, and the head too, so you may have two or three victims or more."

Daria winced and glanced away. "Junk? Dope? Gunshot wounds? Torture? Human trafficking?"

Bozzo shook his head. "I don't know, I can't tell yet without opening the bag to the bottom and pulling out all the pieces. He's pretty far gone, if he's a he and not a she, and if the two or three main parts are even from the same corpse. It's pretty bad. Like botched autopsies tossed together in a salad."

Daria winced again at the image and tapped a finger on her fleshy lips, wondering how much to reveal to Bozzo and how to get him on her side. "At first glance," she said conspiratorially, "what I see reminds me of the dissection lab at Yale. In Padua they could never get enough corpses. The Church..." Her voice trailed off as she waited for a signal from him. Was he a fervent Catholic or on the political right? She did not think so. But these days, you never knew how anyone might react to criticism of the Church.

Bozzo nodded grimly. "Same thing in Genoa," he whispered. "No bodies available. Only the unclaimed vagrants go to science. Luckily things have changed now. You no longer have to go abroad to learn dissection. And there are always the monkeys. Lots of monkeys."

"Well, you see, progress does exist," she remarked, relieved to confirm Bozzo had no reactionary bias. "Unless you object to animal-based dissection," she added.

"Some of us seem more like great apes than humans," Bozzo remarked sardonically. "Except the apes are not nearly as vicious and destructive."

"Call me?"

"Sure," he said, extending his limp, damp hand again.

"And send me the high-resolution images?" she continued, turning to the silent, reluctant Pino Brignole. It wasn't a question.

The photographer glanced at the Carabinieri, waited for De Filippo's acquiescing shrug, then nodded his agreement. Bozzo and Brignole began to shuffle toward their unmarked stripper, a dented white Fiat compact at least five years old.

Her mind trotting ahead of them, Daria had an inspiration. Leaving De Filippo behind and out of earshot, she walked alongside Emilio Bozzo and spoke in a casual undertone, opening the car door for him. "Isn't it unusual for you to be out here, at a crime scene?"

Bozzo looked blearily into her large hazel-green eyes. "As unusual as it is for you to be out here."

"There is no such thing as usual or unusual anymore," she remarked. "It's like the climate."

"Exactly. So, you heard about the others?" Bozzo paused, waiting for her nod. It came. He began talking again. "Same M. O. each time. When you get three bags of mixed rotting meat on one morning," he mused, his voice wavering now with genuine emotion, "and the morning happens to be April 23rd, the anniversary of the start of the Insurrection of Genoa in 1945, and the bags are in commemorative sites from our glorious Fascist past or near a Nazi bunker like this one, well, if you're like me, you get into your car and you drive out in the stinking heat to take a look at the mess and you're not surprised to see Commissario Daria Vinci show up sooner or later and start asking questions." Bozzo sighed, but Daria remained silent. "Have you been to the other sites already?" he inquired.

Daria batted her eyes with a nodding affirmative. "I got the call for the first one at 5:00 a.m.," she said. "The one in Nervi, where they're doing the sewer repairs in the piazza in front of the commemorative plaque. The other call came in afterwards, for the bag at Villa Migone. This is the last."

"For now," Emilio Bozzo said, interrupting. "And this was supposed to be a long weekend?" He glanced around suspiciously, beckoning her to lean closer. "Everything is closed," he whispered, "schools, universities, administrative offices, small businesses, clinics, even the cemetery and crematorium and morgue are theoretically closed, but we, we have to work in this stinking heat." Bozzo appeared to have exhausted himself. She felt sorry for him.

"They knew I was booked onto the 6:10 a.m. express train to Rome," Daria whispered back, trying to sound empathetic. "My mother was expecting to see me. I never have time for her and she's nearly ninety. My brothers," she paused and sighed, splaying her hands, the thought of her siblings filling her with frustration. "They do nothing. The Vice Questor was smarter than we are," she added, forcing herself to lighten up. Daria laughed quietly. "He already left on vacation last night. He must be on a beach in Morocco by now, laughing and living it up. We're down to a skeleton crew."

"Bad comparison," Emilio Bozzo said, smiling at the unintentional pun despite himself. "If it's any consolation," he continued, "it must be even hotter and drier down in Morocco. Ruggieri goes south while all of Africa is leaving, heading our way. God bless them." He straightened himself. "I'm not sure how we missed each other earlier," he added, mopping his brow and trying to sound upbeat. "At the other crime scenes, I mean." He looked dejected again. "What's the point?" he wondered out loud. "The war ended over seventy-five years ago. Can't we let go of the past?"

Daria shut the car door. The white Fiat pulled out and drove slowly downhill toward the coast with Brignole, the photographer, at the wheel, a swirling police light suction-cupped to the roof.

Glancing around the turnout, taking in the scene again as she made her way back to the glinting gray Alfa Romeo, Daria stopped and stared at the mud and wrinkled her prominent, sculpted nose before burying it in a handkerchief and blowing louder than anyone, including the Carabinieri, expected. They started and turned. "Gigi," she said, "any idea why there's all this mud in a drought? It hasn't rained in months."

Marshal De Filippo stepped up from where he had been lurking behind her. "There's a spring back there," he pointed. "By the path to the bunker. It feeds the creek in the bottom of the valley. The farmers say it never runs dry. I'll bet that's why the Germans built the bunker here."

Daria pretended to agree. "Yes, you're certainly right. Or maybe the choice of the site had something to do with the need to fire anti-aircraft guns at RAF and USAF bombers coming down the valley, trying to blow up the railroad viaducts at Recco and Rapallo and crush the Nazi-Fascist regime so that we might live in democratic freedom?" She watched his uncomprehending face darken as the irony penetrated and spread. She let it go. "Any usable tire tracks, footprints, or signs of dragging?"

De Filippo shrugged as only a southern Italian can, a legacy of tragedy, fatigue, fatalism, and pointlessness distilled into the simplest of human gestures. "Commissario, without wishing to be indelicate," he said, his syllables and double consonants tripping and melting into each other, "I must tell you this spot is used day and night by men who need to ease and relieve themselves urgently, and young couples equally in need of satisfying their passions. There are dozens, hundreds, of footprints and tire tracks here. Some are more or less fresh. We will make a few casts and we have the photographs. But..." He left the thought dangling.

"Those look like delivery truck tire marks, for instance, don't they?" Daria motioned.

"Could be."

Either he knew something she did not or was playing the usual Carabinieri-versus–Polizia di Stato game, Daria realized. "Do you think you might take casts of them?"

"Certainly," he said. "Anything to please il commissario."

Daria strained to remain polite. "Any sign anyone tried to cover their movements?"

"Yes," he said. "Naturally. There's nothing around the bag other than the boar and dog tracks. Whoever it was, he knew what he was doing."

"Very good," Daria said, certain now De Filippo knew nothing of the other bodies and bags found that morning, or was purposely misleading her. She prepared herself for the sham of the share request. It always felt like begging. "I would be most appreciative if you could email me your report as soon as it is convenient, and keep me up to date." She watched De Filippo eye her again. They bowed slightly to each other. "One last thing," Daria said, swiveling. "Was he a black man, by chance?"

De Filippo sucked his large, yellow teeth and let the weight of his arms fall on the submachine gun slung around his neck. "The skin is blackened by decomposition, as you can see, but we think he was North African. He had a cappuccino complexion once upon a time, not a black African skin color. We think this corpse belonged to an illegal immigrant, possibly Moroccan or Algerian or Tunisian."

"Or Libyan?"

"Or Libyan," De Filippo acknowledged. "But not Egyptian, it's not the right racial type."

"So, you knew him?"

"If it's the man the people in the farmhouse think it is. Everyone around here has a pet African they feed." He paused to chuckle. "We took him in more than once last winter."

"But you let him go?"

De Filippo shrugged again, then turned and signaled to the ambulance crew. Sweating and cursing from under their protective plastic overalls and face masks, they began lifting the body parts and removing the bag, using a stretcher so as not to further tear the plastic. Daria saluted. Her parting words to Luigi De Filippo were inaudible. She had lost her voice.

Four

Sliding into the cool interior of the specially equipped Alfa Romeo Giulia sports sedan, Daria Vinci surreptitiously glanced at herself in the wing mirror. With deft treatment each morning, her taut, angular features, high cheekbones, and what some called a patrician nose, made her appear younger than her forty-nine years—and less mannish. Not that anyone seemed to notice or take interest except predators like Gigi De Filippo. Am I destined to be an old maid, she wondered? The term itself seemed impossibly old, obsolete, and out of date.

Popping a mint in her wide, sensuous mouth, Daria bit it and took a melancholy breath, cleared her throat, then leaned forward from the back seat and into the real world. "Okay, Osvaldo," she said as evenly as she could, "let's go. I'm sorry to be sitting back here like a capo but I need to study this file." Daria exhaled, filling the passenger compartment with the scent of mint candy. Then she leaned back again, realizing just how hot and tired she felt. "Why does this guy's name ring a bell?" she asked Lieutenant Morbido absentmindedly, waving the file like a fan. "Joseph Gary? Joseph Gary Baldi?"

Osvaldo Morbido grunted. "Bannon, the elections in March, 2018, Signor Gary met the Stephen Bannon entourage and entertained them and exponents of several extreme right-wing political groups at his villa near Santa Margherita. It was in all the papers."

"That's it," she said. "How could I have forgotten?"

"Because it was over in a flash, like lightning striking a cemetery, and it was the Questor himself who attended the meeting, not you." Morbido glanced meaningfully at her in the mirror. "Speaking of the Questor," Morbido continued, "HQ has confirmed it was the same delivery van that dropped the first two bags of body parts. The vehicle was picked up by the security cameras in both locations. The name on the van and the tire marks were also the same. So, it stands to reason, it probably dropped this bag, too."

Daria nodded, drumming her lips with her fingers, an unconscious nervous tick that alarmed her whenever she realized she was in its grip. "The van was from and found where, and in what condition—torched, I assume?"

Morbido shook his large, jowly head. "Found in the alley by the public rest rooms next to the Rapallo train station at approximately 6:45 a.m. Time of drop-off unknown. The door had been forced and the ignition hot wired. It was easy to steal—a fifteen-year-old clapped-out red Fiat Ducato bakery delivery van, already stolen twice. It's unmarked except for the name of the business. There are wear marks on two tires, the ones you spotted at Villa Migone and in Nervi in the mud and dust, and Gigi De Filippo missed. Otherwise it's undamaged. So far, no prints, no DNA, and no traces of blood, just lots of flour and crumbs. They must've worn sterile outfits and gloves and wiped everything down. The body parts were in waterproof, sealed plastic bags."

Daria absorbed Morbido's shorthand report but felt unsatisfied. "Anything else?"

Morbido grinned. He looked like a purple jack-o'-lantern. "Just something essential, a bombshell sure to delight the Questor." He paused to eye her. "The bakery's delivery list from yesterday was written on a sheet of butcher paper on a clipboard. Scrawled across the list with the baker's grease pencil that's always attached to the clipboard was a handwritten message in capital letters."

Daria leaned forward. "And what does the message say?"

"It says JUSTICE ALWAYS PREVAILS, in capital letters. And then it's repeated in what I am guessing must be Latin: *Jus Stat*."

Daria emitted an unladylike grunt. "Well, let's hope they're right," she blurted. "That's the kind of wishful thinking carved on the facades of administrative buildings." She paused and touched a finger to her lips, then caught herself. "The rest of the Latin motto is missing. *Hora fugit*," she said sententiously, "*Jus stat*."

"If you say so," Morbido muttered skeptically, looking and sounding increasingly like a bulldog or bullfrog. Daria laughed out loud, a light, silly laugh, imagining Osvaldo Morbido, the tough lieutenant, as the Frog Prince and Churchill rolled into one large, croaking mass of flesh. "That means *time flies, justice remains*?" he asked, blushing at her laughter and wondering if he should feel offended. Morbido watched warily as she nodded. "So, the stolen vehicle is a bakery van, like I was saying, from Quarto dei Mille, in the eastern outskirts of Genoa."

"Osvaldo, for goodness' sake, I have been here long enough to know where Quarto dei Mille is." Daria spoke more emphatically than she meant to, interrupting him with another burst of laughter.

As a Roman with an American mother, Daria Vinci knew she would always be a foreign interloper in the eyes of local Ligurians. No matter what their political stripe, most Riviera natives were traditionalists and regionalists. They spoke incomprehensible dialects, ate peculiar foods seasoned with strange herbs, and had the chippie sense of injustice the ancient Ligurians, a conquered nation, had always felt. They even looked like the descendants of the short, wiry, Celtic tribal peoples the ancient Romans had defeated over two thousand years ago. The words "hidebound," "quarrelsome," and "ornery" sprang to mind. Daria banished them. Certainly, she said to herself, Osvaldo Morbido was the opposite of at least half the stereotypes, and he could not be more Genoese. Perhaps he was an import of recent centuries, say, only five or six hundred years ago?

"It goes without saying, commissario," Morbido croaked, "that you know Quarto. And everyone in the world knows who Giuseppe Garibaldi's famous Mille were—our great freedom fighters, patriots, and heroes, most of them Genoese or otherwise Ligurian."

"I also happen to know," Daria added in her most conciliatory tone, "the year that Giuseppe Garibaldi and his thousand patriots left from Quarto to unify Italy. What was it, 1860, sometime in the spring?"

"They embarked on May 5th and 6th," Morbido said with unabashed pride, raising a finger and rising to Daria's bait. "Without Genoa's contribution to the independence movement, the country would never have been freed from foreign oppression then—or later, for that matter, during the Second World War. It was the Red Shirts who unified Italy and then the reds of Genoa who drove out Mussolini and the Black Shirts." He glanced at her in the rearview mirror, his face flushed, realizing too late that she had roused and riled him on purpose.

"Genova la Rossa," she teased. "Is it still a red city?"

"More black and blue than red nowadays," Morbido muttered, regretting that he had allowed himself to be baited. "Remember the bruising the political left took during the G8 Summit in 2001? Look it up on the Internet, commissario. I was there. I saw it with my own eyes. The worst violations of human rights in Europe since the end of the war were committed, the kind of brutality the Nazis and Black Shirts loved, and this, perpetrated by our esteemed colleagues, several of them promoted, to boot. In this context I will not mention the name of the Questor. But you know Marshal De Filippo was there? We were both young..." Morbido paused and drew breath and seemed to also regret his vehemence. "What was it all for?" he asked rhetorically, echoing the words of Emilio Bozzo, the pathologist. "What do our idealistic children do? They vote for right-wing crackpots or they don't vote at all and the crackpots get in. The only thing the young seem to care about are smartphones, junk food, and avoiding work. My kids have no backbone—they're nice but have no moxie."

Daria made an empathetic noise and glanced out the window. "Getting back to the delivery van," she suggested.

Morbido watched her in the mirror as he spoke. "Sì, commissario. It was reported missing this morning at approximately 5:30 a.m., presumably stolen at some point between midnight, when the bakery knocked off, and 3:15 a.m., if the first bag with body parts was dropped at 3:42 a.m. in front of Villa Migone, as the video footage indicates. The bakery owner and delivery driver have both given statements already. We also talked to the taxi driver who reported finding the van in Rapallo at 6:45 a.m., as I said. It was there when he arrived at the stand and then went to the men's room before starting his shift. He saw nothing unusual. And no, there are no surveillance cameras in the area, and no license plate identification cameras either."

"What's the name of the bakery?" she asked.

Morbido cracked a rueful smile. "Garibaldi."

Daria metabolized the information. "Gary Baldi?" she asked. "Or Garibaldi? Do you think someone is sending us a subtle message?"

"Too subtle for me," Morbido grunted. "What is the message, commissario? And who is it addressed to?"

"Garbled. Recipient unknown."

"Exactly what I mean. It's like clumsy Russian disinformation. It's so ham-fisted it works. We're confused."

"Speaking of ham," she said, "we're going to be late for lunch. The Dutch eat early. You remember the address?"

"Sì, commissario," he said eagerly, "Villa Pinky, above Zoagli on that corkscrew, dead-end alley."

She raised an eyebrow at the mention of the facetious name those in the know had given the ambassador's family mansion, Villa Adele. "You will drop me and return for me one hour later?"

"Sì, commissario."

"There's a café at the bottom of the hill on the Via Aurelia," she added in the same apologetic tone. "They make very good sandwiches. And cut the sì commissario stuff, Osvaldo. You know I would invite you to join us, but my godfather is eccentric and he wants to speak to me in private, doubtless about some family matter."

"Having to do with the family of Joseph Gary Baldi, alias Giuseppe Garibaldi, or is it the other way around?" Morbido's delivery was deadpan. "Don't worry, Daria," he said in his affable basso voice, his face twitching, betraying the lingering nausea that had seized him earlier that morning near the bags full of butchered bodies. "The heat has taken away my appetite."

Daria shut her eyes, counting to ten. Then she forced them open and turned to the pile of printed, single-spaced sheets on the back seat, picking up where she had left off, trying to focus on Joseph Gary, alias Gary Baldi, Joe Gary Baldi, and Giuseppe Garibaldi, his birth name, an international operator of a high order, it was clear.

As she read, she felt Morbido's eyes on her, watching her reflection in the mirror. She guessed from several things he had said that he had read or at least scanned the Joseph Gary dossier when downloading and printing it out.

Name: Joseph Gary. Born Giuseppe Garibaldi, Prati di Bovecchia, Province of La Spezia, March 24, 1927, the report began. *Changed name and renounced Italian citizenship, 1946. Granted refugee status, Toronto, Canada. Naturalized Canadian then U.S. citizen, 1948 and 1954, respectively. Korean War veteran, general discharge. Subsequently U.S. Navy Intelligence. Joined FBI under J. Edgar Hoover, 1961, contract terminated, 1969. CIA operative, dates unknown. Various covers. Import-export manager, Caracas, Venezuela. Principal, Sequester Free, a private security firm specializing in freeing kidnap and blackmail victims. Political adviser, Washington, DC, and, later, K Street lobbyist for Monsanto, Gazprom, the Libyan National Oil*

Corporation, the NRA, Boeing, Finmeccanica, and others. Real estate developer with interests in Bahrain, Barbados, Bucharest, Dubai, Naples, Panama, Florida and New York City. Now officially retired but unofficially an active "security consultant" and "trade promoter," otherwise known as a "fixer." Friend of Trump, Putin, Erdogan, et al.

Daria skipped ahead, wondering why the discharge had been general and not honorable, why Hoover had fired Gary from the FBI back in the late 1960s, and whether he was still communicating with the CIA, and, lastly, what kind of defense systems he had helped Finmeccanica, Italy's largest arms exporter, sell to the Pentagon and possibly others.

Estimated worth, she read, *$100–$140 million or approximately €80–€120 million.*

So, she said to herself, he isn't a billionaire, merely super rich.

Gary had been married four times, the report confirmed, and divorced four times. He had four children. One had predeceased him. The three survivors were scattered across the globe. All were adult males aged between fifty and seventy, the younger two estranged from Gary and disinherited. They had so far engendered fourteen grandchildren...

Daria ran her finger down the page and found what she was looking for. Currently, Joseph Gary was living with a certain Signora Lepa Sneguljčica, alias Morgana Stella, a self-described aroma therapist, aged forty, of Slovenian nationality, holding a valid long-term Italian residency permit issued in Genoa in 2009. *Stella met subject Gary in 2017. Moved into Villa Glicine with Gary in 2018*, the report specified.

Daria paused and reread the paragraph that followed. It made clear that Joseph Gary was not registered at the prefecture of Genoa with a long-term residency permit. He had entered the country via Luxembourg and France two years earlier as a tourist. His official residence for tax purposes was Barbados. Gary had traveled back and forth to Luxembourg in the interim and to Switzerland at least six times in the last year.

Daria smiled. The Guardia di Finanza, Italy's tax enforcement authority, might be curious to learn the details. Perhaps they already knew them?

A red flag shot up. If the tax police knew about Gary and had not intervened? This was a question for the higher-ups. Since Vice Questor Ruggieri was away on vacation, should she jump the chain of command and refer the case directly to the Questor, Carlo Alberto Lomelli-Centauri? But Centauri had attended a political meeting with Joseph Gary at Villa Glicine. That suggested a conflict of interest. Centauri's extreme-right bent was a matter of public record. After the beatings and murders at the G8 Summit, Centauri had been nicknamed Spartacus, the great hero of the Italian political right.

Daria hung her head and rubbed her eyes. Clearly, Joe Gary was a model citizen. Probably protected and almost certainly untouchable. The perfect profile for Portofino. She closed her eyes again and let the pages fall back to the seat. Why had Willem Bremach told her to dig out his dossier—and why now?

With lights swirling and siren screaming, the Alfa Romeo raced downhill on the serpentine country road into the cluttered, heavily built-up valley. A streaking bullet-proof rocket, it passed the freeway off ramp and sped through the blight of Rapallo's postwar outskirts, picking up the busy Via Aurelia coast highway again in the medieval center of town. After battling through traffic near the train station, the car pulled free of the pocket-size downtown area and continued south by southeast on the scenic, winding highway. Soon it was slaloming through citrus and olive groves, amid Art Nouveau and Art Deco villas teetering on rocky cliffs.

Wherever she looked, willing her eyes open to avoid motion sickness, Daria seemed to see suffocating masses of blood-red bougainvillea and purple morning glory knotted around the guardrails along the road or hanging from the fleshy-leaved, pungent pittosporum trees. The pittosporum grew in suffocating profusion, their dark, musty branches clotted with tiny, cloying white and yellow blossoms oozing translucent honey. The windows of the Alfa Romeo were closed, but the sickly sweet smell reached her. She coughed, almost gagging.

"Thank God for air conditioning," Daria said aloud, filling the void.

"I hate spring," Morbido grumbled, accelerating around a car, bus, and truck in one smooth but risky maneuver. "Winter is the only good season." Though she admired the way Morbido drove, like a Formula One champion, she wished he would slow down. "I hate air conditioning," he added, "but sometimes it's useful."

To Daria's mind, the air conditioning transformed the speeding vehicle into a climate-controlled spaceship flying across an enchanting April morning. The cool temperature matched the slide show of seductive images in her head, vintage Technicolor images of the Italian Riviera in a picture-postcard springtime from days gone by, the days of her youth, when she and her parents had spent entire weeks at Villa Adele with her godfather Willem Bremach and his wife Priscilla, a.k.a. Pinky.

But Daria was not seduced by the Riviera. She knew things rank and steamy were uncoiling amid the riot of dripping honeyed blossoms and blood-hued flowers. It was not fear that caused her to shiver imperceptibly. It was a sense of dread, of looming tragedy.

Swerving south and weaving from lane to lane, the unmarked police car reached the tangle of narrow roads rising up the seafront hillside to the hamlets suspended above the scenic resort town of Zoagli and neighboring Chiavari, a small, prosperous city of the eastern Riviera di Levante.

You had to be a billionaire to live in Portofino, Daria reflected, unwilling to admit to herself that she disliked the famous seaside hamlet despite its staggeringly beautiful setting. Even here, ten miles away from Portofino as the crow flies, unless you were lucky enough to be born on the terraced slopes, you still needed millions to buy even a fisherman's shack. Willem Bremach was among the lucky few, grandfathered into paradise.

Daria had long thought of her enigmatic godfather as the Flying Dutchman, an unlikely chance Italian. Still standing six feet three inches tall at ninety-three years old, he was the scion of a Dutch trading dynasty based since the 1890s in the teeming alleys of old Genoa. That was why he had been born in the heart of the city of Christopher Columbus, in a bedroom the size of a tennis court, hidden within the massive, fortress-like seventeenth-century frescoed Palazzo Spinola.

Now a national house museum hung with priceless Renaissance and Baroque paintings, and stuffed with rare porcelain, tapestries, and furniture, Palazzo Spinola had lured Daria into its labyrinth of rooms half a dozen times since her transfer to Genoa from Rome six years ago. She loved everything about the palace—the smell, the suffused light, even the dust. She had gotten to know the museum's director, dottoressa Simonetta Farina. She had even introduced Farina to Willem Bremach, who, after revisiting his birthplace in the charming director's company, had told Simonetta Farina everything he remembered about life in the palazzo before World War Two.

It was after the war, in the booming fifties and the wild, swinging sixties, that Willem Bremach had become Daria Vinci's father's closest friend and associate. As secretive as he was jocular, the Dutchman remained an unapologetic cold warrior, like Daria's long-dead father. Also like him, Bremach had not always served his country in the capacity of a bland, guarded diplomat. Because Willem's mother had been English, giving him dual nationality, and because he had lied about his age, the plucky Bremach had become a fighter pilot for the RAF when still a teenager at the end of World War Two. The propeller of his Spitfire, shot down over La Spezia in April 1945, adorned the wall of his study. Ever since she was a small child, Daria had wondered at the strange fact that the propeller was made not of steel or aluminum but of laminated wood.

Under diplomatic cover, Bremach's duties and postings had been various and colorful, like her father's—like the variegated vegetation she could see now beyond the car's windows—and equally tangled. Bremach had retired eons ago, but, it was said, kept his hand in, a mirthful eminence grise who could pick up a telephone and speak with government ministers, heads of secret services, and the industrial elite who flocked to places like Davos each year to set the world's agenda. That's what made him such a useful, if willful, ally and sometime informant.

Waking now from her daydream, she braced herself as the car skidded to a halt in front of Bremach's sprawling, turn-of-the-century residence, Villa Adele. It was known to friends and family members as Villa Pinky in part because the faded rose-hued stucco mansion was surrounded by pink roses and pink hydrangeas. Around the garden grew clumps of scented pittosporum. The terraced olive groves and rows of flame cypress trees covered dozens of acres and reached halfway down to the sea.

Feeling dizzy again, Daria handed the Joseph Gary file to Morbido and tried to clear her mental cache. Something told her she was about to learn a thing or two from her beloved godfather, things she could not learn from the DIGOS printout, and perhaps not from anyone else still alive to tell. "Thank you, Osvaldo," she murmured as the car idled in the driveway. "Enjoy your lunchtime reading."

Five

"Where is your dear Communistic friend?" Willem Bremach asked Daria with a wicked wink, feigning surprise at the absence of her perpetual sidekick, Inspector Morbido. Bremach rose shakily from his wheelchair, gave Daria a lingering hug, and kissed her on both cheeks.

Freeing herself, she lowered him back to safety, then pulled Priscilla into a warm embrace, pecking her cool, powdery cheeks. Daria always thought of Priscilla's cheeks as made of porcelain and smelling of perfumes a grandmother might wear. "Morbido will be back in an hour to pick me up," Daria said, pushing Bremach's wheelchair toward the living room.

"So soon?" he protested. "Well, we have no time to waste. A drop of elixir, Daria? You may need it."

She shook her head, knowing what would happen if she consumed an alcoholic beverage at lunch in the heat after getting up at five. "Let me wash up, then I'll help Priscilla get lunch together."

Priscilla wagged her index finger. "You two stay out of the way and talk. Everything is cold. It's already on the table. Angela and I will take care of things."

"The angelic Angela," Willem sang, his shrubby white eyebrows quivering. "You'll never break through the glass ceiling if you behave so civilly, Daria," he added, scolding. "You must let your subalterns do the work so that you may enjoy the glory."

With a nod and a friendly tweak of the shoulders, Priscilla redirected Daria down a side hallway. "Use the kitchen bathroom, please," she said. "The guest rooms and bathrooms are occupied and the occupants are still sleeping or showering."

"'Tis the season for migratory nieces and nephews," Willem said, raising his voice, "not to mention children, grandchildren, and their friends and cousins, the entire populations of the Netherlands and several Nordic countries, in fact, plus New Zealand and Australia. We're a proper Hotel California just now."

"Don't be an old crab," Priscilla said. "You were young and idealistic once."

"Idealistic? Tut-tut, Pinky. You mean young and hedonistic, young and narcissistic, young and hormonal, young and so on. They come by the droves in spring to hike the Sink-we Terry, as they call the Cinque Terre, and go to nightclubs, and then crawl home in the wee hours making sure to wake us up, or, worse, have us pick them up at indecent hours," he snorted. "They are highly idealistic."

"That's unfair," Priscilla said, "they protest, they sign petitions, they march against gun violence and sexual harassment or to save the planet and liberate themselves from racism and gender oppression."

"All very heroic," Willem clucked. "When I was their age..."

"Oh, when you were their age," she cut him off, "the world was young, men were men, and everyone was a hero, as long as they were white males!"

Willem and Pinky continued their mock battle as Daria shut the bathroom door behind her. She could hear him raising his voice again, making sure he could be heard through the door and over the splashing water. She wondered, not for the first time, if all old couples inevitably bickered, battled, and played childish games with each other. Maybe, she decided, maybe it was a different form of love, a form she would never understand or experience because she was doomed to be single.

"Now Daria is different," Willem roared from beyond the bathroom. "She's the true idealist, because she is operating from the inside, not throwing stones and running away." He paused, then shouted. "You should be a Vice Questor by now, my dear Davinci. I must make inquiries. When will that wretched Centauri retire?"

Once Daria had returned to the living room, her cheeks pink and damp, Willem Bremach beckoned her to follow him as he rolled himself ponderously toward the wide verandah. "Tennis," he said, "in case you're curious. Not serious, not worth discussing. My man Vittorio pushes and drives me around, and Angela feeds me chocolates and whiskey when Pinky isn't looking, so all is well."

"I meant to ask what happened," Daria said, contrite.

"Tut-tut," Willem shushed her, "you're a busy professional and I am one step from the boneyard." He handed her the Zeiss binoculars and raised the battered vintage pair to his eyes. "I took these off a Kraut in the spring of 1945," he chortled, lowering them again to tell the tale. "Best deal I ever made. An ounce of hot lead for the Kriegsmarine's finest optics." Willem smiled toothily and waited for Daria to react. "E. Leitz Wetzlar 7 × 50 magnification," he added. "After I crashed the Spitfire and made my escape. You've heard the story before?" Daria nodded. "Well," he said, only a little crestfallen, "I'd better cut to the chase, as your mother likes to say. How is your sainted mother, by the way?"

"Stainless."

"Steel?" he laughed. "Well, well, well, let us hope we are all made of such stern stuff. Do you ever get back to Rome to see the poor creature? I know she misses you terribly and wishes you hadn't moved away. We hear from her once in a great while," he added, "whenever she needs something."

"Barbie the Barracuda," Daria laughed, using her mother's nickname and trembling imperceptibly at the mere thought of her. "She is just fine." Daria blushed and felt guilty. She had not meant to sound unloving. Surviving her mother had been a full-time job. "Why none of her five strapping sons, meaning my brothers, can find the time or resources to entertain her is a mystery to me," Daria added, inwardly hoping her words would work sympathetic magic.

"It's always the daughter," Willem said thoughtfully, "and in addition to being the only female of the prodigious brood, you are the youngest, the great last hope, Barbie's very own darling child, the unexpected girl, the beautiful look-alike, and, coincidentally, you're the only one residing in this country and therefore exploitable."

Daria nodded, relieved Willem Bremach understood and was on her side. He had always been on her side, a protector and nurturer, the perfect godfather. "I'm also the only one free of grumpy spouse and annoying children," Daria found herself adding.

"But she *is* such a loving grandmother, isn't she? Doesn't Barbie rush around the globe giving hugs and kisses to the little ones?" He chortled again. But both realized simultaneously they had reached the end of the bantering session.

"Have we cut to the chase yet?" Daria asked.

"Tempus fugit," he fended.

"I believe it's also hora fugit," she retorted warily, recalling the six grueling years of Latin and ancient Greek she had struggled through as a girl. "Time flies but justice remains?"

"Oh, good for you, Daria! You have out-quoted your feeble old godfather."

"Justice is running out of time," she quipped, "and patience." Puzzled more than ever by Willem Bremach's summons, she perched on the bench on the verandah and crossed her legs, her antennae up and waving. Had he already learned of the scrawled message left in the bakery van, she wondered? He must have. But how? With Willem Bremach, the question of *how* was nearly always unanswerable.

"Before we go any further," he cautioned, "I want you to look out there at the promontory and find that wooden speedboat."

He walked Daria through the same visual itinerary he had sketched out for Priscilla earlier. "Did you get a chance to read up on old Giuseppe Garibaldi?" He asked the question nonchalantly as she followed his instructions.

"Mmmmm," she said, unwilling to editorialize.

"By the by, I called Colonel Rossi at SISMI and told him I hoped the honorable, worthy, incomparable Italian military secret services would be generous if an information request just happened to come in this morning from DIGOS in Genoa. I gather you or Lieutenant Morbido made that request? I certainly hope you did. Your DIGOS profiles are never quite up to scratch, are they?"

Daria lowered the binoculars and stared at her godfather. Rossi at SISMI? That was the pinnacle, the *nec plus ultra* of the Italian clandestine universe. Willem was astonishing. Beyond the bluff, anti-PC sense of humor that rubbed so many young people and women the wrong way, he was disconcertingly well informed and well connected, especially for someone his age, a quarter century after "retirement." This explained why the file on Joe Gary was so complete and up to date. "I saw enough to make me car sick," Daria said.

"It is rather sick-making, isn't it?" Bremach grinned a long-toothed grin and raised his long index finger again, pointing. "That's Joe Gary's boat you're looking at, the famous Riva Aquarama." He consulted his watch. "It's been bobbing around out there since Garibaldi disappeared. Two and a half hours ago."

Daria gazed through the binoculars, scanning the surface of the sea. "Disappeared?"

"We must assume he drowned, or was snatched, unless he was struck or scooped up by a helicopter or a water bomber. In that unlikely scenario, he would have been dumped somewhere inland, presumably on a fire, presumably unwittingly. It would not be the first time, at least not in literature."

"Let me get this straight," she said, flushing at the news, "you think it was an accident?"

Bremach grimaced but said nothing, staring out to sea. Daria waited in silence. Her godfather was known for his oblique references and peculiar manner of delivery. She expected him to flinch, but he did not. She caved and spoke first.

"Willem, are you pulling my leg?"

"Any gentleman would be very lucky to pull your leg, my dear girl, but I am your padrino and dandled you when an infant so it would be immoral and obscene for me to do so. I also know you're rather too busy these days for a wrestling match." He paused, admiring her dark blue linen pantsuit with an appreciative eye. It was creased and slightly soiled. "Been gardening this morning?" he asked in his signature teasing voice.

Daria, startled, glanced at the cuffs of her pants, then bent down to brush off the spots of dried mud from the roadside turn-out. "I should not have worn linen," she blurted unguardedly, "it's far too hot today, and it wrinkles so easily."

Bremach's eyebrows danced. "What was all that about dead bodies in bags, by the way?" he continued in his jocular way. "Found in a mud bath? Sounds dreadful."

Daria shook her head. "First let's do Joseph Gary."

"Yes, that's wise," he muttered. "People say I have become an old gossip." He cleared his throat. "Now, before I tell you exactly what I saw and what I know, you might wish to consider alerting your own people at DIGOS or the cousins, if you prefer to play second fiddle to the Carabinieri or, even better, the Guardia di Finanza." Daria shot him a startled glance and was about to respond, but he raised a hand and continued.

"In your place," he said in an oracular tone, "I might speculate, for purposes of shared consumption, that you received a tip from an eyewitness—to wit, me—the gist of which is that what occurred was an accident, almost certainly, and that the authorities should get the underwater brigade in and start looking for him. You might want to put out an APB in the unlikely case he has been abducted. If you want Garibaldi to be your case, Daria, you'll have to act. Soon." Bremach studied her face. It remained impassive. Again, she did not have time to respond.

"I happen to know that Gary's rather disagreeable factotum

and manservant must already be on the alert," he continued, more forcefully this time, "and that his charming lady friend, the self-styled Morgana Stella, will sound the alarm if her sugar daddy is any later. You see, Garibaldi is never late. *Was* never late. Now the clock is ticking for you, Daria. They may have reported his disappearance or rather his no-show already."

Daria hesitated. "Two words, Willem," she said. "Tell me in two words how you know whose boat that is and why you have such an interest in Joseph Gary."

Bremach consented. "Fair enough. I met him again two years ago at the Rapallo yacht club. He needed a recommendation to join. Since for some mysterious reason he'd already been accepted by the blue-blood geriatrics at the Galleria Club and Jardin Club in Genoa and I knew, therefore, that Pinky and I would not be able to avoid him socially, I consented. During the vetting process, I asked certain sources for information. Pinky thought I should give the committee a thumbs-down. She doesn't like the smell of him. It amused me to think of old Joe at the yacht club. We sympathized on a certain level once upon a time, though he was a swine. And I will admit, I only gave him a recommendation because I thought I could keep a closer eye on him this way.

"You see, Daria, I knew Signor Garibaldi very slightly a very long time ago, before you were born—a professional relationship, you understand. Your father knew him too." He paused, weighing his words. "Do you remember the Aldo Moro kidnapping and assassination by the Red Brigades, those clumsy left-wing terrorists? How could you, you were a mere child, or perhaps you weren't born yet. Moro, you know, of course, was the famous prime minister of Italy who attempted to engineer the 'historic compromise' between the Christian Democrats and the Communists. Around the table of men who decided to let Moro die at the hands of the Red Brigades was a certain former Navy Intelligence officer and one-time FBI agent who had switched and was batting for the CIA." He paused significantly. "I've already said more than two words." He paused again.

"Go on."

"I've never known anyone so egregiously misnamed as Joe Gary Baldi," Bremach continued, his voice warming to the task. "Granted, Giuseppe as a name is standard issue and Garibaldi is one of the most common surnames on the Riviera, as you know, especially around here. Open the phone book and you'll find scores of Garibaldis. But this fellow was about as like the original Red-Shirted revolutionary Giuseppe Garibaldi as Pinky is like Lady Macbeth or Eva Braun. And then there was the famous heroic Red Communistic Garibaldi Brigade of the partisans in World War Two, and he certainly did not belong to them, au contraire.

"As to knowing that's his boat," Bremach added, "we have been out on it with him several times, over Pinky's strenuous objections. You've read by now that Gary was a Navy Seal? He swam every day, even in winter. I often watched him go out there, always at 10:00 a.m., rain or shine. Not much rain since he moved here, lots of shine. I've been stuck in this contraption now for two weeks since I wrenched my knee playing tennis and have had occasion to observe him closely every morning. Suddenly he disappeared. It's as simple as that.

"Except it isn't simple at all, dear Daria," he said, rolling on, the power and passion in his voice increasing. "Joe was a delectable gentleman. That's why Pinky picked up his scent. I never said a thing about his glorious past to her. She's terribly upright, you know, with a fine sense of smell. I'm more like Joe, a natural-born ruffian."

Willem Bremach handed her a page torn from his notebook. On it were a neatly written series of airplane registration numbers, observation times, and short descriptions. "Seaplanes," he said, "water bombers, commonly known by their trademark name, Canadair, though that is misleading since a dozen manufacturers make similar aircraft nowadays. In fact, I believe at least two of the ones out today were not built by Canadair but rather by Russian and Chinese consortiums, one of each. You would be able to find that out easily enough. Might one of these have accidentally or deliberately scooped up our Signor Garibaldi?"

Bremach raised himself slightly and pulled a wrinkled magazine out of the side of the wheelchair, then offered it to Daria. "*Aviation Weekly*," he said. "I read it religiously. Once a flyer, always a flyer. As you'll see, in this issue there just happens to be a rather long and boring article about the new generation of seaplanes. Naturally enough, the Chinese are making them bigger and better and cheaper than anyone else, and they are trying to win the lucrative southern European market, since the entire Mediterranean Basin seems to burn perpetually and be flooded with stranded migrants in need of search and rescue services. The Russians are also competitive.

"Both these countries' latest planes carry a lot more water than the old Canadair models, but they have the disadvantage of being less responsive." Willem paused for effect, his hands gripping an imaginary steering wheel. "In case you're wondering, the reason the article is in this issue of the magazine is simple. There's a three-day international air show going on right now in Albenga. Yes, Albenga, the Ligurian capital of artichokes way out west on the Riviera di Ponente. All the world's seaplanes for search and rescue and firefighting are there, and if I hadn't wrecked my knee I would be too. The air show might explain why I spotted several unusual-looking aircraft out this morning. I've placed asterisks by the registration numbers I could make out." He smiled, pleased by his disquisition. "They were in transit, I suppose, or had been pressed into service because of all those fires you mentioned. That too will be easy to discover. Whatever you do, just remember the old ditty, 'flyers are liars.'"

"Oh, Willem, stop that," shouted Priscilla, who was eavesdropping, pretending to rearrange plates on the table in the dining room.

Daria took the handwritten sheet and the magazine, glancing at them and pursing her lips, wondering what she was getting herself into. After a moment's hesitation, she walked to the end of the terrace and used her smartphone to call headquarters in Genoa. Speaking in concise, telegraphic sentences, she gave detailed instructions to a first voice, then waited and spoke deferentially and at length to someone else, doing her best to ensure neither Willem nor Priscilla could hear her. Bremach guessed the second speaker was her boss, the loathsome Questor, Carlo Alberto Lomelli-Centauri III, a pompous, useless reactionary ass from Genoa's old-money nobility. Willem Bremach had crossed swords more than once with his nemesis's grandfather, Carlo Alberto Lomelli-Centauri I, way back, during the Second World War, and with his father, Centauri II, during the Cold War, then, less belligerently, with the useless whippersnapper Centauri III, this time over a green felt-topped card table at the Galleria Club. The Centauris were among the club's longest-standing members.

Several minutes later, Daria strode back to where Willem Bremach waited, pocketing her phone. "Okay," she said, trying not to sound dramatic or hardboiled but calm, controlled, and professional. "Any incoming caller using the national emergency numbers to report the disappearance will be told the incident has already been reported," she explained. "So, the case is ours. Our Carabinieri cousins can't claim it. The scuba divers should be in Portofino in about ninety minutes. They're coming from Genoa-Voltri. Our local Polizia di Stato and the Carabinieri from Santa Margherita will arrive shortly after. By then, Lieutenant Morbido and I will be ready to greet them."

"Excellent," Bremach said, making a tent of his fingertips and grinning toothily. "Now, your turn, about those bags and bodies..."

Daria was unsure how much to reveal. The phrase *quid pro quo* sprang to mind. More Latin. But this time even those who had never studied ancient languages could understand. She hesitated, drumming her lips, then caught herself and plunged forward. "The Minister of the Interior has already spoken to the Questor about this," she reasoned aloud, "meaning Centauri is under pressure to deliver, therefore I am under pressure to deliver to Centauri," she said. "The Minister is demanding results, saying it is a national outrage to have the anniversary of the Liberation

of Italy besmirched by murders and mutilated bodies left in strategic sites in and around Genoa—in garbage bags. They say it is a
left-wing conspiracy."

"Do tell," Willem said with undisguised delight, his bushy eyebrows rising.

The discovery of the bags would be on the mainstream
news stations soon, Daria knew, and was already trending on
social media. She glanced at her watch. With Facebook, Twitter,
Instagram, and the like, nothing could be kept quiet. Would they
also report about the handwritten message left in the bakery van?
That too may have leaked. It must have leaked already. How else
would Willem have known?

"I might as well share what I know," she said at last, relieved
again to be able to trust someone, "in case you have some insight
into the matter."

Giving Bremach an edited rundown, she started with the bag
of body parts left in front of Villa Migone, the celebrated mansion in downtown Genoa where the Nazi surrender was signed
on April 25, 1945, ending the Second World War in Italy. Then
she moved on to bag number two, left in the piazza in the eastern suburb of Nervi, where the Insurrection of Genoa had begun
two days earlier on April 23. She finished with a description of
the muddy turnout behind Rapallo, fifteen miles or so east of the
second bag. This time the bag had been deposited directly below
a machine gun nest and bunker complex where, apparently, a
dozen Communist partisans from the Garibaldi Brigade had been
murdered in a summary execution by the Nazis and members of
the Fascist Mussolini Brigade on April 24, 1945.

"Something of the kind was inevitable," Bremach said with
surprising alacrity. "The Krauts and Fascists lost the war but won
the peace. Just look at our political parties and apprentice tyrants
today. If Il Duce hadn't been shot and hung upside down on a
meat hook in Milan, he would be elected by a landslide today, or in
a rigged farce of an election, like that imbecile across the Atlantic.
Therefore, it would not be surprising to me if the bodies in the

bags were those of neo-Fascists executed by a new Red Brigades or suchlike."

Daria frowned. "That might be," she said diplomatically. "Except they look more like unfortunate African immigrants than extreme right-wing activists."

"Well then, perhaps that's the message. Stop the immigrants, bring back the Fascists?"

"Maybe," she said, wondering what Willem Bremach really thought and what he was holding back.

"Think," Bremach added triumphantly, using his favorite jocular tone, "what would a cabalist say? Let us calculate. You have three bags and nine fires? Three is a very important number, the Holy Trinity, and nine is three times the Trinity. Three times nine is twenty-seven. Take the numerals two and seven and add them together and you get nine again. So, clearly, it is some kind of cabal, don't you think?" He grinned. "Now you'll have to count up the pieces in the bags and see if they also come to twenty-seven."

"Willem," she began to protest. He held up his hand to check her.

"I'm afraid I have no other great perceptions about this rather dismal-sounding case," he sighed. "Perhaps something will come up, some clue." He paused, then said, "Might there be a connection with our man, Joe Gary Baldi?"

"Come to the table," Priscilla commanded from the dining room, "otherwise the food will get hot." She laughed suddenly and smiled. It was so rare for Priscilla to pun, quip, or laugh that all three of them were stunned.

Bremach's eyes sparkled. "Coming," he called back. Placing one large, mottled hand on Daria's arm, he whispered, his breath scented by his morning whisky. "Remember, with Joseph Gary, *cherchez la femme*. He is, or was, a womanizer. Your American counterparts are cruder, telling you to follow the money. In this case the politics, the women, and the dollars, or rubles, who knows, may be one and the same." He winked.

Daria began pushing him toward the table, where a bowl of pasta salad with cherry tomatoes and thimble-sized mozzarella balls awaited, flanked by a platter of thinly sliced cold veal topped with creamy tuna sauce.

"What about the Mob?" she asked in a whisper. "Everything in his profile points to the Mafia."

"You know better than I," he added, "that the Mob wears a cloak of invisibility, or a carnival mask, or a tailored linen suit, and speaks all of Mammon's languages, even Bitcoin. My last word to you, dear Daria, is go to Albenga, to the airport, to see about the seaplanes, and then seek out Andrew Striker, the head of the x-ray security team at the container port in Voltri. A damn fine pilot he is, by the way, though reckless. Tell him I sent you. They have some all-knowing algorithm, it is claimed. If Joe Gary was scooped up by a seaplane, they will know it and they will find him."

Daria glanced down at Willem Bremach, her heart thumping at the mention of Andrew Striker. She composed herself. "They?" she asked. "Meaning Homeland Security?"

He nodded. "You know Andrew Striker?"

Daria frowned and flushed. "Willem, you know I knew him well," she blurted out. "Too well."

Bremach's face twitched. He struck his palm to his forehead. "Of course, how could I forget, *I* introduced *you* to *him*. And you left him heartbroken because he was a blackguard. My apologies, Daria dear, I am getting old after all, old and senile, like that blighter Centauri, the damned Questor."

Six

Daria knew in her heart, stomach, and soul that this was her lucky day. After car sickness in the morning on the Via Aurelia, she was now experiencing seasickness live, on camera, in one of the world's more spectacular settings, Portofino. She had not meant to be the star of the show.

Surrounding Daria on sea and land were sea gods, goddesses, and heavily armed, blue-cheeked policemen who appeared to be enjoying the cruise as if it were a school outing. Only she, the commissioner, was seasick.

Away across the waves from Daria, scores of pedestrians, joggers, and rubbernecking drivers gaped at the police authorities from the snaking seaside road. Illegal immigrants moved among them, selling sunglasses, paper tissues, handheld electric fans, and bottles of cold water. A fender-bender had already caused the temporary closure of the narrow two-lane coast highway. The vans and cars of the press corps stood bumper to bumper, further complicating the job of the traffic cops, among them the familiar, disconcertingly handsome, Sergeant Gianni Giannini.

Overhead and at water level, drones and powerboats sent

by local and national TV news stations hovered and sharked. They and the dozen or more speedboats owned by curious local residents and Riviera visitors were kept at bay by a motley flotilla of boats from the Coast Guard and Guardia di Finanza—the customs and tax police—not to mention the state and municipal police, the Carabinieri, several local fire departments, and the harbor masters of Portofino, Santa Margherita Ligure, and Rapallo. Daria knew why she was dizzy and nauseated, and it was not simply a matter of the swelling, sultry sea.

How had the disappearance of Joseph Gary degenerated into a circus so quickly? Daria knew the two-word answer: social media.

But she consoled herself with a positive thought. There was a potential upside to Facebook et al.: a superabundance of photos and videos to analyze. Despite the holidays, tech teams at the provincial DIGOS headquarters in Genoa and at the mother ship Ministry of the Interior in Rome had been on the case for several hours, tracking images purportedly capturing the scene of what looked increasingly like a crime. The postings so far offered variations on the theme of "the American secret agent" and "foreign billionaire, friend of oligarchs and potentates," who had, it was claimed, been murdered, kidnapped, poisoned with nerve gas, or drowned, with or without a glamorous former porn star named Morgana Stella in his arms, in the bay off Europe's most exclusive seaside resort. What had Joe Gary done, who was getting revenge or would stand to profit, which crime family might be involved, and where was the body to be found—these were the questions with the longest comment chains.

Other equally accurate and intelligent posts speculated on the retail value, top speed, horsepower, and desirability of the victim's Riva Aquarama motorboat and the victim's comparably vintage Maserati parked in Rapallo's yacht harbor, guarded by municipal police officers.

On land, three teams of Polizia di Stato and Carabinieri, including two men pulled from Gigi De Filippo's squad, were going door to door along the coast road between Santa Margherita and Portofino, asking for eyewitness accounts. So far, no one had noticed anything suspicious about the speedboat or the lost swimmer. Why would they? Like the Aquarama, dozens of handsome motor yachts and boats of all kinds were out on this perfect spring morning. Like Gary, hundreds of waders, water skiers, and swimmers could be seen splashing, slaloming, and cavorting in the sun. Besides, everyone knew that the oligarchs, Mafiosi, and felonious politicians came a dime a dozen on the Riviera, so why notice them?

Peering down into the depthless crystalline waters of the Gulf of Tigullio directly off Portofino, Daria leaned perilously on the thin stainless-steel railing of the harbor master's motor launch. Holding her handkerchief over her mouth, she knew what the color green felt like. She regretted losing the lunch Priscilla Bremach had gone to such trouble to prepare and wished she had not been caught on camera being sick.

The harbor master was Rapallo's most affable aquatic hunk. He seemed hesitant to give advice to a DIGOS commissioner. The deeply tanned former weight-lifting champion kept watch from the helm of the launch, ready to fish Daria out if she fell in.

Given past precedent, why she had agreed to ride in the high-powered patrol boat she could not now imagine. The inevitable self-questioning began. Was it a sense of duty?

Earlier in the afternoon, Daria had merely cluttered the scene of the crime and gotten in the way as the fingerprint team and detail men from headquarters worked over Joe Gary's gleaming, rocking Riva. Every inch of the speedboat including its many locked compartments had been unlocked, checked, and photographed. Gary's smartphone had been bagged, plus a pocket-sized paper note pad and gold-plated pen. His leather boat shoes had also been wrapped in plastic and taken away. Containers filled with an assortment of sun screens, lotions, makeup, chap stick, and lip balm, rubbing alcohol, hydrogen peroxide, and bandages, as well as high-impact bins holding waterproof flashlights, flares, smoke grenades, and other emergency equipment, were labeled and removed for inspection.

Something among the jumbled items called out to Daria, something unusual, but in her muddled, queasy state of mind and body she could not form an articulate thought about what that something might be. She also had the vague notion that behind the controls of one of the countless official-looking boats on the scene she had glimpsed the unmistakable profile of Andrew Striker. When she had turned to look back, that tall, lean figure with a vampire widow's peak and a jutting jaw had vanished.

Only after the routine and fruitless checks had been completed had Daria rejoined the harbor master on his lethal launch and vomited repeatedly as they toured the scene. The boat rocked gently now, almost at a standstill, following the boiling bubbles of the three fire brigade scuba divers below. They were searching the bottom, so far without results.

A hundred yards north of the launch, Joe Gary's toy boat, as Pinky Bremach had called it, tugged gently at a buoy. Two uniformed police officers from the Santa Margherita station sat with their submachine guns cradled in their laps and looked distinctly out of place in the tuck-'n'-roll upholstered interior. They watched Inspector Morbido pull alongside and clamber out of another launch, then teeter on board in his pointy black leather shoes. For a meatball on legs, Morbido was surprisingly agile. Accompanying him was a sullen-looking, muscular, deeply tanned, middle-aged man wearing expensive designer sports clothes, a thick gold chain, and mirrored sunglasses. He might have been the cheerful harbor master's twin but for his evident grumpiness and the fact that the first joint of his right index finger was missing.

Daria shaded her aching eyes and watched Morbido and the new arrival. She knew the man's name to be Maurizio Capurro. He was a local jack-of-all-trades with just a shade of murk in his past, enough to have caused the loss of his trigger finger. Somehow, he had risen from short-haul skipper and small-time smuggler to become Joe Gary's live-in personal assistant. According to Daria's other sidekick, Lieutenant Gambero, who had interviewed Capurro at the Gary villa earlier that day, Capurro and his handsome young wife were highly paid and greatly appreciated by their employer—their former employer, by the looks of it. They occupied a bungalow on the villa's grounds.

Maurizio Capurro's job was to take care of the Riva and Maserati, do the day-to-day maintenance on the villa, and supervise everyone else—the outsourced dog-walkers, swimming-pool people, mow-and-blow teams, and construction crews called in periodically to add an elevator or gazebo or rebuild a bathroom in the already obscenely large, rambling villa.

Maurizio's wife, Imelda Capurro, née Cruz, a naturalized Italian from Manila, handled the grocery shopping, extra cleaning, catering, and cooking, under the dancing baton of her exigent mistress, Morgana Stella, the recycled starlet of Eastern European pornographic cinema, now an aromatherapist.

Stella had also given a statement to Gambero, preferring to remain at the villa for the time being and avoid the zoo at the scene of the disappearance. Besides, she had said, the dogs were traumatized by Gary's sudden absence.

Judging by his scowls, Maurizio Capurro seemed to be aware that this was likely going to be his last trip piloting the vintage speedboat back to Rapallo's yacht harbor or driving the Maserati along the corkscrew highway to Gary's garage. Everything in his demeanor telegraphed the same sour message. *The good times are over. Stop.* What did he know that made him so sure Joe Gary would not pop up like the proverbial jack-in-the-box? Daria was confident she would soon find out.

Steadying herself, she wondered how much longer the search for the body would last, then realized it was up to her to make the decision to call it off. Surely the divers would run out of air? Secretly she hoped that, for purely technical reasons, the day would soon be over, she would not be blamed for weakness, and she and her team could rest and regroup.

What confused her most was why Joe Gary's body had eluded detection for so long. He should have been found by now, face up, on or near the surface, or on the bottom, within swimming distance of his boat, somewhere along the narrow sea lane he followed. There was no wind, no tide to speak of, no undertow, and the water temperature was a mild 23 degrees Centigrade—73.4 degrees Fahrenheit. The gulf looked and felt like a tepid bathtub.

Reportedly, Gary swam in the same direction every morning, out to sea about a quarter mile, then back again, two or three or even five times, following an imaginary line drawn from the buoy and boat to the lighthouse at Portofino. He was a small, lightweight man short in the arms and legs. That meant his body caused little or no drag and would naturally tend to turn on its back, face up, and remain stationary.

If he had suffered a sudden, massive heart attack or been struck on the head, she reasoned, he might not have had time to inhale water, meaning he would not sink. In that case, someone—Willem Bremach and his binoculars for instance—would have seen him floating. If instead he had died from sucking water into his lungs, he would have sunk quickly and remained stationary on the bottom for the time being.

Gary always wore extra-long, high-performance buoyant rubber flippers, according to the sulky Maurizio Capurro and the petulant Morgana Stella. The fins doubled as flotation devices and probably would have kept Gary suspended at least partway between the bottom and the surface. They were also highly visible in clear water and should have been spotted already.

Most human bodies sink quickly, Daria reminded herself with a shudder of pity and disgust. They only float back up once bacteria in the cavities form gases. Then they remain on top for days or weeks before sinking to the bottom again. That was why the dead were weighted down when buried at sea, she knew, and why victims, whether alive or dead, when dumped in the water by organized criminals and other murderers, wore the proverbial cement overshoes. With time, depending on the salinity and temperature of the water and the tides, a body might rise and sink more than once before decomposing or washing up on shore. Sooner or later, Joe Gary would bob up and be spotted.

But not if he had been struck by the hull of an amphibious plane and dragged off his normal course, decapitated, or lifted in the air and dumped on a distant fire.

Checking her wristwatch, Daria was about to call off the search and tell the harbor master to take her back to shore when she found a fold-down bench and perched wearily on its edge. Her phone rang and she answered reluctantly, afraid she might be sick again or, worse, that it might be Carlo Alberto Lomelli-Centauri III, the Questor, demanding another update.

She was relieved when it proved to be Lieutenant Morbido, waving at her from the deck of the Riva. He was close enough that she could see his thick, rubbery frog lips moving when he spoke to her.

"The personal assistant, Signor Capurro, says his boss always wore a close-fitting gold chain with a Saint Christopher medal, a large gold signet ring, and a waterproof Rolex with a GPS tracker dot embedded in the backing," Morbido barked. "We need to reach the divers and tell them to use the underwater metal detectors. That might speed things up."

"Good," Daria said. "We need to find out who's tracking the GPS dot, presumably Capurro or the woman, Morgana Stella?"

"Negative. That's where it gets complicated," Morbido said. "Capurro claims he used to have the app and code to track his boss, but he says his mobile was stolen last week and he and Gary failed to install the app on the new phone. I checked with the local Carabinieri, and they confirm Capurro reported the theft of the phone. Capurro says he has no idea if his boss wrote down the codes elsewhere or who else would have them. He's never noticed a laptop or other computer in the house."

She pondered. "What about Morgana Stella?"

"No," Morbido replied. "Capurro says Gary didn't want her to know where he was or be able to track him down. Clearly, the Viagra worked."

"I see," Daria muttered, the vision of an overly tanned nonagenarian having sex with a woman fifty years his junior increasing her queasiness. "Then the app and code would be on the victim's mobile, the one we bagged from the boat?" Daria managed to ask. Morbido grunted and said that was probably correct. "And that phone is locked?" Daria questioned, following up. Morbido again said yes. "Then please ask HQ to find someone who can unlock it," she said.

"I already have," Morbido answered wearily. "It's not easy and everyone in the tech section is gone. They're on vacation. Back next week. Even then, it is no picnic to break into one of these phones, as you know very well. Remember the case in America with Apple. We should probably send it to Rome or ask Homeland Security for help."

Daria raised her head suddenly, then shook it. "No, not Homeland Security," she said, thinking, yet again, of Andrew Striker.

Morbido shrugged philosophically. "I might point out, commissario, that there's also an old-fashioned paper note pad. Maybe something was noted in there. I'll get the fingerprint team to bring the note pad upstairs to your office. They're already back in Genoa at headquarters with it."

Daria tapped her lips and frowned. "Okay," she said, buying time. "Get them to scan each page of the notebook, upload them, send them to the research department in Rome, and email a copy to me. I want every name and number in that pad analyzed before the day is out."

"Sì, commissario."

Daria took a deep breath and felt her head pounding. "I'll tell the harbor master to alert the divers about the gold items and getting metal detectors," she said, trying to be systematic, "then I'll meet you at the car in half an hour. Anything else?"

"You know Gambero is at the villa?" Morbido queried, reluctant now. "It seems the fiancée, Signora Stella Morgana, is distraught and hysterical and wants you or the Questor to come over in person—otherwise she says she will phone the minister, a personal friend of her husband's."

"Which minister," Daria asked, exasperated, the nausea mounting again. "Our Minister of the Interior?"

"No, the Minister of Defense," Morbido muttered. "Carabinieri," he added with irritation. "The woman says if Gary's not in the water or on the boat or in his car then he may have been kidnapped. That's why he had the GPS dot embedded in the Rolex, she says, not because he thought he might misplace the watch. He never took it off. She seems to know a lot about the kidnapping business."

"Well, *he* certainly did," Daria remarked, recalling the report she had read that morning in the car, and the company Gary had managed, Sequester Free. "There are no signs on the boat of violence or forcible abduction, is that right?" she asked. Morbido made a grunting sound in the affirmative. "Okay. So, since he was in the water when he disappeared, according to the only eyewitness we have, meaning Ambassador Bremach, the kidnappers would have had to grab Gary from another boat with a fishing net, or from a submarine, or perhaps on water skis, like James Bond? Let's be real, Osvaldo."

The sarcasm in her voice caused Morbido to emit a guttural, basso laugh. "What about a helicopter?" he asked. "007 loves helicopters."

Daria scoffed but acknowledged that was not impossible. Helicopters equipped with water barrels on steel cables had been used more than once to fight wildfires locally. She would need to find out if that had been the case this morning.

"He could have been scooped up," Morbido said, "by one of those seaplanes."

"Osvaldo," she muttered, "the chances are one in a billion. But we'll check on it. See you in half an hour." She disconnected and shaded her eyes again, then waved the harbor master over to her seat.

"Yes, commissario, are you well enough to travel back to Rapallo?"

"Am I mistaken," Daria asked, "or have the water bombers and helicopters gone home?"

"I guess the fires are out," he said with skepticism, glancing at the hills. "That was uncharacteristically efficient."

The commissioner raised an eyebrow. "Did those fires look strange to you?" she asked.

"How do you mean, 'strange'?"

"Just, strange, I'm not sure how else to put it."

"They seemed to make lots of smoke, without much flame, and the flame was a very blue color, not orange, if that's what you mean."

"That's exactly what I mean," she said. "You're very observant, my compliments. Did you also observe by chance if the airborne brigades were using helicopters to fight the fires today?"

The harbor master pursed his lips, shook his head, and ejaculated the typical Italian sound for baffled uncertainty, a percussive *bo*.

"One more thing," she said, snapping her fingers in remembrance. "I get why Signor Gary would have the flares in his boat, but why the smoke grenades? I saw them earlier, in one of those floating plastic containers."

The harbor master smiled indulgently. "That's easy. They're a great way to attract attention if you have a breakdown in daylight hours. Flares work early in the morning and at night, but it's so bright here during the day most of the year that you can't spot a flare, so you use smoke bombs. Sometimes they're colored."

Daria nodded, a penny dropping into a mental slot located somewhere behind her throbbing temples. "Cobalt blue?" she asked.

"Yes, that's a popular color," he confirmed.

Seven

On the bucking run back to Rapallo in the patrol boat, Daria tried to think positive thoughts about the late-afternoon sunshine and unseasonable heat, the speeding speedboat, and the muscular man at the helm, as her smartphone rang incessantly and vibrated in her clutched hand. The real problem was she could no longer think. She had to lie down again. If only she could get horizontal, everything would be all right, she told herself, cursing her physical weakness. She closed her eyes for a split second. When she opened them, she saw her dark blue linen pantsuit now thoroughly creased, reflected in the rear-view mirror of a car, her long thin body stretched out on the back seat of the Alfa Romeo. Morbido sat at the wheel.

"How long have I been out?" she asked, sitting up and staring incredulously at the mottled orange sunset sky.

"Long enough for more hell to break loose," he said mildly, his best toad expression wrapped around his wide, saturnine face.

Lieutenant Morbido spoke slowly and clearly, in case his superior officer might still be dazed. He explained that the scuba divers had been sent home. They had run low on air, were tired, and had found nothing. The afternoon was nearly over, the light was going. No metal detectors were available. They would have to try again in the morning.

His tone, words, and expression made it clear he too was tired and fed up but resigned to go forward, as he knew they would have to.

While rooting in her purse, Daria listened and acknowledged the probable correctness of everything Morbido was saying. She found her breath mints, popping two into her mouth and offering the package to the stolid inspector.

"I'm on a diet," he grumbled, shaking his jowls as he handed her a bottle of spring water. "Where to?"

Before speaking, Daria thanked him, then gulped down the entire bottle of water. She scanned the two dozen text, voice, and encrypted app messages on her phone, toggling back and forth between professional and personal accounts. Triage was the only way forward. She skipped the three messages from her mother, for a start, more than mildly annoyed that one message wasn't enough and the pushy, unstoppable stainless-steel Barbie the Barracuda was breathing down her neck again.

"To Gary's place, Villa Glicine," Daria blurted, raising her eyes. "I'll be all right." She said the words more to reassure herself than to persuade the lieutenant. Pausing, still unconvinced, she asked, "What about you?"

"Oh, I'm as fresh as a rose, commissario," he grunted, switching on the swirling light and siren, then bumping over several curbs and out of the parking lot of Rapallo's yacht harbor. He raised his bellowing voice over the roar. "Life on the Riviera is a never-ending holiday."

She wanted to laugh but couldn't. "The fires are under control?"

"Sì, commissario," he shouted, "but they are all in very remote locations, apparently all of them in World War Two bunkers, like the one near Rapallo this morning, so no one has been up to them yet. The Questor is delighted."

"Not even Gigi's men made it up to them?"

"Certainly not Gigi's men. They couldn't climb in body armor, especially in this heat."

"What about that traffic cop, I think his name was Gianni, did he get up to that big bunker?"

"You *think* his name is Gianni? Don't be coy, Daria. You know it is. Gianni Adonis Giannini. He has not reported back yet, as far as I know, but Gigi may not be in a mood to share his info with us, after the way you mocked him and led him astray this morning. Finding the dogs and wild boars, and the origin of the plastic leaf bags— really, Daria, sometimes you overdo it."

She ignored the remark and the innuendo about the unnaturally handsome traffic cop but felt the heat race to her cheeks nonetheless. "Can't we send in some firemen and people from the Civil Defense Department to check the bunkers?" she asked, regretting her reference to Gianni Giannini.

"It will be dark soon," Lieutenant Morbido replied calmly.

"But we have night-vision goggles."

He chuckled. "Oh yes. One set of them, commissario, the Carabinieri have the others, like the metal detectors."

Daria laughed out loud, a bitter, sardonic laugh. Her head was throbbing from heat, motion sickness, and dehydration. "Tomorrow at first light, then," she suggested.

"Sì, commissario," Morbido agreed, watching her. When she raised her eyes again from the screen of her phone, he spoke. "With your permission, I have two important things to say to you before we arrive at the villa. Primo, Rome is sending reinforcements from Savona and La Spezia, because the Questor wants your head and the Minister wants results yesterday."

"Good, so do I," she replied in a clipped, cool tone. "Let's detail the extra men to go up to the sites of the fires, accompanied by local firemen or Civil Defense volunteers. We also need to get someone over to the airport in Albenga, about the seaplanes. I'll explain later."

Morbido nodded. "Secondo," he added in his booming basso

voice. "Emilio Bozzo, the coroner, phoned. He says he has news for you. He called you but you didn't answer, so he sent you a text message."

"Osvaldo," Daria said, leaning forward and cupping her hands, "can you kill the siren?"

Relative silence returned. The car paced itself past stalled traffic, leaving Rapallo, this time on the busy two-lane shoreline road to San Michele di Pagana, a luxury seaside village. It lay halfway between Rapallo and Santa Margherita. The values of certain isolated properties here, like Joe Gary's celebrated Villa Glicine, hidden among olive and citrus groves, rivaled those of Portofino.

Daria raised her phone to her ear and listened to the first voice message. It was from Willem Bremach. "I was watching the TV news just now and had an epiphany of sorts, Daria. Regarding those delightful little parcels left for you this morning in the plastic bags, I am reminded of the Brindisi Bronzes. Might that solve at least part of the riddle? Ta-ta, my dear."

More perplexed than before, Daria replayed Bremach's cryptic words. It was typical of him to speak in riddles, in part because of his unshakable paranoia about eavesdropping and wiretapping, a leftover from predigital days. She loved and respected her godfather, and had idolized him when she was young, but sometimes he irritated her almost as much as her mother.

What could Willem possibly mean by referring to the Brindisi Bronzes? She could not remember anything about the bronzes found near the southern Adriatic coast city of Brindisi decades ago, when she was a child, other than the fact that they were a clutter of hundreds of broken Greek and Roman statues made of bronze, scattered underwater around a shipwreck. What could they have to do with bodies in plastic bags?

The additional strain on her brain caused by this enigma made her dizzy again. Hoping that Willem Bremach had made himself clearer the second time around, she listened to another message from him. "Sorry to trouble you again, Daria," he chirped. "You must know by now that despite our efforts to keep her out of your hair, your blessed mother got on the noon train from Rome and will detrain in Rapallo this afternoon. We are picking her up. She will spend the weekend with us, as per her request. She said if the mountain won't go to Mohammed, Mohammed will go to the mountain. I expect she means the impregnable natural fortress of the Monte di Portofino, unless she's referring to you. In any case, we hope you will join us tomorrow night for an indecently early dinner at the Galleria Club, say, 7:30 p.m.? I am reserving and treating. That makes three for Mohammed plus one mountain. Ta-ta."

Feeling the sweat breaking out on her brow, Daria growled and forced herself to blank out the vision of her mother, the manipulative matriarch, unstoppable at age eighty-nine. Refreshing her mental cache, she scrolled down and read the coroner's encrypted text message, the small, smudged screen jostling in her hands. Then she phoned him back. "It's me, Emilio," she said, "What've you got?"

Eight

Smoking a cigarette in the semi-darkness of Villa Glicine's lush garden, Lieutenant Italo Gambero was leaning his long, wispy, slightly sinister silhouette on the police cruiser. The unmarked gray special series BMW sports sedan sat sideways under the orange and olive trees lining the cobbled driveway of the villa, as if it had slid to a stop. The property appeared to be true to its name—*glicine* meaning wisteria in Italian. From ground level up, the front and side walls on both of the villa's two wide stories were cloaked by twining, sinuous wisteria vines dripping with delicately scented mauve grape-bunch clusters. Daria nosed the air blowing in the car window and found the scent divine, though she would not dare say so to either of her vulcanized lieutenants.

Joseph Gary's pair of Rhodesian ridgebacks had heard the police car approaching. They were busy barking, jumping, and snarling behind a six-foot chain-link fence. Gambero ground out the butt of his cigarette and saluted as Daria and Morbido stepped out of the Alfa Romeo and strode over. Even in the low light, she could see Gambero's thin black eyebrows arched high on his forehead, so high that his streaming, puckered red eyes seemed ready to pop out of his head. He looked as if he had been punched or scratched by sharp fingernails or both.

"Thank God you're here," he muttered, blowing his nose.

Daria glanced at Morbido, who bowed, swept his arm, and said, "After you, commissario."

The villa's heavy oaken door swung inwards. Standing on the threshold was Imelda Capurro, the Filipina housemaid married to Joe Gary's personal assistant. She wore an old-fashioned, frilly, powder-blue outfit. It looked to Daria at least one size too small for her. A toothsome woman of perhaps thirty—her age was hard to guess—Imelda dipped her head silently, her dark eyes not meeting theirs. No blush of fear or expression of nervousness marred her dusky cheeks or stiffened her smooth, muscular movements, Daria remarked, always fascinated by the nuances of human body language.

Imelda led the three DIGOS officers through a wide atrium, then down a long corridor. It was glassed in on one side and brightly lit by golden sconces shaped like torches. The floors were of colorful variegated marble. Beyond the windows lay an Olympic-size pool and a hidden patio clearly conceived to keep out prying eyes. It was hedged by closely planted eight-foot-tall oleanders blooming riotously in shades of white, pink, and blood red.

They stepped into an enclosed verandah hung with heavy chintz curtains woven and flecked with gold. The curtains were pulled closed, presumably to prevent paparazzi from seeing inside. The verandah was also overlit by golden torches. The light bounced off the golden legs of the crystal-topped coffee table and was picked up by the gold trim and gold-patterned upholstery of the outsized couches and armchairs ranged around the vast room. A pair of long-haired Persian cats, one white, the other black, sat on gold cushions on miniature throne-like chairs in one corner.

The combined scent of wisteria, citrus, and pittosporum filled Daria's nostrils. It was underlaid by the smell of cats and large dogs and overlaid by yet other scents—of a woman's powerful perfume and, Daria thought, lavender deodorizers hidden under the furniture, presumably by Imelda Capurro. The cumulative effect was overpowering. One after the other, Gambero, Morbido, and Daria sneezed. Gambero tried to speak but could only cough, his eyes streaming.

"Aromatherapy," he spluttered.

Imelda invited them to sit, left the room, and returned almost immediately followed by a tall, slim, remarkably buxom woman of middle age, wrapped in translucent golden veils, her fingers and neck sparkling with diamonds and gold. She teetered on golden high heels under a mass of coiled platinum blonde hair. The woman grimaced, frowned, and struck a pose, as if on a runway. She watched the police officers rise to their feet.

Had she been equipped with black hair, and had she been wearing black instead of gold haute couture clothing, Daria couldn't help thinking, Morgana Stella would look like the cat in the celebrated Chat Noir posters, her back unnaturally arched, perhaps in pique at seeing a woman police officer.

Morgana Stella's Trump Tower Miss Universe look evoked a starveling Slavic variation on Marilyn Monroe, Anita Ekberg, and Stormy Daniels—each on a bad day. The blue-tinted bulging contact lenses on her small, heavily mascaraed eyes seemed hard and dry. In her gestures and expressions, she did not convey a sense of grief, sadness, or anxiety, but rather of annoyance, anger, and arrogance.

"Which one of you is the commissioner?" she demanded of Daria and Morbido, waving them back onto the couches. Her voice was shrill, a penetrating soprano, her spoken Italian almost unaccented, except for the slurred double consonants. "I said specifically I wished to see the Questor or at least a commissario. And I demand to know what progress has been made. Have you found Joseph yet, and if not, why not?"

The dogs barked ferociously from somewhere behind the villa. A man's voice shouted at them to shut up. Daria waited a beat, then rose to her feet again, her cheeks coloring. "Signora Stella," she said with icy calm, "in my experience it is the role of the investigator to ask the questions. If you sincerely desire to aid in the search for Signor Gary, you will be kind enough to cooperate and provide the information essential to our effort."

"Are you suggesting I do not want Joseph to be found?" she shrilled. "That's preposterous. I have told your lieutenant here everything I know, over and over, and see what good it has done! You are forcing my hand. I will phone the Minister this minute."

Morbido and Gambero glanced at each other, their jaws tensing. Daria smiled poisonously. "Please do," she said. "I will be very happy to give him a progress report. However, you might prefer to speak with the Minister of Finance, whose operatives, la Guardia di Finanza, are working closely with us on our investigation and are eager to speak to you. They will be very interested to learn that Signor Gary has resided in Italy for the last two years and has not left the European Union in the last ten months, yet possesses no residency permit and, above all, does not declare or pay his taxes in Italy or anywhere else in the EU.

"Naturally," Daria continued, slowly and ominously, "you understand, Signora Stella, once Signor Gary is found alive and well, he will be able to resolve this deplorable situation without difficulty, perhaps with advice and encouragement from his personal friends at a variety of ministries. However, in case something has befallen him, his current illegal status will complicate the investigation and freeze for an open-ended period of time the probate period of his will. Anyone benefiting from Signor Gary's testamentary wishes will doubtless want to avoid such an unfortunate series of eventualities." She paused to gauge whether Morgana Stella was following her elliptical, bureaucratic phrasing.

"Indeed, signora," Daria began again, a dark, toxic liquid racing through her veins, "everyone in Signor Gary's household could very well be subject to prolonged scrutiny by more than one branch of the administrative and police authorities."

Barely concealed rage twisted Morgana Stella's remade face into a demonic doll mask. But with what was clearly a superhuman effort, she metamorphosed moments later into a golden bird of prey, perching on the arm of an overstuffed chair. "What do you want to know," she hissed at Daria, now transforming herself into a snake. "Imelda," she hissed again, "call Maurizio. Let's get this over with."

Nine

Was the deception willful? Daria thought so. Morgana Stella had proven singularly incapable of shining light on Joseph Gary's whereabouts or the means to find them. For reasons not yet apparent to her, Gary seemed to have dug a moat around his companion. Morgana Stella claimed to know nothing of his business dealings or his movements when not at home or with her and the dogs on their daily excursions. These consisted of shopping for designer clothes and accessories in Portofino and Santa Margherita, boating in the Riva, motoring in the Maserati, or lunching at the yacht club, Galleria Club, or Jardin Club in Genoa. They rarely entertained at home.

Gary had what seemed to be casual friendships everywhere, Stella claimed. She did not know his close friends or relatives and said she thought that he did not have any. To the best of her knowledge, she stated, Gary was an intensely private, elderly, well-off American and had no relations in Italy. She claimed to be surprised when told his birth name was Giuseppe Garibaldi, and that he had grown up in dire poverty twenty miles south of the villa in the mountains behind the Cinque Terre. Daria had

77

immediately asked whether they frequented the Cinque Terre and knew anyone in that area.

"Oh, we never go there," Stella had exclaimed, in earnest, at last, "but we were planning to visit the Cinque Terre tomorrow, for the first time."

Her claim that she did not know he was Italian was sufficiently farfetched, Daria thought. Morgana Stella also claimed she had never seen a will or spoken to Gary about a legacy. The commissioner listened, her face expressionless. She felt reasonably sure Stella was telling the truth, but not the whole truth. Wasn't it more probable the legacy had been paid in advance for services rendered? The Guardia di Finanza would have fun tracing this one, Daria said to herself. Where might the money trail lead? To Luxembourg, Belgium, Switzerland, or someplace farther afield? The Bahamas, Barbados, Libya? The best method would be to find Stella's family in Slovenia, then trace the remittances back to the source. But that would only happen if the Questor pushed for it.

With apprehension, and only after prolonged negotiations, Stella had conducted the three DIGOS agents into Joseph Gary's remarkably impersonal, maniacally tidy, almost entirely empty office area, ordering Maurizio and Imelda Capurro to follow them and video their every move using their smartphones. But nothing had been found. Joseph Gary, she reasoned, did his business by telephone and via encrypted text messaging. There were no note pads and no laptop. Someone someplace else, possibly an entire network of associates, did the heavy lifting for him, out of reach of the Italian and other European financial and tax authorities. There was only one way to find out anything about his activities: interrogate Gary, if he was still alive. Perhaps, as they hoped, the key to the embedded GPS dot in his Rolex would be found in the analogue note pad they had discovered in the Riva, or on his smartphone?

The only useful lead Stella had provided turned out to be half a clue. Gary's attorney resided in the Bahamas, she had said. He might know how to trace him, she had added. However, neither she nor Maurizio Capurro could provide the attorney's full name, address, or telephone number. "Joseph called him Don," Stella said peevishly. "That's all I ever knew. It was none of my business," she insisted, now speaking in a girlish Marylyn Monroe voice, no longer a snake or a bird of prey.

The din of the jumping, snapping, snarling, barking Rhodesian ridgebacks followed the police officers back to their cars. "Pity the burglar who tries to break in here," muttered Morbido.

"Ever read *The Hound of the Baskervilles*?" asked Gambero, unable to repress a deep yawn.

Morbido shook his jowls in reply. "I don't read unless I have to," he joked. "Commissario Vinci reads enough for all three of us."

Worn out by a long day's work and in desperate need of anti-histamines, Lieutenant Gambero asked to be relieved of duty. The pair of DIGOS cars followed each other down the highway until Gambero pulled over at the first pharmacy they found. He said he would drive back to headquarters on his own, taking the auto-strada turnpike direct from Rapallo to Genoa. The lieutenant had a young wife and an infant child. Daria knew the twelve- to four-teen-hour shifts routine in the service were hard on him.

Before leaving the Portofino Peninsula, Daria and Lieutenant Morbido stopped in the easternmost of Santa Margherita's two curving coves. There they wolfed down several slices of the local cheese focaccia. It was not as good here as in Recco, the capi-tal of Ligurian gastronomy, over the hills toward Genoa, Morbido said, providing Daria with a short history of the delicacy, while the cheese and olive oil dribbled down his large and now stubbly chin. Given the circumstances however, he had hastened to add, the focaccia they were eating seemed more than good enough.

The night air had cooled, but the sweat on Morbido's bulg-ing forehead still stood out, glistening in the florescent light of the seaside pizza joint. On the wide beach front sidewalk, under the motionless palm trees where they had parked the Alfa Romeo, Daria wondered out loud where Joseph Gary might be. Had he floated to the surface already, or was he somewhere else entirely, a captive or a corpse?

The steep hills up and down the curving, rugged Riviera twinkled with pinpoints of fire light. The smell of burning brush mingled with the floral scents wafting from the luxuriant gardens of the tony seaside resort towns that ran continuously for hundreds of miles along the arching coastline from Tuscany to France. Were they new fires, Daria wondered, or old fires that had flared up again from embers? But she was too tired to think it through. Not my table, she said to herself. To be continued. Tomorrow.

Except tomorrow was already today, now, this evening, and it was also yesterday, because time was a circle without beginning or end, she felt with sudden clarity. The continuum could not be over yet, she said to herself with a philosophical shrug of the shoulders. For one thing, she had agreed to meet the coroner, Emilio Bozzo, near the morgue on the way back to town. Like Willem Bremach earlier in the day, Bozzo had said he had things not only to *tell* her, confidentially, but to *show* her, urgently. He never spoke freely on the telephone.

This time Daria sat in the front passenger seat. It was a relief. She felt the difference in rank and social background melt away. Osvaldo Morbido happened to be one of the smartest, and, given the opportunity, funniest police inspectors she knew. Why had he been skipped over and never risen above the rank of lieutenant? Was it his politics or his looks? His manners? Was it because he lacked the most basic social graces?

She knew Morbido had little grasp of or interest in history and culture, for instance, and did not seem able to get beyond his family's blue-collar past. He had every reason to be proud of his father, she reflected, a steelworker and Communist union organizer at the giant Ansaldo steel mill and shipyards in the city's eastern suburbs. But the mill and shipyards were gone, the political party and union Morbido Senior had represented were moribund, and he, the father, Benedetto Morbido, was long dead. The 1970s were dead and gone, Daria told herself, glancing out of the windows at the magical nighttime view. Except they lived on in the hearts and minds of millions of men and women like Osvaldo Morbido, people forged during the Age of Ideology.

It struck her as right and fitting that she and Morbido had so far worked together in apolitical harmony. He never questioned her decision to join DIGOS, for example, a notoriously right-wing branch of the national police, when she clearly did not have right-wing tendencies. He had never asked her how she voted. Surely, he had read the abundant material available publicly about her father, Roberto Vinci. Yet Morbido never spoke of him to her, probably out of respect, she reasoned. Everyone knew what had befallen Roberto Vinci. A high-level government functionary, diplomat, and, it was claimed, a longtime intelligence agent, the dashing, mustachioed Roberto had spent the greater part of his career keeping tabs on Italy's Communist unions and left-wing political groupings while liaising with his virulently anti-Communist American and European counterparts. In other words, he had spied on the organization Morbido's father had represented from the shop floor.

On his last posting, undercover in Asia posing as a commercial attaché at the Ministry of Foreign Affairs, Roberto Vinci had been stabbed to death in his hotel room in Jakarta by an unknown assailant. The year was 1995, the year Daria had dropped out of Yale and moved home to be with her widowed mother. She blinked now at the view beyond the windows of the speeding Alfa Romeo, but also glanced inward. How far from the paternal tree had she fallen, after all? Though they had grown up on opposite sides of the spectrum, how different was she really from Osvaldo Morbido? They were both dedicated public servants, both idealists case hardened by decades on the force, and both wary of politics and an excess of self-questioning, self-doubt, and self-analysis.

As the car sped west through the heavily built-up suburbs of Genoa, Daria's phone rang. Again. And again. She did not recognize the number. No name was associated with it.

"Am I speaking with Colonel Vinci?" said a hesitant male voice, a light, musical tenor.

"Who is it?" Daria growled, instantly suspicious. "Who gave you this number?"

"Sergeant Gianni Giannini here, from Rapallo. Gigi, I mean Marshal Luigi De Filippo, said I should report to you."

"Ah, yes, good evening, Giannini. I am a captain, by the way, not a colonel. What did you find?" Daria sat upright and unconsciously straightened her pantsuit and rearranged her hair. She remembered Gianni Giannini's baby blue eyes and gentle smile, the smile of a Boy Scout leader, a grade-school teacher, a young father, a poet—not a traffic cop.

"It was strange, commissario capitano," Gianni Giannini said respectfully, "the hike up that hill behind the turnout where the bag was found is very, very steep and the trail overgrown. When I finally reached the top, there was no trace of fire and no heat from flames, but I saw a sparkling light and there were great clouds of smoke pouring out of the bunker, so I could not enter the shore battery complex, because of the smoke. I was forced to turn back. Apologies for taking so long to report to you. It has been a busy day."

Daria pondered this, tapping her lips. "That is interesting," she said. "Very interesting."

"I could accompany you there tomorrow, if the commissario capitano wishes," he added.

"Yes, that would be nice," she answered readily—too readily. "That is to say, it might be useful, sergeant. May I call you tomorrow morning, first thing, at this number, to arrange a meeting?"

"Sì, commissario," he said, "with pleasure."

"Good night, Sergeant Giannini," she said and disconnected, her heart beating faster than it should.

Glancing over, she caught a glimpse of Morbido's bullfrog grin. "Do you mind taking Corso Europa instead of the turnpike?" she asked, regaining her composure and willing away the heat in her cheeks. "There shouldn't be any traffic now going into the city."

Morbido assented silently, the grin by now uniting his large, pendulous earlobes.

When the Via Aurelia coast highway widened into the Corso Europa four-lane expressway, on the eastern edge of suburban Nervi, Lieutenant Morbido accelerated into the center lane reserved for buses and emergency vehicles. Determined to drive the image of Gianni Giannini out of her visual cortex, Daria began compiling a mental checklist of what she knew, what she didn't, and what steps had to be taken next.

There were times when she felt like an organist with both hands and feet on the pedals and keyboard, simultaneously reading and playing the music, and pulling out and pushing in the stops. At other times she felt like the reluctant young Yale premed student she had been a quarter century before, making up lists and methodically moving down them, her own predigital pull-down menus.

Whichever metaphor she chose, mastering her current task list felt daunting. Unsure why, she found herself dreading the impending encounter with Emilio Bozzo, the coroner. Was it because the bodies had been butchered into so many pieces? Was it because it reminded her of the remains of her own father? Roberto Vinci had not only been stabbed to death. His attacker had then hacked him apart, packed him into suitcases, and dumped the suitcases in the river. To this day, she still did not understand why she and not one of her elder brothers had been made to leave school, fly out to meet her mother, and identify the remains. Why hadn't she insisted one of them handle the emergency, or at least come with her? What was it that made her brothers and so many of the males in her life behave like princelings surrounded by female attendants?

Willing away the memory, Daria moaned unintentionally, then covered her mouth and pretended the moan was a yawn.

"Okay," she said with more emphasis than she had intended, breaking the silence that had filled the passenger compartment. "Tonight, in theory, I will find out more about the bags and mutilated bodies," she continued, raising her fingers to use them as counters. "Tomorrow morning, we have Gary's note pad and his attorney and the GPS dot. We have the Guardia di Finanza and Gary's tax status. We have the sites of the fires, and the airport in Albenga where the water bombers are based. We have people representing the Veterans Administration and the Ministry of Culture for the commemorative ceremony at Villa Migone for the anniversary of the liberation, and we need to brief them before the Questor's speech the day after tomorrow. And we have the scuba divers and metal detectors and the small task of finding Gary's body, unless he is still alive. Then we have to make sense of it all."

"That's it?" Morbido croaked ironically.

"What's on your wish list?"

He chuckled. "Well, you've got the fires, with Sergeant Adonis, and you're the one who speaks English, so you've got the note pad and the call to the attorney in Barbados or wherever he is, unless you want someone in Rome to handle it. That leaves the Guardia di Finanza, Albenga, Villa Migone, and the divers and Carabinieri and the body. Gambero can take his pick. A breeze."

"Deal," she said. She pulled a leather portfolio from underneath the front passenger seat and flipped it open. Reaching back, she picked up the Joseph Gary file from the rear seat. She opened it and carefully slid in the sheet of handwritten notepaper and the aviation magazine Willem Bremach had given her that morning.

That morning? It seemed a week ago. She explained to Morbido what the two documents were and asked him to make a copy of Bremach's notes and the flagged magazine article about seaplanes, scan and email them to her, and take the original with him to Albenga, or give them to Italo Gambero if he needed them to identify the water bombers Bremach had spotted. An air show was under way, she explained, or may have just ended, she wasn't sure and was too tired to google it now. Someone at the small regional airport set among the artichoke fields of Albenga would be able to answer questions about water bombers, and detail where they had come from, who had flown them yesterday, where exactly they had been operating, and when. "It's a very long shot," she said, "but crazier things have happened."

Morbido assented. He cleared his throat and seemed reluctant to speak. "I picked up a novel once," he began, taking her by surprise.

"You did what?"

"Yes, occasionally I read novels. It was maybe twenty years ago? Something by a Canadian author. Translated into Italian. It took place in Canada, on a lake. I can't remember much of anything about it except that a swimmer is scooped up by one of those Canadair planes."

Daria swiveled in her seat and stared at him, astonished. A smile stretched her lips wide. "That's excellent, Osvaldo," she exclaimed, pausing to study his flushed face. "That must be what my godfather meant. I'll ask him. Maybe this is some kind of crazy copycat crime and that's what he was hinting at. Willem is amazing. He's terrifying in a way." She paused again, reluctant to press her luck with further questions. But Morbido's words had reminded her of something else Bremach had said. "Do you remember anything about the Brindisi Bronzes?"

Morbido shook his head. "The Riace Bronzes I remember," he said. "I saw an illustrated book about them. Beautiful craftsmanship. Ancient Greek, not Roman, I think."

Revived and curious, Daria had her phone out and was tapping the screen, then scrolling as the car raced up the last hill into central Genoa. "Here it is," she said. "The Province of Brindisi website says..." Her eyes scanned the entry. She paused at the section titled "The Archaeological Dig." "So," she summarized. "The archeologists think the sculptures were either substandard or too broken to be fixed, and they were being shipped to a foundry to be melted when the ship transporting them sank."

Morbido shook his jowls in bafflement. "I don't get it."

"Not important," she said. But now she understood. "Incinerated," she muttered, "cremation for bronze, except with bronze it melts, you can recycle it, you see, and with human body parts you can't, unless you're Doctor Frankenstein."

Morbido glanced at her warily. "If you say so," he remarked. "Sometimes you make my head ache."

"I'm getting out here," Daria said, pointing.

A small, rusted sign a few yards off Corso Europa indicated the coroner's office and morgue. *Camere mortuarie*, it read, *Via Giovanni Battista Marsano*.

Morbido tapped the brakes, put on the swirling roof lights and emergency blinkers, and pulled the Alfa Romeo over to the right, nudging it up and onto the sidewalk. Thanking him and jumping out, Daria walked swiftly the remaining half block to the meeting place. She could already see the coroner, Emilio Bozzo, at a two-top table in the café, alone by the window, facing her way, his lean figure bent over a pile of papers. Bozzo was too old to be putting in such long hours, she said to herself. But he was unattached, an old bachelor, and dedicated to his career, like Morbido, like herself. She had long sensed she and Bozzo shared more philosophically and even politically than met the eye. A hidden world view, perhaps, a hidden avenging angel agenda?

Usually inured to blight and misery, as Daria approached the café, she wondered wearily why all of a sudden tonight she was noticing how cracked, pitted, and remarkably filthy the sidewalk of Corso Europa was. The condition of the area fronting what had to be the most hideous, badly built, and run-down set of apartment buildings in the city was worthy of a war-torn Third World country, she said to herself. Tilting her head up, she recognized the buildings as notorious tenements. Large billboards on the facades advertised cheap rooms for short-term rent. A foyer for immigrants kept two of the apartment houses full year-round, despite the appalling noise and suffocating air pollution from the expressway.

It was a cursed spot. Behind the apartment complex spread the grounds of Genoa's main public hospital, San Martino. Among ruins left over from the Second World War rose the looming, dark silhouette of the crematorium's chimney. From some of the apartments in the complex, you could reach out and almost touch it. She shivered despite the mildness of the night and trotted the last twenty yards to the café.

Ten

There were good reasons why Daria had agreed to meet Emilio Bozzo not in his clinical office at the morgue but nearby, outside the hospital grounds, on the corner of Corso Europa, at what regulars jokingly called the "Orange Nightmare." The café had been given its nickname for the remarkably unsettling color scheme of the walls, last painted circa 1980, and the torturous orange plastic bucket seating. A student hangout, the Orange Nightmare overflowed morning, noon, and night when classes were in session. Anxious future health care professionals, fagged-out nurses and orderlies, and even full-fledged doctors desperate for a change of scenery from the clinical white of the hospital to the grimy orange of the café loitered outside, smoking and littering. Others crowded three deep to the bar. But today was a public holiday in Genoa, the start of the commemorations of the Insurrection of 1945. The long weekend or "bridge," had begun. There were no students. The café was nearly empty.

The establishment's only objective attraction Daria could discern was its strategic location flanking not only the crematorium, mortuary, autopsy, and anatomy facilities, but also Genoa's municipal school of medicine. The threadbare premises of these state-run institutions clustered along the same dreary pot-holed street edging the vast, unkempt, unmade, premodern San Martino hospital grounds, the city's largest and busiest.

Over the desultory scream of sirens raging like madmen in the night, Bozzo rose to limply shake Daria's hand, then plopped back down into his chair, visibly exhausted. "It's self-service," he said, his voice raspy. He made a move to rise again to get her a drink, but Daria gestured him down, suddenly feeling spry compared to the coroner. She took a bottle of sparkling water from a nearby standing fridge, then sat across from him at his table, studying his haggard face. Silently, warily, glancing around the empty terrace room where they sat, Bozzo handed her a white A4 envelope. He watched her open it and flip through the contents. She stared with a pained expression at a series of disturbing photographs and suddenly wondered how she had wound up doing what she did and how much longer she could stand it.

"Taken in the morgue, two years ago," Bozzo whispered. "We record everything that comes through." Then he touched the screen of his phone lying on the table. An image appeared. He rotated the phone so she could see it. "Taken two hours ago, also in the morgue. Compare the two."

Daria put the print next to the smartphone and glanced back and forth. The print was blurred and not a close-up. It showed a cadaver from the waist to the head. She looked at the digital image again. It showed a severed arm, a man's arm, judging by the development of the muscles. That arm had once belonged to that body. The incisions made on the arm by intentional scarring were unmistakable.

"Scarification," Bozzo whispered. Then he made a logical jump that Daria at first found hard to follow. "Imagine what this will do to medical science in Italy," he said. "Once certain people in the government and the Church get ahold of this story, no more bodies will be given for science, no more dissections will take place in Italian universities, no more cremation will be possible.

We are heading back to the 1930s. They are already banging the Bible the way the Americans do. What's next?"

Daria did not know what was next. But she had an inkling and did not like it. She pursed her lips tighter and nodded her head.

What she did know with exactitude was what Emilio Bozzo meant without saying it. He was pleading with her to help him keep the details of the case quiet. To avoid scandal. The beleaguered hospital, medical school, and morgue do not need further knocks, his stale, panting breath and glistening brow told her. The budget had already been slashed by the latest incoming reactionary government. Everyone knew that. Privatization was the mantra. Politicians and the wealthy went to private clinics, not state-run facilities. Any excuse to run public services into the ground and outsource, take universal medical coverage away and break up the welfare state, that was what was next. But did he really expect her to assist in a cover-up?

"Let me tell you how it happened," he began in what was evidently a goodwill gesture. "Because of the long weekend, everything is shut up tight except the emergency room and the main hospital. I got the super to let me into the medical school on the pretext that I needed to check the cold rooms and certain cadavers. They know me of course. I also teach here."

"Of course."

"Four things are worth noting, commissario. First, I was able to go in and out without a key. Anyone can. All you have to do is enter by the tunnel from the Institute of Anatomy, and probably any of the other adjoining, communicating buildings including the hospital—of that I am certain. You can also lift the barrier by hand and drive into and out of the parking lot behind the morgue. That barrier is supposed to be locked but never is. The lock broke two years ago or more.

"Second, two of the five cold chambers at the medical school used for storing bodies and body parts are broken and therefore are sealed shut. They call it 'deferred maintenance.' Except one of them wasn't sealed shut. It was being used in violation of all health norms and statutes. I found it unlocked, the door ajar. It was filled with the year-old body parts from the dissection labs scheduled for incineration. These were body parts that weren't incinerated because of scheduling problems, problems with the incinerator last week, a chronic backlog, plus the long weekend.

"Third, I discovered that, because of budgetary restrictions, the security team in the hospital now also guards the adjoining medical school and morgue. It does not have a videotape or whatever it's called nowadays covering the period last night when the events in question happened. Why? Because they only have enough digital storage space in the system to keep data for twelve hours. Twelve hours. Can you believe it?

"One of them remembers seeing a disposal crew come in at around three in the morning, but he isn't sure of the exact time. He had actually been asleep and only woke up because he had to use the men's room. So on the way back from the toilets, he glanced up, and on the cameras in the cold room area, he saw two men in hospital whites with the usual white head coverings and white cloth masks. They were removing body parts from the broken cold room, dropping them in plastic bags. He didn't think it was unusual and did not alert anyone. The disposal people come at all hours of the day or night, and, as I say, there was a backlog and a terrible stench, because the cold rooms were full and two are broken.

"The security guard toggled to the outside cameras and saw an unmarked van, its doors open. He assumed it was a substitute removals service working during the holiday break. Who would steal rotten, chopped-up monkeys, and pieces of John and Jane Doe?"

Daria realized she had been nodding her head the whole time, like one of those spring-loaded toy dogs placed on the package tray of a car. Her neck ached. She spoke to Bozzo in an undertone, telling him to avoid the press. Use one of the tunnels into the basement of the hospital when coming and going and leave from the emergency room, she suggested. It's always crowded. There is safety in numbers. Wear a hat and sunglasses. Don't let anyone catch your eye. If you are known to follow the same route habitually, change your habits and change your route. Don't answer the phone without screening calls. Don't talk to anyone else in the police department or the Carabinieri—call me first.

"So," she said slowly, whispering now like Bozzo, "just to be clear, the human body parts we found in those bags were mixed with parts of monkeys used for studying dissection, and everything in the three bags originated here and was scheduled for incineration?"

Bozzo rubbed his eyes and blinked. "Yes. Can you stand to see it again?"

Daria hesitated, then dipped her head, nodding slowly. She knew her nod concealed a lie and that in all likelihood she would lose the focaccia and sparkling water that were keeping her on her feet. But she also knew she had to see the evidence.

What had clinched his suspicions, Bozzo said, as they kicked their way through mounds of cigarette butts and piles of trash, walking down the dog's-leg street past the medical school to the morgue, was what everyone else called "the tattoo" on the severed right arm. It wasn't actually a tattoo, he explained, but rather a specific form of scarification practiced by certain Sub-Saharan tribes. He had rarely seen it at the morgue and only once in that area of the upper arm. In life, it had been a very strong and inky, almost purple-black arm.

Later, Bozzo had been able to confirm that the body of the African was that of an illegal immigrant who had died of natural causes, from extreme privation and exposure. The body had passed through the morgue two years ago. Like many other unclaimed corpses, after autopsy and a lengthy process of investigation to try to find its identity, it was sent to the medical school. Under normal circumstances, it should have been incinerated a year ago—one year was the statutory time limit for scientific uses of cadavers. But because it was such an unusual specimen, at Bozzo's request a meeting of the medical committee had been called. It decided the scarified arm should be preserved in embalming fluid and used for teaching purposes for an additional year, until the state of disaggregation of the tissues became too extreme.

"It was at the bottom on the third bag," Bozzo explained. "I didn't see it until I was back here. Most of the other parts in the bags I had never encountered before," he said. "They probably came from other regions of Italy and wound up here at the request of the medical school. Unclaimed corpses do a lot of traveling in this crazy country."

It was not the first time Daria had been inside the morgue. In some sections, the walls were tiled in white floor to ceiling. In others, they were clad in stainless steel. The air was cold. A sour smell like the smell of a butcher shop, no matter how scrupulous the butcher, clung to everything. One side of the long, narrow room where the cadavers were kept was lined by a double row of refrigerated steel cells. They looked like the giant sliding drawers in a high-tech industrial kitchen.

Emilio Bozzo tugged at a handle, and one of the drawers, measuring about a yard square, slid open. Arrayed on layers of thick, disposable, absorbent cotton fiber paper were some of the body parts from the bags. Even though Bozzo had lowered the conservation temperature to half a degree above freezing, the stench was still strong.

"Starving, desperate, homeless Africans all look alike to most people around here," Bozzo sighed. "But this time, that couple from the farmhouse up near the turnout were right. It was the man who slept under the viaduct, except they got the timing wrong. This man died two years ago. Who knows how many others have come and gone since then?"

"So, he was not North African, he was black African? What about that head I saw? Was that his?"

Bozzo grunted. "No, that was someone else. I found a photo of that body with the head attached. But to return to the arm..." Vinci followed the tip of the pen Bozzo unclipped from his shirt.

"Like I said," he observed, "the scarification is unmistakable." He slid the drawer back in. "I don't think we have photos of the monkeys, so you'll have to trust me on that. If either one of us starts phoning around trying to identify the other human body parts," he added, pausing to swallow hard, "everyone in the country will learn what happened. I can guarantee you that all of the unfortunate human beings in those bags died at least one year ago and passed through the dissection labs here. This is not a case of murder, commissario. It's a case of someone—some group, perhaps—for some reason, trying to use these poor unclaimed people for political purposes, unless it's a sick hoax, a hazing rite of some kind."

Bozzo slid another door open, let Daria glance at the arms, legs, and heads, then shoved the drawer back in. "I would like to send what's left of these people to the crematorium right now. That would be the ethical thing to do. But I can't and I won't because I realize your investigation might need them as evidence. What I will do is keep things under wraps on my end for as long as I can, in hopes you can figure out what is going on and bring the body-snatchers to justice. If you do that swiftly, the impact of the theft and the sacrilegious treatment of the remains will be dampened. If the case drags on, and the press gets ahold of the details, it will be catastrophic to the state of medical science in Italy."

Tired and depressed, the pathologist accompanied her down another tunnel and out of the morgue to a parking lot at the side of the building. They shook hands. Feeling ill at ease, she turned to him and asked a final question. It was ridiculous but it had been nagging at her ever since she'd seen Willem Bremach. "Do you know precisely how many human and monkey body parts were in the bags?" she asked. The coroner seemed perplexed. He thought for a minute or two before answering. "I inventoried and labeled each one, just in case," he said, glancing wearily at his smartphone. "Unless I'm misremembering, there were nearly thirty. Why do you ask?"

"Nearly thirty? How many, precisely?"

Bozzo hesitated, glanced at the screen, then said, "Twenty-seven, unless you count certain jointed parts separately, in which case there are thirty-three."

Blanching despite herself, Daria mumbled something inaudible about the Brindisi Bronzes, nodded, thanked him again, and walked swiftly away across the parking lot, her heart thumping and the hair prickling on her arms.

Eleven

I t was a neighborhood suffused with pain and suffering. As Daria strode through the parking lot, she recognized the somber surroundings from having been to the morgue countless times in the past six years, since her transfer to Genoa from Rome, a change about which she still had mixed feelings. She had escaped her mother and a dead-end relationship but had left her favorite city and her childhood friends behind, possibly forever.

Leaving the parking lot, she tested the barrier, lifting it easily with her bare hands and confirming it was unlocked, as Bozzo had reported. Anyone in the know could drive in and out at any time of day or night.

Glancing across the narrow, tree-lined street beyond the rusty fences encircling the morgue, Daria noticed for the first time a small florist's shop. Its front was almost entirely masked by parked cars and the spreading branches of old trees. That explained why she had not seen it on previous visits. The shop looked as if it had been in business for a century. A light was on inside, the only light in the street. Feeling like a powerless moth, Daria floated toward it. She peered through the window, then found herself knocking on the door. It swung open under the pressure of her rapping knuckles. She stepped in, light-headed, stretching out an arm to steady herself. The scent of lilies rose up. An elderly woman sat hidden in the closet-sized room, bent double over a pile of papers, writing in an accounting ledger.

"Good evening," the woman said without looking up, her voice solemn, "may I help you?"

Daria hesitated. She had not meant to come in. Did she want to question the woman? About what? She suddenly realized she did not want to know whether the woman had seen the van of the body-snatchers. She wished the van did not exist, that the case would go away, that she could wake up in her old bed in her mother's old apartment in Rome. "Please forgive me," Daria said softly, "I should not have disturbed you."

"You haven't disturbed me," the woman answered quietly. "It's life that disturbs us. Then it's over. Then we rest." She stood, shuffled over, stared for a disconcertingly long time through milky gray cataracts into Daria's hazel-green eyes, then plucked a lily from a vase. She handed it to Daria in a strange, mystical silence.

Startled, Daria snapped out of what felt like a trance. Taking the flower, she whispered her baffled thanks and quietly shut the rickety door behind her.

As she stood under the thick cover of branches, Daria felt tears filling her tired, burning eyes. She wiped them away, then sniffed at the intoxicating sweetness of the lily.

The night air was cool and clean and tonic. Taking a deep breath, Daria considered whether to pick up a taxi at the hospital's emergency room or walk home. It might take an hour or more on foot, she knew. But she could continue researching along the way and also clear her head. Her legs made the decision for her.

Pausing to nose the lily again, Daria puzzled over how to delay reporting the details of the theft of the body parts. She could sleep on it. That would buy her six to eight hours. At the very least, she could think things through as she strode across town toward her apartment. Part of her wished she could click her heels and be safe at home, her new home, her impregnable citadel.

Home? It was a cramped, impractical crow's nest of a studio apartment in a centuries-old building, a hulking, haunted reconverted fortress-tower astride the eleventh-century castellated walls of the city. But she had come to love it, even though the neighborhood was at best transitional. In the last two years, the area had become unappealingly trendy, an edgy place of dark shadows and strong smells only recently pried away from the drug dealers, prostitutes, and traffickers of migrants.

Yes, she said to herself, recognizing that she was more than tired, yes, a long, vigorous walk will do me good. She knew it would. Fear was not an issue. Daria had never feared her fellow humans. When young, she had trained as a gymnast, kick-boxer, and practitioner of Okinawan karate. She was also armed with a police ordnance pistol and was a very good shot.

Striding down the verdant zigzags of Via Giovanni Battista Marsano, past the Soviet-style postwar housing projects and into the valley below, two shop signs on the same premodern corner caught her eye. One advertised a trattoria serving home-cooked Ligurian specialties such as pasta al pesto at affordable prices. The other offered the services of a funeral home. She hoped a thick wall separated the two and the kitchen was not shared.

Jogging left on the nondescript Via Donghi, a residential street at the bottom of the hill, her eye was caught again, this time by an electric votive candle flickering on a tall, ugly modern building. She paused, glancing around to make sure no one was watching, then placed the lily in a wire flower rack below a commemorative plaque.

There were dozens, perhaps hundreds, of similar street-corner shrines and plaques in Genoa and up and down the Italian Riviera. Each recalled the heroism of a partisan shot by the Fascists or Nazis. The numbers of dead seemed daunting, even by the colossal standards of World War Two.

Numbers brought her mind back to the business at hand. Were the criminals who had stolen the body parts college pranksters, or did they belong to some crazy cabalistic Catholic group, adepts of numerology, she wondered? Twenty-seven was three times nine, she said to herself, three times three times three, and the number two added to the number seven made nine, as Willem Bremach had joked. Had he *joked*? Thirty-three was another of those sacred numbers, she knew, the age of Christ crucified but also two threes set side by side. Daria shook her head. Nonsense, it had to be a coincidence, or some kind of prank.

Still thinking of numbers, but reviewing the coroner's chronology in her mind now, she turned right on another apparently banal street, Via Giovanni Torti, and began reconstructing the events of the previous night as accurately as she could.

The bakery van is stolen from Quarto dei Mille at some point between 2:00 and 2:30 a.m., she told herself, guesstimating. It arrives at approximately 3:00 a.m. at the medical school's shipping dock. Two people are in it—presumably males, but since they wore white smocks, hats, and masks and there's no video footage, that cannot be assumed.

The perpetrators fill the plastic bags with twenty-seven or thirty-three body parts, she continued, depending on how you count them, and load the bags into the van, presumably between 3:00 and 3:30 a.m. They follow Via Giovanni Battista Marsano down the hill, jog left on Via Donghi, not respecting the fifty yards or so of one-way street, because, after all, who would be watching at that early an hour in the morning? Then they go right on Via Giovanni Torti, drive four blocks, and reverse the van down Via San Fruttuoso, a blind alleyway fronting Villa Migone.

Daria picked up her pace. In five minutes, she had reached the dark, leafy alleyway footing the hilly park of the magnificent Renaissance-period Villa Imperiale, now a public library, and its neighbor, the smaller but no less historic Villa Migone.

At the end of the alleyway, by the traffic barrier, she told herself, coming to a halt now, the thieves stop to drop the bag of body parts at the base of the caretaker's house flanking the gates to Villa Migone. Their target is a plaque on the wall of the gate house commemorating the end of World War Two in Italy—a plaque, she now saw, that is dirty, encrusted with moss, and unlit. Daria sighed audibly. Where had the reverence gone for the heroes of that war and the founding of a modern, secular, democratic republic?

Staring up, scrutinizing the marble plaque in the low light, Daria tried to decipher the pompous verbiage lauding the war's heroes. So, the treaty ending hostilities had been signed here? Yes. That made perfect sense. She looked through the ornate, wrought-iron gateway up the steep driveway to the isolated villa.

To her overwrought mind, there was something magical about the mottled light and intertwining branches that made an archway over the mossy pavement. It seemed impossible such a place could lie hidden among the city's blighted clutter of high-rise, blistered housing projects and battered, badly built postwar apartment complexes. How could any planning commission have allowed low-income projects to be placed here, she wondered, their massive cubist shapes cutting off Villa Migone from the city and a view of the sea? But she knew the answer. It was a five-letter word starting with "M" and ending in "a," with "afi" sandwiched between.

The Mafia was not the whole story, she also knew. More than half of Genoa had been destroyed by five years' worth of Allied bombing raids and naval barrages. When the war had ended in 1945, real estate speculation had raged like the wildfires now destroying the region's hinterlands. Reconstruction was the mantra. Quality and aesthetics went out the window. Anything would do.

As she turned to leave, a pair of powerful floodlights attached to the security cameras on the driveway flashed on. Shielding her eyes, Daria spontaneously stepped up to the video intercom and spoke clearly.

"Commissioner Daria Vinci, DIGOS." From an inner pocket, she produced a badge and held it up to the camera lens.

"How may I help you?" croaked a voice, the voice of an elderly man, Daria guessed.

"Forgive me for troubling you," she said, "I merely wished to see the premises from the outside in order to form an idea of how many agents to send over the day after tomorrow, during the commemorative ceremony, should that prove necessary."

The voice made reassuring noises through the intercom. It asked if she wanted to come in and familiarize herself with the villa and grounds.

Blinded by the floodlights, Daria blinked and listened carefully to the man's accent, his manner of speech and choice of words. He spoke like an aristocrat, not a gatekeeper or superintendent or security guard. She guessed he must be one of the villa's tenants—an owner, possibly a member of the Migone family.

"Will you be joining us this evening?" the man inquired in his grave, vibrating voice. "You are accompanying the Questor to dinner, I assume?"

Daria drew a sharp breath. "My apologies," she said, "I was not aware Questor Lomelli-Centauri was expected here tonight. Mine is a routine security check, given the events of the day, about which you will have heard, no doubt, the lamentable discovery of the bag in front of your gate, and the heightened political tensions since the elections. We anticipate a rally or protest march on April 25th."

"No need to apologize," said the voice, "you are doing your duty. May I help you in any other way?"

"No, no thank you. Again, I apologize. Good evening to you."

Striding away, Daria felt the tingling sensation of having narrowly escaped something. It filled her with apprehension, causing her to walk even faster than usual.

A unit of local Polizia di Stato sat in a van wedged into the mouth of the alleyway. They had been called, no doubt, in anticipation of the Questor's arrival for dinner. Recognizing each other, the officers on duty gave Daria salutes that struck her as insubordinately slack. She nodded back disapprovingly and continued on her way.

For the Questor and the millions of right-wing Italians like him, was April 25th a *celebration* or a *commemoration*? A sad remembrance and reminder of the end of a lost war, the end of Fascism and authoritarian rule, or a joyful date marking the dawn of democracy? Daria knew the answer and it troubled her.

She paused on the corner of Via Giovanni Torti to recap, returning in her mind to the chronology she had begun earlier. So, where was I? The security cameras of Villa Migone pick up the van and pair of men dropping the first bag onto the mud at the bottom of the driveway below the plaque. The body-snatchers then retrace their route. Instead of turning left on Via Donghi, they continue up the hill until they reach the expressway. They drive east approximately five miles, taking fifteen to twenty minutes, exiting in the suburbs at Nervi. Then they leave the second bag of body parts under the commemorative plaque on the corner building facing the traffic circle, where Via Oberdan intersects with Via Felice Gazzolo. At this point, it is 4:14 a.m.—we know that from the security camera footage from Nervi.

Daria walked slowly west toward her apartment, pondering, the chronology coming together in her mind and beginning to make sense. After dropping the second bag, she said to herself, the body-snatchers take the on-ramp back onto Corso Europa, leaving Nervi and heading toward Rapallo. Almost immediately, the expressway narrows, turning into the two-lane, roller-coaster Via Aurelia coast highway. At some point before reaching Rapallo, probably before entering the tunnel in Ruta, approximately eight miles southeast of Nervi, they turn left and follow Highway SP31 to Santa Maria del Campo.

Why would they do that?, she asked herself aloud. The answer was obvious. To avoid driving into downtown Rapallo, where they might encounter a random roadside blockade by the Carabinieri or be picked up by security cameras on the various public buildings, banks, and other commercial real estate downtown. Once beyond the tiny hamlet and church of Santa Maria del Campo, they cross the valley under the autostrada turnpike, then drive east into the hills, depositing the third bag on the muddy turnout below the Nazi machine gun nest where she had parlayed with Marshal Gigi De Filippo and Sergeant Gianni Giannini. By then it's about 5:15 a.m.

The final leg takes the conspirators down the hill and into central Rapallo, where they ditch the van in the alley by the public bathrooms flanking the train station, at some point before six. Either they are met by accomplices, possibly in a car, or, if they are amateurs, they take a taxi, and we will soon have them. Other possible exit strategies are, one, they get on a train, which makes sense given their choice of the drop site, or, two, they walk into Rapallo and disappear, or, three, they take some other means of transportation they have left ahead of time: two motorcycles, for instance, or two cars, or even two bicycles. Another, remote, possibility is they live in Rapallo and simply go home.

What about the white clinical outfits they were wearing?, she asked herself. Are they still wearing them? Have they dumped them along the way, along the Via Aurelia or up in the hills?

As Daria walked across a wide, animated square not far from the railway viaduct, scores of local residents sat out on benches amid refreshment stands selling cold drinks and ice cream. She paused to watch a motorcade of unmarked police cars approach then turn and drive in the direction she had just come from. She recognized the cars but could not see the drivers or passengers through the deeply tinted windows. The Questor, she whispered to herself. Why is Carlo Alberto Lomelli-Centauri III dining at Villa Migone tonight? A rehearsal dinner? Rehearsing what? Perhaps he is a personal friend of the Migone family?

Shrugging the tension out of her shoulders as she walked across the gritty city, she added new elements to her mental laundry list. She needed to accomplish the following: thorough checks of the Rapallo train station security system, if there was one, the ticketing machines, the surveillance cameras in downtown Rapallo and anywhere else along the van's route. Surely, the white clinical outfits would have been thrown into a ravine, a dumpster, or a trash can somewhere? Would the trash have been picked up? It was a holiday weekend. Could the trash be checked in time, before it was taken to the dump and incinerated?

These routine checks could be entrusted to the reinforcements coming from La Spezia and Savona. Once home she would email HQ. An officer on night duty would put the machinery in motion. She needed to reserve Lieutenants Morbido and Gambero for the crucial, strategic tasks.

More important was the question of who and why. Who were the body-snatchers? What was their motive? Was it to get the government and Church up in arms over the treatment of unclaimed corpses and monkeys presumably used for experiments or dissection? Was it to stir up animal rights activists? Or denounce the return of Fascism? Or halt the invasion of Italy by illegal immigrants, while simultaneously equating them with monkeys? To decry the lack of funding for public services, from the mortuary and medical school to public safety and the security infrastructure?

She stopped at a red light on the city's broad, straight main thoroughfare, Via Venti Settembre. What if it wasn't any of the above? What if the bags were a ruse, a diversionary tactic? In that case, to cover what? The kidnapping or murder of Joseph Gary? Why put them in front of commemorative plaques where they were sure to be seen? Was there a wartime connection? That seemed unlikely. Gary would have been a teenager during the war. But Willem Bremach had also been young and an active participant. What had Gary done, and why had he renounced his Italian citizenship after fleeing right after the war to Canada then America?

Questions, questions, questions, she said to herself, darting along streets laid out centuries ago then rebuilt after the devastation of the Second World War. Each question was an island. What she needed were answers—at least one or two answers.

With them, she could build bridges and move from island to island, getting nearer to the truth.

A familiar refrain sprang to mind. Might this be the doing of the Honorable Society, alias Cosa Nostra, 'Ndrangheta, la Camorra, la Mano Nera, la Mafia—none of which were honorable, all of which were murderous, the antithesis of justice, unless you considered summary justice and frontier justice, revenge and vendetta, legitimate forms of justice?

The self-styled avengers typically affiliated with these criminal groups had memories as long as their proverbial knives, though nowadays guns were their weapon of choice. Their modus operandi was nearly always the same. They could wait months, years, even decades to settle a score. The more she thought of it, the more she felt sure the gruesome body parts and attention-grabbing kidnapping or murder of Joseph Gary Baldi smacked of one of the families of organized crime.

Yet in all the years she had been stationed on the Riviera, she had rarely had contact with them outside the flourishing realm of human trafficking. That was a growth industry, but one unlikely to have involved a man of Gary's caliber and wealth—unless... unless smuggling humans was merely one part of a more complex mechanism, a form of payment in kind or barter. She shook her head, unable to join the dots. Morgana Stella certainly looked like a Mafioso's moll, she reflected, and Maurizio Capurro was the archetype of the small-time mobster. They had even branded him by snipping off his trigger finger.

Daria's legs were aching by the time she reached the cobbled ramp tilting up from the turn-of-the-century section of town into the medieval core of Genoa. On her right she passed the Casa di Colombo, the unlikely stone-and-brick hovel where Christopher Columbus had supposedly been born or grown up, she couldn't remember which. Just beyond and behind the tumbledown house rose the reconstructed medieval cloister of Sant'Andrea. Its pale, weathered marble jigsaw of stones looked like upended bones thrown down on a card table by some otherworldly hand.

Looming gloomily over everything were the tall, twin cren-
ellated towers of Porta Soprana, the upper gate of this ancient
Oz, its mouth gaping wide and seemingly wriggling with human
bodies. They were the bodies, she now recognized, of the tireless
party people who had taken over the neighborhood, keeping it
awake until dawn day in, day out, despite police raids, fines, and
attacks by irate neighbors.

The towers of Porta Soprana had already been three or four
hundred years old when Columbus had sailed the ocean blue in
the year 1492, then sailed the deep blue sea in the year 1493.

The ditty became an earworm lodged in Daria's exhausted
mind. If he could return to life, she thought, Columbus, a bigot
and reactionary even by the abysmal standards of his day, would
doubtless hate his old neighborhood now. It was a handsome part
of town and sizzling with atmosphere but has been utterly dena-
tured, transformed into a playground for spoiled bobos with no
respect for the law.

Wending her way past the city gate then farther up and to
the west, then up again still higher, and higher, through teeming,
twisting alleyways an arm-span wide, past crowds of drunken tren-
dies, fashionistas, and foodistas milling and dancing in the streets,
she entered a quiet maze of even narrower alleys and reached
the refuge of her building. Unlocking the heavy back door, she
crossed a courtyard into the main foyer, emptied the contents of
her neglected mailbox into her arms, and began trudging up the
165 stairs to her seventh-floor walk-up aerie.

Similarly obsessed by secrecy, in Paris, nineteenth-century
novelist Honoré de Balzac had chosen his unlikely lair in the Passy
neighborhood for many of the same reasons. Like Balzac's, Daria's
building possessed two entrances, one of them known only to the
tenants. This secret back door gave onto multiple easy escape
routes down unlit back alleys.

Flinging open the French windows in the airless apartment's
living room area, Daria stood on the stone balcony breathing
deeply and gazing over the crazy crumpled quilt of her adopted

city. Its dozens of hills rose steeply, plunging into the sea amid a chaos of puckering, peeling, frescoed facades on helter-skelter knife-slit alleys. Leaning belfries, sloping slate roofs, teetering crumbling campanili, and lantern-topped domes hovered over terrace upon terrace of cyclopean stone walls. To the south and west towered the massive cranes of Genoa's port, one of the world's biggest and busiest.

Turning east, she stared at the sinister outsized silhouette of the Monte di Portofino, a titan's castle of conglomerate stone infinitely older than Genoa or even Rome, dropped on the jagged edge of the Mediterranean almost precisely at its northern apex. Somewhere out there beyond, or perhaps atop that forbidding rock, lay the body of the late Giuseppe Garibaldi. Daria knew it in her tired, aching bones. Gary had not been kidnapped. He had been murdered.

Twelve

Why scramble up a thousand vertical feet?, Sergeant Gianni Giannini had asked Daria. The better way of reaching the Nazi bunker behind Rapallo was to drive to the pass and hike back on the ridgetop trail bearing west by northwest.

It was nearly 7:15 a.m. when the Alfa Romeo, Daria at the wheel, crested the Passo della Crocetta, having negotiated the archetypal corkscrew two-lane road up from the coast.

Sergeant Giannini had shown admirable sangfroid as she screeched around the hairpins and slid toward the guardrails on loose gravel. They had skidded to a halt and backed up twice, first to allow a miniature passenger bus and later a delivery truck to get by. At the top, Daria had pulled onto the gravel shoulder by a small roadside shrine, leaving the car at the intersection of an even narrower road, hopeful passing traffic could go by unhindered. Enchanted by the boundless view from two thousand feet above sea level, Daria's eyes swept over Rapallo, then out across the rugged Portofino Peninsula and Gulf of Genoa. She could see the flotilla of police and Carabinieri boats, Coast Guard cutters, fire boats, and harbor masters' skiffs and launches, already back at work searching for Joe Gary's body. Had she really seen Andrew Striker among them yesterday, or had he merely been a figment of her nauseated imagination, stimulated by Willem Bremach's puzzling words?

Daria knew it was too soon for Morbido to have heard from Lieutenant Gambero at the airport in Albenga, but she was tempted to call him again anyway. The three had met at head-quarters that morning at six, divvied up tasks, reviewed their strategy, then spoken again just before seven, when she had met Sergeant Giannini at the Rapallo train station.

Given the extreme isolation of the mountain pass, Daria was startled by the arrival of a cluster of wobbling cyclists, seniors dressed in colorful athletic wear, peddling up on racing bikes from the opposite valley, dismounting at the summit, then march-ing like robotic penguins on their stiff riding shoes while gulping water and talking a mile a minute. A moment later, half a dozen graying backpackers appeared on the ridge, their aluminum Nordic walking sticks swinging and clicking. They had come from the direction of the Sanctuary of Montallegro a mile or so east, they bleated joyfully to the cyclists.

"Popular spot," Daria remarked.

"It's the weather," Gianni confirmed, "and the long weekend."

They allowed the trekkers to go ahead of them on the ridgetop trail. Shouting loudly, as if born with megaphones in their mouths, the group bounced off, tricked out in high-tech hiking gear, ready to set geriatric speed records. Daria could not keep up with them. She already regretted having donned her uncomfortably stiff blue DIGOS military-style summer uniform. Worse were her loose black leather shoes with soft rubber soles. They gave no ankle support.

Scrambling up the steep, slippery gravel scree, Gianni led the way west. They spoke little. Beyond his sunny personality and tune-ful tenor voice, Daria also admired the man's stamina and stride. Though encumbered by his ridiculous traffic cop outfit crowned by an impractical upswept white military-style hat, Sergeant Giannini had the physique of an alpine trekker. When Daria made a remark about the pace, he admitted to having done his compulsory military service in the famous Italian Alpine Brigade.

Compulsory was the key word, she knew. Feeling it a dereliction of duty to think of such immaterial subjects, nonetheless she couldn't help doing a quick calculation. The military draft had been abolished in Italy in 2005—over fifteen years ago. Men were usually twenty when they did their compulsory military service, though they might be anywhere from eighteen to twenty-five. That meant Giannini was at least thirty-three to forty years old, about ten years her junior, though he might be five years older than that and therefore closer to her age.

If it had been the other way around, she told herself with a philosophical shrug, no one would bother. She wondered if Italy would ever evolve from patriarchal medievalism toward a progressive, egalitarian, gender-respectful society. Perhaps if a prime minister or president had an older wife or lover, like President Emmanuel Macron of France, or if a woman were finally put in charge of the government, things would begin to change. But probably not. There would always be the Vatican, and thousands of years of male domination and ingrained machismo. She could not repress a loud scoff. Gianni turned to look back at her and asked if she were all right.

Glancing furtively at his large, muscular hands, she tried to remember if she had seen him wearing a wedding band. But the hands were in motion, swinging like pendulums as he strode toward the bunker complex. She had looked at his ring finger before, she chided herself now, and had *seen* but had not *observed* if it bore a band. The time had come to pay closer attention. She rewound the mental videotape of her encounters with Gianni over the last two or three years. There had been several, all brief and businesslike but somehow memorable. She shivered despite the heat.

Veering off the main hiking trail, they took an offshoot due west, wading through the scented Mediterranean scrub of yellow broom, white rock rose, tree heather, and spiky-fruited arbutus. Gianni came to a sudden halt. He raised his arms high, warning her to stay back. She heard a grunt and a squeal, unholstered her pistol, and seconds later jumped to the side as a feral sow and its piglets rushed by. Daria couldn't help laughing out loud from nervousness and childlike hilarity.

"That's probably the most dangerous thing we'll experience today," he chuckled good-naturedly.

"I certainly hope so," Daria said, her large, ripe mouth glistening.

Criminals were one thing, she remarked, and she was used to dealing with them. But wild pigs in the middle of nowhere? The only way out if you were injured was by helicopter.

The bunker complex turned out to be much bigger than she had expected. This was no simple machine gun nest but rather a full-blown shore battery fifty yards long and built of reinforced concrete. How the Fascists and then the Nazis who took over from them in late 1943 had gotten their heavy cannons up here and supplied the bunker with food, water, and ammunition in the days before helicopters was beyond her imagination.

On the other hand, she knew from having walked along parts of the so-called Gothic Line—the Nazis' rampart against the approaching Allies, running east to west across the Italian peninsula, from the southern outskirts of La Spezia to Pesaro on the Adriatic Sea—that it had over two thousand machine gun nests and nearly five hundred heavy gun positions along its length. Many of them were just as elaborate and even more isolated than this one. War, violence, bloodletting—they were so much a part of human nature that she wondered if peace and harmony were no more than pipe dreams, and her vocation futile.

"Watch out for vipers," Gianni shouted as they pushed through the last barrier of scruffy vegetation. "It's so hot they might already have come out of hibernation."

"You make it sound like we're in the Wild West," Daria said, wide eyed, "except the Nazis never made it out to California."

"No," he laughed, "they seem to have settled in Washington, D.C."

Daria glanced at him, astonished by his candor.

Jumping down onto the roof of the ruined bunker, Gianni swiveled and reached out his hands, offering to help her down. She hesitated, decided she really did not want to twist an ankle, and accepted reluctantly. A strange tingling sensation passed through her fingertips and up her arms. She shuddered imperceptibly. To mask what she was feeling, she said in an unintentionally suffocated voice, "At least they had a nice view." Dusting herself off and following him around and down into the gutted gun position, she paused. "Sergeant Giannini," she said. He turned and looked at her.

"Please call me Gianni," he said. "No one can hear us."

Daria felt her heart skip several beats. Her flesh tingled again and her knees were rubber. She fumbled for words. It had been so long. The last one she'd truly loved had been that rat Andrew Striker. She had forgotten the sensations. "Gianni," she shaped his name in her mouth, "have you noticed anything?"

He looked at her meaningfully. "Many things, commissario."

"You may call me Vinci," she said. "Or Daria, call me Daria, but only when we're alone."

Gianni nodded and did not take his eyes off hers. "Let me help you downstairs again," he said, his big, baby blue eyes twinkling in the sunlight.

Feeling vulnerable, something she was unused to and did not like, Daria withheld her hand. "What I mean," she said, confused by the onslaught of emotions, yet drawn forward by professionalism and the call of duty, "what I mean is, have you noticed that nothing is burned on the ridge or around the bunker? The ground is still wet and stained red from the water bombers, but there was no fire here."

"As I told you yesterday," he said smiling, still holding out his hands. "Lots of smoke, no fire."

A long semicircular slit about a foot and a half high in the concrete face of the building let in bright sunlight. This was where one of the big cannons in the shore battery must have been, she reasoned.

"It's only because I'm wearing these stupid shoes," Daria protested, still hesitating, "otherwise I would be perfectly capable," she began to explain. Then she jumped down, almost into his arms. She did not pull her hands away this time.

"Of course, you would be more than capable, commissario," he said softly. "I mean, Daria. You are in amazing condition."

"For an older woman, you mean?" Turning to face Gianni, she stepped closer, but before leaning in to meet his lips, her eyes darted around warily, a defensive reaction that had become second nature. Her glance fell upon a knee-high heap of burned-out flares and smoke grenades. Then she spotted another mound of flares and smoke bombs in a dark corner at the other end of the bunker. Stepping back abruptly, she pointed and blurted out, "There's your explanation."

Gianni blinked and leaned back, aware the magical moment had passed. They had missed it. He coughed and reached out unthinkingly to touch the burned materiel. Daria ordered him back. "Don't!" she snapped. Peering down at the mound, she counted a dozen or more flares and just as many smoke bombs. They appeared to have been wired to a timer mechanism.

"We need to check for prints," she said, "and we need the bomb squad and specialists in here. You must never tamper with evidence, Sergeant Giannini," she scolded. But there was something playful in her tone. "Especially if you hope to transfer to the regular Polizia di Stato and rise up the ranks." Not waiting for him to react, she took his hands in hers, tugged him toward her and kissed him gently on the lips. Gianni neither resisted nor seemed surprised. She was in command. But only temporarily. Folding her in his arms, he pressed his superior officer to his chest and kissed her deeply, seriously, dangerously. Daria gasped for breath and wriggled free. "It's too fast," she said hoarsely, "it's too much, too soon..."

"Is someone down there?" shouted a man's voice from above and outside the bunker.

Daria muttered an incredulous, incomprehensible impreca-
tion, ran her fingers through her tousled hair, then straightened
her uniform and shouted back. "Who is it?"

"We're a group of hikers," the voice shouted again. "Are you
stuck in there? Do you need help?"

"No, stay back," called Gianni. "This is the police. Do not enter.
Get back to the ridge trail and wait for us."

She and Gianni looked at each other in silence. He raised his
eyebrows and smiled ruefully.

Following close behind him, Daria climbed to the roof of the
bunker unassisted. "Please, Gianni, tell the hikers the site is off
limits," she said, stepping away. "I'm putting in a call to headquarters, if there's any connectivity up here. Let's check around the
bunker to see if we find the body."

"What body?" he asked. He seemed perplexed.

"Joe Gary Baldi's body." She paused. "Didn't you know that's
what I was looking for?"

Thirteen

Daria cringed as she heard the tale unfold. Speaking to her via a GPS connection, Lieutenant Italo Gambero gave her the details unedited, in a calm, even voice that she heard very clearly over her smartphone while she and Gianni marched single file along the ridge, back to the Alfa Romeo.

It was so typically, so wonderfully, so grotesquely Italian. Here was a small, overcrowded peninsula jutting into the Mediterranean that nonetheless ranked among the top-ten industrial powers, a country with no natural resources but an overabundance of talent, energy, and creativity, the cradle of ancient Roman civilization, the builder of the Colosseum and the inventor of law and the Latin language, the seat of the Roman Catholic Church, the birthplace of the Renaissance, humanism, and modern science, of da Vinci, Michelangelo, and Galileo, Vivaldi and the opera, the godhead of architecture, urban planning, modern banking and insurance, and countless inventions from pasta and espresso to the radio.

Italy, the California-sized country that single-handedly had given humanity more than half the sites on UNESCO's World Heritage Site list, and yet, and yet, Italy had also produced

Caligula and Nero, perfected the Inquisition, invented the papacy and the Borgias, suckled Machiavelli, nurtured the Mafia, and produced the monster Mussolini, not to mention Silvio Berlusconi and the notorious Northern League and other neo-Fascist populists. It was a chaotic, filthy, polluted, incurable, sclerotic, inefficient, suffocating, tangled, backward, corrupt, impoverished, Mob-infected, cynical, vitiated, maddening bureaucratic mess of unparalleled beauty.

Daria kept herself from shouting out loud at Gambero by biting her lower lip, watching her feet, and reminding herself not to shoot the messenger.

First of all, Gambero had said, he was calling from the Albenga airport. That accounted for the helicopter and airplane noise in the background. So, he explained, the three-day international search and rescue and water bomber air show had ended yesterday evening as planned.

"Planned" was the key word. Everything had been planned and had worked to perfection, according to the organizers and the deputy director Gambero had spoken to, the man in charge of the coastal farm town's small, rural airport.

As always, since the 1990s, the triennial air show had been planned a year ahead and permission duly given by the Albenga municipal authorities to hold it. This year, the organizers had wanted to put the competing seaplanes through the paces by having them carry out real-life rescue operations of migrants stranded off the coast and, for the water bombers, put out fires scattered around the interior.

"Of course," Gambero had reasoned, "given the critical fire risk caused by the drought and heat, they couldn't set real fires."

So, they had asked for permission to light fire-safe, spark-free flares and also set off smoke bombs in a series of isolated, safe sites distributed along the ridges above the Riviera.

"Of course," Daria had muttered, taking Gianni's hand as they slipped side by side down a gravel scree. "What could be more natural?"

"Well," Gambero had continued, "the ideal spots were the old machine gun nests and bunkers, made of reinforced concrete and therefore free of vegetation and in isolated locations. The pilots were not told where they would be expected to drop the water bombs. It was up to them to respond. The test was to see which planes could pinpoint the blazes, scoop up the water, and extinguish the source of the smoke fastest and most thoroughly."

Daria nodded bleakly and said yes, she understood. "But why were we and the Carabinieri not informed?"

"That's the tricky part," Gambero said brightly. He explained that, as Captain Vinci knew, permission to carry out such activities would have to be obtained from the prefecture of the province and the municipality where the nest or bunker was located. Since there were four prefectures involved—from west to east, respectively, Imperia, Savona, Genoa, and La Spezia—applications would have to be filed with each. If there were nine bunkers or nests chosen as targets, as was the case in point, each of the municipalities where the sites were found would also need to give the go-ahead. In three cases, he added, the bunkers or gun nests actually straddled the city limits of more than one municipality, and five were in municipal, provincial, or regional parklands. Each of the park authorities would also have to reply.

"Then once all of the permissions were granted, the dossier would need to be submitted to the sub-secretariat of the National Fire Prevention Authority in Rome."

"Naturally," Daria said as they neared the Alfa Romeo. She clicked her key and watched as Gianni unbidden opened the doors to let the infernal heat out of the passenger compartment.

"Since the air show had been organized so far ahead, and planes had come in from Canada, the U.S., Britain, China, and Russia," Gambero continued, "and the countersigned permissions had not arrived yet, the organizers decided to go ahead and pay any fines the authorities might later impose. It was cheaper than canceling the air show, you see."

"Of course, I see, it's only human. And let me guess," Daria continued, unsure whether to laugh or cry, "the organizers assumed the airport and municipal authorities would have contacted the local police departments up and down the Riviera to make sure no hikers were in the vicinity, and the municipal authorities and local police departments naturally thought the provinces and prefectures would do that, so nothing was done, and no one even thought of telling us or the Carabinieri, not to mention the various fire departments that might be involved?"

"Correct," Gambero said. "Who told you?"

"Are you kidding, Italo?"

The upshot was, Italo Gambero concluded, startled by his boss's vehemence, that no one had been hurt, no fires had spread, the places were all very remote, everything had gone off perfectly, the local Canadair pilots from Albenga had outperformed the others—as expected—but the Chinese and Russians had done a fine job and dropped more metric tons of water and flame retardant than the Canadair planes...

Daria interrupted Gambero with a sharp, "Okay, all right, that's great, that's just too much information." Then feeling guilty again for biting his head off, she got control of herself and asked a second later if Gambero had been able to confirm the registration numbers and information on the seaplanes and pilots. He answered in the affirmative, adding that, in fact, there were twelve airplanes involved, not eight, as Daria and Ambassador Bremach had assumed. "Excellent," she replied, "now, does anyone at the airport have any idea which of those planes might have been flying around Rapallo, Santa Margherita, and Portofino yesterday around 10:00 a.m. and might have struck or scooped up Joe Gary?"

Gambero cleared his throat and said, "No, commissario. You see, the whole idea was for the competition to be a free-for-all—who could get to the fires first and put them out."

"But they weren't fires."

"Well, no, but everything was filmed by helicopters and performance was tabulated..."

"Ah," she interrupted. "Now Italo, what you must do is get the video footage from them so we can see which planes did what, where, when."

There was a long pause. "I asked for that," he said. "But there is a problem."

"What problem?"

"The airplane manufacturers and the Chinese and Russian organizers of the air show paid for the helicopters and the filming, and they say this is proprietary information related to the performance of the seaplanes. They will not release it without a warrant."

Daria laughed aloud. "They must be joking," she said. "Do they realize that one of the pilots may have committed involuntary manslaughter or murder? I want you to ground or impound the seaplanes that are still in Albenga. We'll get onto Interpol for the ones that have already flown abroad. Put the deputy director of the airport on, please."

She waited impatiently, dangling the key of the Alfa Romeo for Gianni to take it. Technically it was against regulations for anyone but a DIGOS operative to drive a DIGOS vehicle, but Daria was in a hurry to get back to Rapallo, Gianni was a policeman, and, unlike most smartphone addicts, she could not talk and drive at the same time even with an earbud—she needed her hands free to gesture and help her speak.

Gianni took the key, started the car and the air conditioning, and waited for her to climb in. Then he began rolling slowly down the hill, creeping around the corkscrews while admiring the way Daria talked and drew holograms with her tendril arms and long fingers.

Flustered and defensive, the airport executive she was talking with argued that it was out of his hands. He did not have the video footage in the first place. The organizers had steadfastly refused to cooperate with his and Gambero's requests—they had spoken to the Chinese and Russians not half an hour earlier. They had already left their hotels in a minibus. "They are flying out of

Genoa this morning," the man added, "we don't get many long-haul flights here."

"Well," Daria snapped, "we will have to detain them at the airport in Genoa. By the way, you are hereby ordered to impound and ground all the planes in Albenga involved in the air show. Please hand me back to Lieutenant Gambero and follow his orders." She drummed the fingers of her right hand on the car door. "Italo? You have the names of the organizers? Good. Call headquarters and have a squad sent to meet you at the airport in Genoa. Call the security detail at the airport, and the Carabinieri, and have them detain those people until you get there. We can use anti-terrorism legislation to hold them. They are suspects in a case of potential manslaughter or kidnapping possibly involving international terrorists—whatever it takes. And Italo, call Rome and have them issue a special warrant anyway. We want that footage, got it?"

Daria disconnected, shut her eyes for a few seconds, feeling the sunshine on her eyelids, then opened them and smiled at Gianni. "What a nice morning," she laughed.

"It *is* a nice morning," he said earnestly, reaching out to touch her hand. She shook her head.

"Later," she said in a hoarse voice. Gianni silently obeyed, nosing the Alfa through a hamlet seemingly suspended from the steep hillside. Half a dozen cars were double parked near a local café. As the Alfa squeezed past, among the parked vehicles Daria thought she spotted an unmarked DIGOS car. "One of ours," she remarked, glad the car's occupants were in the café and not out where they might spot her with the sergeant.

Asking Gianni to pull over as they reached the bottom of the corkscrew road, she took the wheel. Before she could pull out and drive the last leg into the center of Rapallo, he leaned over and kissed her. Momentarily stunned by the electrical charge bucking through her body, she kissed back, thirstily, spinning into a vortex until she was out of breath. "This is crazy," she said, pushing him back.

"What's crazy?"

She took a deep breath, held it, and looked out of the windshield. "This. Us. You." She paused and swallowed. "Let me guess," she said slowly, her heart beating fast. "You have two teenage children, one girl, one boy, and you're separated from your wife, heading for divorce..."

"Who told you?" he asked, genuinely surprised. "Gigi?"

Daria scoffed. "I don't talk to Gigi if I don't have to," she said. "I'm just making an educated guess, Gianni. You're too handsome and too gentle and too well-spoken not to be attached or have been attached. I'm also guessing you're a few years younger than I am, so your children are not adults yet."

He smiled, reaching out to take her hands. "You have most of it right, except my kids are both girls and I'm not separated, I'm widowed. My wife died three years ago, suddenly, of ovarian cancer. It ran in her family." He paused and smiled sadly, then continued. "Luckily, my daughters are wonderful and we're making do. The grandparents help a lot. The kids practically live with them."

"I'm so sorry," Daria whispered, hanging her head. She squeezed his hands, leaning over and kissing him again, softly, resignedly, knowing she would be the nail to drive out the nail of his dead wife, and, when he was fully recovered, she would in turn be driven out by another nail, a younger nail, the keeper. So be it, she told herself. It is my destiny to be the first nail, the stepping-stone, the bridge, for wounded men.

"It's strange," he whispered after another long kiss. "I haven't felt so much in love since I was a teenager, when I met my wife. We were in high school, at the *liceo classico*. We both became teachers. I taught philosophy, but I knew I would never get a full-time tenured position in a college and I couldn't afford to be a contract employee and substitute. So, I wound up a civil servant, a cop. Lousy pay, decent benefits, and pretty much a guaranteed job for life."

Detaching herself from his embrace, Daria took another deep breath and sat upright at the wheel. "It's an infatuation, Gianni, you think you are in love with me but it's just an idea of me, not me, because you don't know me, you can't know me."

"Who says?"

"I do."

"Well," he laughed, "this may be insubordination but I must say, you're not always right, captain, no one is, and you're wrong in this case. My daughters are infatuated with fatuous rock stars and movie stars. I'm all grown up. I've seen you around for years and I've dreamed of you but have never had the courage to approach you until now. This is love. Everyone else in the department knows it and snickers behind our backs."

Daria was shocked. She caught her breath then hiccupped— she was not only emotionally overwhelmed but also starving. "Gianni, please..." she began to say, "this is incredible, it's scandalous they do that, we barely know each other."

"Can we meet again tonight?" he interrupted. "I could come to your apartment in Genoa. That would be safer for the time being."

"No," she said, then realized she had barked an order. "There's nothing wrong with recreational sex—that's what they used to call it at Yale—and I'm no prude, it's just that...the timing isn't great now. Let me wrap up this case and put my mother back on a train to Rome first."

"Your mother is here?"

She nodded. "And if you knew my mother. Mamma mia!"

Gianni nodded, smiling. A moment later he looked serious again. "Okay," he muttered and opened his mouth to continue. She sensed what was coming and spoke again before he could.

"We must proceed cautiously," she whispered. "Before we do the Italian thing and get families involved, I mean. You realize your mother especially and your late wife's mother will probably hate me, and your daughters too, unless they simply resent and dislike or distrust me? No one can replace their own mother. It is so difficult to succeed in a relationship when children come attached, especially if the children are only on one side. I speak from experience, Gianni."

He nodded again, leaned over and kissed her softly, and watched her put the Alfa in gear. She drove calmly and methodically toward the train station. "It isn't the time or the place," she added in a gentle voice. "My mind is elsewhere. This case, it's so strange, it's unlike anything I've investigated before."

"It sounds pretty complicated," he said resignedly.

"If you only knew."

"I hate to further complicate things for you," he added. "But before you take off, there's someone you should meet. He's not exactly an informant. Sometimes he sees things and shares what he sees with me."

Daria's eyebrows twitched. "Who is he and what has he seen?"

"If you park the car here and come with me across the square, I'll introduce you. His name is Clement," Gianni said. "No last name yet. But we're getting there. He's an illegal, from Congo. Soon he'll have papers, if things go my way. For the time being, he sleeps rough, in the park on the edge of the bus depot across from the station. I got him a tent a few months ago and we've become friends, I guess you could say."

"Your pet African?" she remarked. "That's what Gigi says."

Gianni hung his head, then looked up at her with his baby blue eyes through his long, sun-bleached eyelashes. "I'm not of Gigi's persuasion," he said. "I talked to Clement this morning before you got here. He's expecting us. It might be important."

Fourteen

Clement the no-last-name African had pitched his green pup tent on a tiny patch of parched grass behind the tatty shrubbery fringing the bus depot and public car parking lot across from Rapallo's train station. The encampment was screened by half a dozen industrial-sized garbage dumpsters and recycling bins. They exhaled the nauseating stench of rot and corruption. Litter blew and danced in the morning breeze. On it wafted clouds of diesel exhaust from the buses idling nearby.

But a bright generous sun smiled down through the foliage of the laurel and cypress trees, and the faces of the two law enforcement officers who stepped out of the Alfa Romeo special series sedan were also smiling. As Daria and Gianni approached on foot, bells rang out 9:30 a.m. from the campanile of an ancient stone church whose name Daria could not remember. An architectural hodgepodge, it looked as if it were about to crumble and bury the spot in a cloud of Romanesque rubble.

A third smile lay upon the remarkably thick lips of the young man named Clement. They spread wide and appeared full of sincerity to Daria. Already youthful-looking, the man's front teeth were missing, making him look even more like a lost child. She judged he was in his late teens or early twenties. Clement wore the requisite uniform of the young of all nations—a bright cotton hoodie and a pair of baggy sagging jeans that looked like falling diapers. In his case, she told herself, the sag was not a slumming-bobo fashion statement but the result of slim pickings. That was why she could not help noticing that his brand-name athletic shoes were new and expensive—she possessed a similar pair.

It also seemed clear Clement liked and trusted Gianni Giannini. Sweeping off his billed cap as a sign of respect, Clement bowed and nodded when the commissioner stepped up to him and with unexpected courtesy offered him her hand.

"So, you are from the Congo?" Daria asked. "Which Congo? Brazzaville or the Democratic Republic?"

"Oh yes, signora, today would be a nice, cool day in my country, Congo-Brazzaville." When he spoke, Clement bounced on the balls of his feet, swaying like a rubber-band boxer. "You have been to Congo, ma'am?"

"Yes," she said, "a long time ago, before you were born."

"That is impossible, ma'am, for you are surely no older than I." His winning smile grew even wider.

Cocking her head, Daria heard a French and English matrix behind his gallant words, spoken in Italian. Could be Congolese, she decided, or Ghanaian or Nigerian. The skin coloration would fit with tribal groupings in any of the three. Ghana was most likely. What was his real story? Gianni had said Clement had no papers and had refused at first to say where he was from, fearing swift deportation if his country of origin was not at war or experiencing major civil strife. Ghana was safe, democratic, successful—a non-starter for anyone seeking refugee status in Italy. Daria decided it didn't matter. Not now.

"Congo is a big, beautiful country," she said, "with endless resources and that incredible river. Why leave? Brazzaville isn't so bad. It's worse across the river in the DRC."

"War, signora, ma'am, violence, killing. My family afraid. My brother dies…"

They walked to a bench in the shade of the cypress trees. It was here, using large gestures and a freewheeling mix of three European languages, that Clement told Daria what he had seen at dawn the day before. "I was in the public bathrooms," he said, "washing up, you see, as I do every morning, between five and six…"

There are two sinks in the bathrooms, plus urinals and four toilets on the men's side, Clement added. No one had ever come in before at that early an hour, he went on, except some of the taxi drivers he knew. But he always prepared for and avoided trouble, and people meant trouble, so he stayed away from people as much as possible. "So, I put up my sign," he said, smiling, "it says 'Out of Order'—Guasto. I like that word, guasto, it sounds like something really broken! I hung my sign on the outside of the toilet door—I do that to protect myself, you see, then I take the sign with me again. Would you like to see it?"

"Not now," Daria said. "Go on."

Clement had heard a car or truck pull up and stop outside. Ducking into a stall, he had perched on the toilet seat and raised his feet and legs so no one could see them. "In comes some man. He walks up and down and pushes on all the toilet doors and looks inside, but can't come into my stall, see? I look down and see strange shoes, like shoes in wrapping paper or cloth."

Daria nodded. "Overshoes. Then what happened?"

The man went into the next stall. The man stripped off a pair of latex surgical gloves and a suit of protective clothing and dropped them to the floor. The gloves and clothes fell partly into Clement's stall. That's how he could see it was latex and a kind of papery, pressed cotton material. Clement also noticed the elasticized booties when they dropped to the floor. They were dirty, with mud and something like talcum powder on them. They had been covering the man's shoes. Now he could see the shoes. "They were running shoes, new shoes, the brand with the big N on them, sideways."

"Nike?"

"No," he laughed, "Nike has the swoosh stripe, don't you know?" He pointed at his own shoes. She nodded. "This was the N of New Balance. It looks almost like a Z." He slapped his thigh. "My favorite shoe!"

Clement went on with his tale. The man gathered up the outfit and stuffed it into something. Then he relieved himself and left the toilets. The whole operation had taken no more than a few minutes. While it was going on, Clement had also heard noises in the women's bathrooms next door—someone walking back and forth, running water, then flushing a toilet.

"So, when the man leaves," Clement said eagerly, "I wait, I open my door and sneak out and stick my head out of the bathrooms and look up and down the alleyway."

What he saw was the backside of a tall young Caucasian male wearing a track suit, with a small pack on his back. "Like a cyclist's pack," Clement explained. "It was red and blue and narrow." He held up his hands in parallel. "The track suit was also red and blue. The man he runs up the alley away from the parking lot, like he running a foot race or jogging."

Then Clement remembered the sound from the women's toilets, so he ducked back into the men's bathroom and waited. A minute later, a young woman walked by. Again, he stuck out his head and watched her. She was wearing sports clothes too, but he didn't know how to describe them. Like something you would wear to play tennis. "And she was carrying a shopper, just like one of the bags I have, from Picasso Doro Supermarket. Do you want to see?"

This time Daria said yes, she would like to see the shopping bag. So the three of them returned to Clement's tent. He ducked in and reappeared with the Out of Order sign—it was spelled *Out ov Ordre*—and a heavy-duty yellow shopping bag with the supermarket's name and logo on it.

"Doro is nationwide, but Picasso is a local chain," Gianni explained, pointing. "The nearest Doro supermarket is two blocks away."

Daria said she would need to know how many Picasso Doro markets there were in the region, and where. "Go on, Clement. Tell us what happened next."

Clement frowned and shook his head. "Not too much," he said. "I'm so very uncomfortable here and so afraid to lose my other teeth if those people come back to beat me again. They are Albanians and Romanians, gypsies. So, I am very tired. I cannot sleep at night. I sleep during the day. It is very hard to remember and tell you, ma'am..."

"That's not what you said this morning," Gianni spoke up. "Why are you holding back?"

Clement smiled a gap-toothed smile and splayed his hands. "Maybe the nice lady can help with my dossier?" He pronounced it the French way. "I been waiting nine months. Getting tired, Gianni. She's a big important lady, I can tell."

Daria smiled wryly. "We'll try to enroll you in the witness protection program," she said. "You'll get papers soon enough. You can also tell us who knocked your teeth out, and who brought you here, the human traffickers. That's my specialty." She paused. "Where are you really from, Clement?"

The young man hung his head, then jerked it up. "Congo," he said, "I swear. But my father, he was from Ghana. My older brother was a priest in DRC in Kinshasa. He said things to the government. The police do not like him for that. They kill him. They chop him up and throw him in the river so his body wash up in Brazzaville. They say they come back and kill all of us in my family. So, I leave, I run. I get to Libya. They make me a slave, they beat me and torture me. I escape and get on the raft. I get to Lampedusa. Then I get another boat and come here. All my money gone. My teeth gone." Somehow Clement managed to smile through the telling.

Daria and Gianni stepped out of earshot. She looked at him and raised an eyebrow. "It might be true," he said. "I checked about the priest and it's true, it happened. But he could have heard about it or read it in the newspapers. We wired the authorities in both Congo-Brazzaville and the Democratic Republic of Congo and sent Clement's particulars, but you know what happens."

"The rubber wall," Daria said, "things bounce right off it."

"Yes, the rubber wall," Gianni repeated. "Just like Italy."

"He might be making up this whole story," Daria sighed, glancing again at the young man's expensive new shoes. "He's a smart kid. He sees the bakery van. He hears about what's going on. Maybe he even reads the newspapers or sees something on the TV in a café." She glanced at Clement. He was undeniably clever, resourceful, good-looking, and had the resilience of the young and desperate. Yet there was something very old and tired and street-savvy about him too, a stray pet pleading to be adopted.

They walked back to where Clement awaited them. "A deal's a deal," Daria said. "You better start studying Italian. What else did you see?"

Clement beamed. With great detail—too much detail, she began to think—Clement described what had transpired next. The man had jogged away, up the alley, disappearing. The woman had followed him a few minutes later, walking fast. Clement had begun heading back to his tent. But as he crossed the bus depot, the woman had reappeared.

"You see," said Clement, pointing, "if you go up that alley and you turn left, you can turn left again a block later and you come out here in the square." Gianni confirmed this. "So, I rush and hide behind a bus and wait and watch her cross the street and the parking lot. Then I follow her."

"Why?"

"Something strange going on, signora," Clement said importantly. "I felt it. Why they leave the bread truck with a broken door and take off clothes and hide clothes and walk and run away separately? So I turn my head and look back to the train station, because the early train for Genoa is coming in, and I see a man, the same man from the bathroom, I think. This time he comes out of the tunnel from under the tracks, he looks around, then he climbs up into the station, and I think he takes the train for Genoa. But there is also a train for La Spezia coming on the other track, so I don't know." Clement paused for effect.

"The woman, she keeps walking across, right near the garbage," he continued, pointing again. "She steps on the pedal and the big bin here opens and into the bin she throws the shopping bag. Then she goes into the alleyway by the market into the middle of the town."

Clement indicated the medieval tangle of alleyways constituting central Rapallo. "Come with me," he said, taking Daria by the hand and pulling her behind, his fear and shyness gone, "I show you."

"What about the bag?" Daria asked, freeing her hand but following Clement.

"Not good," Clement said, shaking his head. "The bag gone, the garbage gone. I tell you later. First, I follow this lady across town, through the market square, where the people are setting up stands already, to sell fruits and vegetables and fishes..."

As he spoke, Clement, Daria, and Gianni trailed across the small square with its vintage ironwork covered market. It was surrounded by animated stalls spilling along adjoining alleyways. The morning crowds had thickened here. The raucous voices of hawkers filled the focaccia-scented air. They shouted and sang out "Ripe strawberries!" "Sweet chard!" "Albenga artichokes!" and "Extra-fresh local oranges!" Customers clutching bushels of sweet basil or heads of garlic stepped back and watched the unusual procession of an African illegal leading a DIGOS officer and a traffic cop.

Continuing west, the three zigzagged across the toy town center of Rapallo through a maze of pastel-painted teetering old apartment buildings, finding themselves at the city's miniature medieval gateway fronting the bay.

"Here," Clement said, pointing to the two-lane seaside road and the palm-lined promenade beyond it. "The woman walks out and across and a car drives up and she gets in and the car drives away. I go back to the garbage bin but it's too late, the trucks are there, the garbage men shove me back, they dump everything in their truck and drive away."

Clement batted his thick, dark eyelashes and looked at Daria, then Gianni, with saucer eyes, wanting to be believed.

Without replying, Daria took out her phone, dialed headquarters, and spoke clearly and briefly with the duty officer. He was to get a detail to the Rapallo garbage dump and get as many garbage men who were there to help go through everything brought in yesterday morning from the train station district—everything, that is, that hadn't already been incinerated. It was a long weekend and a long shot. Maybe they were stockpiling and not burning, she reasoned, remembering the crematorium. Describing the yellow Picasso Doro shopping bag and then signing off, she turned back to study Clement's expressions and body language.

"Okay," Daria said at last, "we need to have you look at some photos and identify people, maybe this afternoon, maybe tomorrow. It's the long weekend, so it's complicated. In the meantime, tell me how you know the man and woman were young and Caucasian, you said that several times. And tell me what kind of getaway car it was on the road back there and who was driving it, if you can. Did you see that?"

Clement smiled his baby smile and bounced along as they crossed town again back to his tent. The two people, he said, walked like young people and dressed like young people. He knew the difference. He had spent nine months on the streets of Italy watching all the old people—they were everywhere—and he knew how they dressed and walked and talked—like people from old movies. So, even though he had not seen the faces of the man and woman in the bathrooms, close up, he knew they were not old. He had seen their hands and they were pale white, therefore Caucasian.

For the car, he added, he was sure it was an old Volvo, though he wasn't sure which model or year, because it was very old. "We like Volvos in Congo," he added, "they are very good cars, they last a long time, not like American junk." Then he concluded by saying he had been studying engineering at the University of Brazzaville and he had dreamed of owning a car one day, a Volvo, Saab, or BMW.

"Color?"

"White," he said. "With a strange license plate."

"Strange? How so?"

Clement said it was bigger than most European plates, had a white background with big black letters and seemed to have a small NZ in the corner, though he couldn't be sure, it might have been an N or an H or a Z. "I see so many cars all day, and so many license plates," he said, "but never this plate, never before."

"The numbers, letters on it?" Gianni asked.

Clement shook his head, then slapped his forehead. "I was looking so hard at the car and the strange plate that I did not see the letters. Maybe a W and a two and a five..."

"The driver? Passengers?"

Clement shook his head again. "It was far away and hard to see. An old woman driver, I think, with white hair, or an old man with a big white beard, bent over the steering wheel."

"Did the young woman who left the bathrooms flag the car down, as if she were hitchhiking, or was the car expecting her, waiting for her?"

Clement sucked his teeth and lips. "I think it was waiting for her in the parking lot down there," he pointed, "and drove up when she came out of the alleyway."

Daria waited a beat, then said skeptically, "Not many cases I know of where an elderly woman or man drives a white getaway car, especially a conspicuous older foreign car with unusual plates that would be easy to identify."

"An unwitting older person might," Gianni suggested. "Someone coming to pick up a young friend or relative?"

Daria shrugged, unconvinced. "I'll believe anything these days," she added, "but only when there's solid evidence, proof, not hearsay and speculation and invention." Studying Clement again from another angle, she wondered out loud how to say "wild goose chase" in whatever his native tongue really was.

Powwowing with Gianni at a discreet distance from the boy, she said she'd call an immigration official in Genoa, once the holiday weekend was over, and see what could be done. In the meantime, Gianni should take Clement to the local police station and get a sworn statement from him detailing the information he had just provided. He should pitch his tent somewhere safe, where the police could see it and protect him 24/7. She would run checks on the supermarkets, trains, and white Volvos or similar cars with oversized foreign plates, and cross-reference with any video footage they could find.

"Have you had breakfast?" Daria asked the young African. When he said no, he hadn't, she swung her head toward a focaccia bakery on the corner.

They loaded up on flatbreads filled with cheese or topped with onions or pesto, pulled bottles of water and soda out of a standing fridge, then feasted, sitting on the park bench near the tent. "Good work," she said to Clement, folding Gianni into the conversation, her eyes locking with his for several seconds. "Now I get to add a whole slew of new things to my task list."

Fifteen

Daria's phone had not stopped ringing and pinging, as calls and messages came in on both SIM cards. Saying goodbye to Clement and Gianni in as neutral a tone as she could muster, she drove west again, back to the Portofino Peninsula and the search for Joseph Gary. The scuba divers had been at work for several hours. Lieutenant Morbido had texted her urging her to hurry. They had found something interesting— extremely interesting.

Four large men, among them Osvaldo Morbido, were packed into the dark recesses of the hot, stuffy mobile TV van jointly operated by DIGOS, the Carabinieri, and the fire departments of Santa Margherita and Rapallo. It was parked halfway up the sidewalk on the highway to Portofino, worsening the monumental traffic jam caused by the holidays and fine weather. The police seemed to be looking into a crystal ball. They stared, mesmerized and slack-jawed at the live images being transmitted to the monitor by divers on the seafloor half a mile away. When Daria stepped up and coughed repeatedly, three of the four backed out of the van to make room for her. The fourth was Gigi De Filippo.

He did not budge. Beckoning Daria to the side, Morbido croaked, "Amazing, it is so beautiful... and be warned, Gigi is pissed off. I think he got someone in Genoa to call his people at the Ministry of Defense in Rome and gripe about you."

Daria entered the van silently and stood behind De Filippo. What she saw on the monitor astonished even her skeptical, tired eyes. Several divers were holding up bright underwater spotlights. They illuminated not only schools of anchovies and other tiny silver and blue fish but also a pyramid formation of what looked like mollusk-encrusted, ancient terra-cotta amphorae and the prow of a wooden ship. How could it be, she wondered? Why hadn't it rotted away or been found before this?

"No Signor Gary in there," De Filippo muttered, addressing Daria without turning around, the ultimate insult for a southern Italian. "Something better, maybe."

"Roman?"

"Looks like it," Morbido said, thrusting his head in, his anger at De Filippo rising. "It's not the first ancient Roman ship they've found off Portofino, but look at how wonderfully preserved it is. And all those amphorae!"

"Maybe they still have wine in them," Gigi De Filippo speculated with irony. "I wonder if the wine was good back then?" He swiveled and grinned maliciously with his yellow teeth at Daria. "The Romans had plenty to celebrate and be proud of. They were victorious, they were powerful, they were proud, they were *just*."

"The conquerors of your ancestors, Osvaldo," Daria said facetiously, not to De Filippo but to Morbido. "Portus Delphini was the Roman name for Portofino," she added. "They had good taste. Not many dolphins left in Portofino, but it's still one of the most beautiful peninsulas anywhere, don't you think?"

"You imagine the Ligurians weren't here before your people from Rome?" said Morbido, chuckling. "We were here way before the Romans took over. And look at the mess Rome has made of poor Italy. Now we have to put up with southern tribes and barbarians like Gigi, people who want to take Italy back to antiquity, even the wine he wants ancient..."

Gigi's moustache whisked back, revealing his lips and large teeth. "You northerners always said we were the Negroes of Italy," he growled. "We were the slaves not of the Romans but of the rich up here. But now we all have *real* Africans, millions of them, invading the whole country, so get ready for the new Italy and the new slavery. Globalized, standardized, black or cappuccino-colored, another America, no faith, no church, everyone the same, men, women, dogs..."

"America has no faith and no church?" Morbido snorted incredulously. "You must be kidding."

"Now, now, boys," Daria interrupted. "We're all proud of our heritage, especially as the creators of the law, and we're all equal before the law, including southerners and Africans."

"And dogs," Morbido croaked, staring at Gigi De Filippo.

De Filippo did not bark but brayed out a sinister guffaw. "The law says that third bag of meat was *mine*. But then DIGOS steps in and everything changes. Where is the equality, Commissario Vinci, where is the justice?"

Morbido bellied up closer. In his bullfrog voice he bellowed, "We found the first two bags long before you found the third bag. The case is ours. The investigation is ongoing. You will receive reports and updates when appropriate."

Swiftly stepping out of the suffocating, testosterone-infused van, Daria strode to the guardrail overlooking the gulf, took a deep breath, and waited for Morbido to join her. The flotilla that had been at work the day before was out, presumably looking for Joe Gary's body, but in reality, distracted and derelict of duty because of the discovery of the Roman shipwreck. Morbido stood next to her, muttering and cursing under his breath.

"It's great they found the wreck," she said, suddenly remembering the Brindisi Bronzes and Willem Bremach's words. It was uncanny. How could Bremach have known a wreck would be found? Another freak coincidence? "It's great," she began again, now thinking of classical bronze statuary and Gianni Giannini's torso, which was thicker and more muscular than Andrew Striker's torso, "but what about Joe Gary? What about the real object of all this?" She waved at the fire department boats, the Coast Guard, harbor masters, Carabinieri, and Guardia di Finanza.

"If you ask me," Morbido grunted, "they're not going to find anything but Roman amphorae and empty Coke cans."

"And why is that?" Daria asked.

"For the same reason you think they won't. Because Gary is not here."

Tapping her lips with her index finger, Daria said, "Okay, I need to bring you up to date on the bunkers and fires and the eyewitness testimony I just heard in Rapallo."

"With Gianni?"

"Yes, with Sergeant Giannini. He's very observant and well connected," Daria said.

"And well put together?" Morbido teased. "I already know about the toothless kid, Clement, from Gianni, early this morning, and I know about the bogus fires from Gambero."

She eyed Morbido. He was still capable of surprises. "Before we get into that," she said, "what's happening at the Genoa airport?"

"Gambero has all of them—the air show organizers and a couple of pilots—in the customs zone lockup and is putting the fear of God into them. But so far, the Russians and Chinese refuse to cooperate. They claim there is nothing on the books that says they have to hand over the video footage of the air show. They are threatening the Italian contingent and the other Europeans with retaliatory actions if they cave in to Gambero."

"They know nothing of European law," she scoffed. "Do they think they're the only police states in the world?" Daria laughed savagely. "Get Gambero to take them to headquarters in Genoa. They can cool their heels there for a few weeks until they change their minds. But don't mention it to the Questor yet."

"Sì, commissario," Morbido said, grinning. "The Questor will be thrilled when he finds out."

Daria glanced at the screen of her vibrating, squealing smart-phone. "Rome," she blurted. Stepping away, she said into the phone, "Vinci here, what is it?"

A call had just come through from the Bahamas, the voice at the Ministry of the Interior in Rome explained. A man claiming to be the legal representative of Joseph Gary Baldi was replying to the urgent messages he had received during the night from DIGOS in Genoa. Once he had confirmed the legitimate origin of the messages, said the voice in Rome, as requested, the lawyer had activated the tracking app Gary had provided and had pin-pointed the GPS dot on Gary's Rolex. It corresponded, said the DIGOS operative, to a hostel for backpackers located on the main street of Biassa, a mountain village above and behind the Cinque Terre, near La Spezia.

"Text me the name and address of the hostel, please," Daria said crisply. "We're on the way. Better send up two cars from La Spezia and an ambulance in case there's trouble. They'll get there first. No sirens. Make sure no one moves in or out of the hostel or the village until we arrive."

She disconnected, trotted back to the TV van, and leaned inside. "Gigi," she shouted, "you're in charge here now. I'm hand-ing over this part of the investigation to you. Don't spend all our resources and manpower on that shipwreck." Pivoting, she strode to the Alfa Romeo. "Climb in," she ordered Morbido. "I'll explain on the way. I'm driving."

Looking more than ever like a cowed bulldog crossed with a boiled bullfrog, Morbido settled warily into the passenger seat. She switched on the swirling roof light and the siren then jerked the car out and around stalled traffic. With one arm waving from the window, she herded cars to the sides and drove at high speed down the middle of the road.

"The watch," she said. "They've located it. We assume Gary is still attached."

"Where?"

"A place called Biassa. Punch that into the GPS system, will you?"

Morbido shook his head bleakly. "That's miles away," he grunted. "You'd better go up to the autostrada and go through La Spezia. I know Biassa, it's a dinky village, nothing there, or maybe I should say it *was* Nowheresville. We used to eat at this little trattoria when I was based in La Spezia, but now I hear everything is crawling with backpackers. What in hell would Joe Gary be doing in Biassa?"

Daria gripped the steering wheel and pushed the car through Santa Margherita, then toward Rapallo and inland to the turnpike entrance, the siren screaming. "We'll soon find out."

Google estimated their travel time at ninety minutes, Morbido observed glumly. That was forgetting the Alfa was a police vehicle and did not have to stay in designated lanes or respect the already terrifying 130-kph speed limit.

As the vehicle rocketed high above the Riviera through an interminable series of tunnels—dark, dank galleries clogged by lumbering trucks and buses and the cars of vacationers—Daria demonstrated that she, too, had excelled at the police academy's emergency driving courses. The term "crash course" popped to mind, in English, making her chuckle in a sinister, unnaturally low register. With something like sadistic pleasure, she watched Morbido grip the armrest on one side and the edge of his seat on the other, squirming visibly when she drove along the emergency lane across a viaduct, then forced cars and trucks to the side as they passed through yet another bleak tunnel.

"Now," she said calmly as the Alfa screamed south, exiting the tenth or twelfth long dark gallery into blinding sunshine, "what you need to do is find out if one of the fake fires set for the air show was in or near Biassa. So, while I drive, you get on the phone to Gambero. Second, we need updates on the garbage dump and that shopping bag, and the license plate and white Volvo. Third, we need Gambero to get research in Rome to find all those seaplanes, and check if there's anything on social media showing a water bomber over the Cinque Terre and Biassa. That ought to keep you busy for the next hour."

"Sì, commissario," Morbido croaked, the sweat rolling down his forehead. "Are you sure you don't want me to drive so you can do all this yourself and feel satisfied everything has been investigated as you would wish?"

Daria could not help laughing out loud. "Put in your earbuds and leave the phone in your lap," she chortled, "that way you can hold onto that armrest while you talk."

Sixteen

he police cruisers and the off-road ambulance of the Soccorso Alpino—a special Alpine Rescue Squad—had arrived from La Spezia about thirty minutes ahead of Daria and Lieutenant Morbido. One of the DIGOS cars had driven through the hillside village of Biassa, placing itself sideways across the narrow road to the summit at Colle del Telegrafo, where the old telegraph tower had once stood. From the tower, the road coiled west and down steeply to Riomaggiore, the southernmost of the Cinque Terre, those five world-renowned fishing and wine-making villages perched like the nests of seagulls on a largely inaccessible strip of the rocky, jagged Ligurian Sea.

The second police cruiser and the ambulance had blocked access to Biassa from below. Four hiking trails ran through the jumble of old stone-built houses. DIGOS agents had taken up positions on each crossroad and were preventing arrivals and departures.

Zigzagging back and forth along the road, the armed officers in bulletproof vests stopped only a handful of cars—Biassa got little motorized traffic. But they were kept busy by dozens of hikers, instructing the trekkers to turn back or wait where they stood, until further notice, either outside or inside the besieged citadel. The three-man alpine ambulance crew in their reflective yellow-and-orange outfits leaned on their matching color-coded four-wheel-drive vehicle, sunning themselves and chatting, unaffected by crowds or emergency situations.

Saluting as they strode forward, Daria and Morbido told the rescue squad to stand ready. "We do not think this is a kidnapping case," Daria said to the commanding police officer, Lieutenant Oreste Ruffini, a tall man aged forty or so with reddish hair and pale blue eyes. "We do not anticipate violence," she added. "But it is best to be cautious."

"Sì, commissario," said the lieutenant, saluting and falling into line behind her and Morbido.

"Has anyone been inside the hostel yet?" she asked. Ruffini said no, they had waited as ordered. "Has anyone left the village?" Again, Ruffini confirmed that no one, to the best of his knowledge, had left on the road or the hiking trails.

"There are several very impatient and unpleasant hikers who want to go. They say we have no right to prevent them," the lieutenant added.

"It is interesting," Daria observed sardonically, "that so many people know so much about Italian anti-terrorism and kidnapping legislation, don't you find, lieutenant?"

Ruffini nodded gravely.

Entering the hostel, they found the lone young woman at the desk surprised and agitated. She struggled to clear away the long lank locks of mouse-brown hair from her pale forehead, trapping them behind her prominent ears. Then she demanded in a petulant, strangled, adenoidal voice to know what was going on. Her young clients were in a panic.

Daria smiled coolly. "Signorina," she said, "we are looking for this man." She held up a photo of Joe Gary. "And this watch." She held up a second image, of the gold Rolex.

"Oh!" the woman exclaimed. "I knew it would turn out to be a headache..."

The watch, said the anxious young hostel manager, leading Daria, Morbido, and Ruffini into the spartan office area, then closing the door, had been left in her custody early that morning, by a young backpacker who claimed to have found it near the hiking trail a few miles northeast of Biassa.

"I told him to take it to the police in Riomaggiore, where he was going this morning," the manager explained, "but he refused. He said he avoids the police and was in a hurry and might not go to Riomaggiore right away. Besides, he told me, he had already done his bit. He could have kept the watch and sold it. He was doing the honest thing and it was over to me to call the authorities or give the watch to the lost and found or throw it away for all he cared."

The three police officers glanced at each other before examining the Rolex, dangling it by the watchband.

"We're not going to find many usable prints on this," Morbido said, shaking his head. "It looks like it's been handled by a thousand sticky fingers already."

The hostel manager confirmed that, in fact, several guests earlier that morning, together with her colleagues running the hostel, had looked carefully at the watch over breakfast, trying to determine if it was real or counterfeit, and if there were any names or markings engraved on it. They had cleaned off what looked like red chalk to see better. The stickiness was strawberry jam, homemade, she added.

"This watch is probably worth tens of thousands of euros," remarked Morbido. "What extraordinarily honest or unwitting person gave it to you?"

"The boy who left it is Australian," the young woman said, tapping the keys of a computer. "His name is Zack... let's see... Zack Armstrong." She looked from one face to the next, blushing. "I know he was hiking to Colle del Telegrafo this morning and then down to Riomaggiore at some point. I think he said he was going to the hostel at the Sanctuary of La Madonna Nera for the night."

From the same drawer where the watch had been kept, she produced a hand-drawn map and showed it to Daria. "The X marks where he says he found the watch. He drew the map for me. It looks like it's near that abandoned farmhouse complex where people camp sometimes."

"Please explain," said Daria. "We are not familiar with the area."

The woman explained that there were several abandoned farmhouses and barns and the ruins of a manor house and church about two miles away in a very remote area, a quarter of a mile or more off the main hiking trail leading to the interior, not the coast. It was not a popular trail. Few people used it, and most of them were locals—mainly hunters and adolescents from La Spezia out for a good time. The main house and church had been damaged in the war and the farms had burned down or fallen into ruin decades ago, she added. They were not in the national park area but rather in a protected buffer zone recently donated to the Italian government. "That is where he found the watch," she said. "We call it Prati, but I have no idea if that is the official name."

Morbido took a snapshot of the hand-drawn map, messaged it to Daria and the research unit in Rome, and pulled up a reserved-use military surveyors' map app on his smartphone. Finding the Biassa area, he zoomed on the hiking trail and scrolled along it northeast. "Is this it?" he asked. The hostel manager glanced at the screen and nodded. "It says Prati di Bovecchia," Morbido added, reading off the screen.

"That's it," she said. "Abandoned farms. That's all I know. I'm not from here."

Getting a detailed description of Zack Armstrong from the manager, they called up Google Images and then Facebook and, after searching for several minutes, summoned the manager again. "That's him," she confirmed, scrolling down then back up his Facebook page. "You see, he even posted photos of the watch and the place he found it, and here's the hostel and Biassa and... me..." She blushed with embarrassment. "I look awful."

Daria tapped her lips and thought for a moment, a sense of the incompleteness of the manager's tale troubling her. The name

Bovecchia sounded strangely familiar, too, but she couldn't work out why. "Osvaldo," she said to Morbido, "send these images to Rome, get them to pinpoint the spot, then send us a map with a dot."

"Already done," he said.

Daria smiled. "Meanwhile," she continued, "you and I and someone from the Alpine Rescue Squad will hike to Prati di Bovecchia, and Ruffini and the other car from La Spezia will separate and find this Armstrong boy and then bring him to us. Get a copter if need be. Oh," she added, snapping her fingers, "let's call Bozzo and see if he's willing to come down here. We might need him. I want our coroner, not that guy in La Spezia—he's too close to the Questor. Definitely get a helicopter on standby for Bozzo. There's a helipad at Colle del Telegrafo, I noticed it on the map. But maybe they can land closer, near the farms."

Morbido nodded and went outside with Ruffini.

"Signorina," Daria said, turning back to the hostel manager. The girl's mouse-brown hair had fallen forward again, half covering her pimply forehead. "Was there anything strange or suspicious about this boy Armstrong?"

The girl grimaced and shook her head. "I don't know what you mean," she said in her pinched, high-pitched voice. "He was just an Australian boy, a teenager, hiking alone, out for a fun time. We see lots like him. He spoke no Italian, and my English isn't great, so we did not share much. He seemed perfectly normal to me, eager to get going, that's all."

"He avoids the police?"

The girl hesitated. "Everyone avoids the police."

Daria let the remark pass. "Do you recall what kind of foot gear he was wearing, and what type of pack he was carrying?"

The young woman seemed baffled. She shook her head vigorously. "Honestly, I don't notice that kind of thing. We get dozens of people through every day. They usually have extra shoes dangling from their packs, and sometimes they have a big pack and a smaller daypack. But with him, I, I don't know."

"He stayed only one night?" Daria inquired. The manager nodded emphatically. "And you had never seen him before?" Daria asked pointedly. The manager nodded again, desperate to pin her hair back behind her ears. She scratched at a pimple on her forehead, then scowled when her fingernail came back bloodied. "He was an attractive young man?"

"If you're asking me whether we had sex," the girl blurted, "the answer is no."

"But he kissed you?"

The young woman blushed and looked away. "Yes," she said.

"And you are planning to meet him tonight, at La Madonna Nera?"

The girl blushed deeply and nodded. Daria nodded back silently, pursing her lips, not out of disapproval or prudishness but as a sign of her perplexity. She rejoined Morbido and Ruffini outside.

"Divide and conquer," Morbido croaked.

"Divide and rule?" Daria suggested instead. "Philip II of Macedon. Much older. Caesar was a copycat."

"I don't want to rule," Morbido grumbled. "I want to conquer, right now, then go home and rest. I haven't seen my wife except asleep in three days. We are no longer children, Daria. I can't take this pace much longer."

"You're right, Caesar," she conceded. "Lead the way."

With a wave of her hand and a few words to Ruffini, Daria lifted the siege of Biassa. The police dispersed.

Leaving clutches of native rubberneckers and disgruntled foreign trekkers behind in the village, then driving north by northwest as far as they could on the kinky paved road, Daria, Morbido, and the Alpine Rescue Squad eventually found a dusty trailhead near Forte Bramapane, an abandoned, tumbledown military outpost. The unlikely pair of police hikers were followed by two of the three-man alpine squad wearing large orange-and-yellow backpacks stuffed with emergency equipment. The third Alpino stayed behind to man the ambulance. Uncomplaining despite the heat and the steepness of the climb, the Alpini also carried a lightweight, collapsible stretcher. They walked at a measured pace, seemingly content to keep to themselves.

In single file with Daria out front, the four trudged up the hot hillside through scrubland, spotty woods, and overgrown meadows. The area must once have been pastures, Daria decided, judging by the trampled, bedraggled look of the terrain, overgrown since who knew when. After millennia of human occupation, it took decades or centuries for the natural world to repair itself, Daria said aloud, inwardly pleased to think so much land would now buffer the overcrowded, loved-to-death national parklands of the Cinque Terre.

"Good thing we have an ambulance crew with us," Morbido wheezed after forty minutes of forced march, breathing and sweating heavily. "How high up are we?"

"Over two thousand feet," Daria answered, pausing to glance at the northeast-facing view of trees, limestone screes, and distant, hovering, half-abandoned villages. "The sign back there at the fort said 668 meters above sea level, and we've been climbing since then."

"We're at 712 meters now," said Leonardo, the heftier of the Alpini, a stalwart giant, checking his altimeter. "Those farmhouses are another half mile away, over there."

"You didn't say you knew where they were," Daria protested. "Why not?"

"You didn't ask," Leonardo replied. "We've been to them before. Last year some kids held a rave party in the ruins and two people almost died. Kids come here sometimes. The place is a pigsty, sprayed all over with graffiti, you know..."

"Sounds promising," Daria muttered.

"I thought we were above the seagull line," Morbido remarked moments later, glancing into the sky.

Daria stared overhead. "They're not seagulls," she said.

"Vultures," remarked the first Alpino. "You don't see many of them in Liguria."

The four glanced at each other. "Road kill?" Daria asked.

"No road here," the second Alpino, a quiet man named Gino, confirmed, tugging at his scraggly black beard. "That's probably why everything was abandoned. No road, no electricity, no water, nothing—so the people left for town."

"Nothing but bad memories," the other Alpino confirmed. "This place does not have a good reputation."

"Very quiet, though," Morbido quipped, his toad face appearing, "except for the cicadas. An ideal spot for retirees."

The Alpini glanced at each other and shrugged. Humor was clearly not their forte.

Finding a pine tree that cast shade across the trail, Daria and Morbido sat on a fallen log and listened to the chirping, thrumming song of the cicadas. She wondered out loud how long it would take for Ruffini and his men to track down the Armstrong boy and bring him along.

"Hours," Morbido said glumly. "Who knows where he went, and if he'll agree to come all the way back here. I wouldn't if I were him."

"Who says he has the choice?" Daria remarked, her sense of duty offended at the thought of juvenile rebellion. She added that they'd better keep going. Sooner or later they would find the secondary trail to the northwest, leading to Prati di Bovecchia.

"It's up there," Gino, the bearded Alpino, said, raising a thick finger and pointing to a copse of beech trees. He appeared unfazed by the climb and ready for anything.

The group began shuffling again toward a fork in the trail. As they walked, the thundering eggbeater wop-wop-wop of a helicopter grew nearer. In less than a minute, the blue-and-white police department machine was hovering directly overhead. It moved slowly along above the trail looking for a place to land, then hovered over a grassy meadow. Rickety hunters' blinds along the edge of woodland shook and flew apart from the rotors' blowback. A moment later, the copter had touched down. Ruffini stepped onto the skids and helped a young man get out. Ducking, they walked toward the group at the edge of the meadow.

Daria greeted Zack Armstrong, speaking English and thanking him for his assistance.

"No worries," he said cheerfully. "How cool can it be? An American policewoman in Italy?"

Daria smiled and shook her head, leading the young man back down the trail, away from the noise of the rotors. "My mother is American," she said. She stared down at the boy's shoes and then at his backpack. "I'm as Italian as pizza and gelato," she added.

"That's even cooler," Zack said enthusiastically. "I love pizza and gelato!" He paused and looked her in the eyes. "My great-great-grandmother or great-great-great-aunt, I can't keep it straight, she's Italian, I think, so I guess we're almost even."

"Great-great-grandmother?" Daria exclaimed, impressed. "She must be very old."

"Oh, yeah, I think she's nearly a hundred. Good genes, I guess."

"And where does she live?"

Armstrong hesitated, blushed, shook his head, and said, "I really don't know. Milan, maybe? I just, like, know from my mother that she's still alive, somewhere in Italy. I guess I should visit her before it's too late?"

Daria nodded sympathetically and allowed Armstrong to orient himself. He turned and looked around carefully, then walked swiftly along the trail to the fork.

The secondary trail was overgrown with blackberry bramble and stinging nettles. The sea was not visible, hidden by a knoll. In a hollow another few hundred yards north, Armstrong paused and began hunting around again. He wandered off the trail.

"I think it was around here," he called out, then walked back to where Daria stood. "I hate to be impolite, officer, but you see, I stopped to answer nature's call, if you get my meaning, and when I turned to get back on this footpath, I reckon I saw the watch on the ground right about here."

Daria pondered, glancing again at the boy's shoes and backpack, listening for something in his voice and watching for something in his plain, open, sunny face. "You slept only one night in Biassa, correct?"

"Yes, that's right," Armstrong said.

"And where did you sleep the night before?"

A perplexed look came over the boy's young features. He blushed. Daria wondered if he had begun to shave yet. His cheeks still had that peachy softness of the adolescent. "Well, I hope you won't arrest me," he joked. "I think it wasn't exactly the thing to do, but I found a little park in the hills behind some town up the coast from here. I climbed over the fence and camped out. It was so warm and beautiful. I camped under the orange trees and the stars. Then I walked down and caught the train to the Cinque Terre and hiked up and got lost and I guess I wound up here before finding the trail to that hostel."

Daria noticed that he pronounced Cinque Terre "sink-we terry" and was thrown momentarily, remembering Willem Bremach talking disparagingly to Pinky about adolescent partiers on the Riviera. She pressed Zack gently for more information.

The town where he had camped, it transpired, was Rapallo. Armstrong had taken an early train, he confirmed, getting off at Monterosso al Mare, the northernmost of the Cinque Terre. The trails up to and over the ridge he claimed not to remember in detail—the analogue print map he had was confusing, and there was no coverage with his smartphone.

She could check later, if need be, Daria decided, wondering if the boy had used the public rest rooms in Rapallo before taking the train, wondering if Clement had unwittingly or intentionally muddied the waters, unless it was another coincidence and this wasn't the person Clement had seen.

The language barrier had kept Daria's monolingual colleagues at a distance. She beckoned them over with her hand. Morbido, Ruffini, and the pair of Alpini stepped nearer, now that she had stopped speaking English. Their body language said, *It's okay, we're safe.*

"The boy says he found the watch here," she explained in

Italian. "Can we get the copter to fly overhead and look from above? Lieutenant Ruffini, you could ride in it and look for Gary's body or the flippers and signal to us if you spot something?"

Ruffini nodded.

"What about getting the dogs?" Gino asked. "If you have something with Signor Gary's scent on it, we have a team of dogs in La Spezia."

Daria shook her head. "I don't think the watch will give dogs the scent, it's been handled by too many people. We'd have to get his clothes from the villa, and it would be dark by then. I should have thought of that earlier."

"No one is perfect," Ruffini remarked.

"Let's fan out," Daria said to Morbido and the Alpini. "But first, the boy. Ruffini, you go in the helicopter with Armstrong, take him back to wherever it was you picked him up, find out where he's going, and get his mobile number so we can reach him if necessary. Please, as discreetly as possible, take photos of any shoes and clothes he has and his backpack—he must have a bigger backpack somewhere, perhaps at the hostel in Riomaggiore? Then send the photos to Lieutenant Morbido and me. Afterwards, come back and fly low, and let us know if you see anything we can't see hidden in the woods."

Ruffini saluted and signaled to the Australian. "Thank you so much," Daria said, shaking the boy's hand. "The lieutenant will accompany you back to where you were. Please give us your contact information. Let the lieutenant know where you're going next."

"That's easy," Zack said. "Poland! I'm flying out of Pisa tonight. Going to hike the big forest up there, before they chop it all down, then join the international protest march."

Daria paused a beat. Then she said, "Thank you for your honesty, Zack. You have helped us a great deal."

"No worries," the boy said again, blushing with what Daria assumed was pride and pleasure.

"One more thing," she asked, as if it were an afterthought, causing Ruffini and Armstrong to pause and turn around. "When you were in Rapallo yesterday morning, did you by chance use the public washrooms in the narrow alley by the train station?"

The boy blushed even deeper and looked at his feet. "Yes, I guess I did, ma'am," he answered. "Was that against the law?"

"Not at all," she said, studying his eyes and facial expressions. "Notice anything unusual?"

Armstrong shifted his weight from one foot to the other, clearly uncomfortable. "As a matter of fact, I did," he said, taking a deep breath and mastering his embarrassment. He ferreted out a smartphone, swiped, tickled and tapped the screen, then smiled, holding it up. "I took a snap of this funny sign. Made me laugh out loud." Daria peered at the sign. She had seen it before. *Out ov Ordre* it said. *Guasto*. Armstrong laughed heartily now. "What seemed even stranger to me was I could tell someone was hiding inside the WC with the sign on it. Their feet weren't on the floor, but I could hear them inside. I figured they might be up to no good at that hour and whatnot, hiding in a broken toilet, so I took care of business so to speak and hurried out."

Daria smiled and nodded. "You weren't by chance in the stall next to the one that was 'out of order'?"

Armstrong shook his head. "No, I used the first one, near the door, on the right, when you come in. The others were unoccupied except the broken one with the sign and the one next to it."

"Someone was in that stall?"

"I'm not sure, I couldn't swear to it, but I think so. The door was closed and there might have been some clothes on the floor. Hanky-panky, I figured. I didn't think much about it at the time. It's only now that you ask, and that funny sign..." He laughed and shrugged the tension out of his shoulders.

Daria smiled wryly, nodded, shook Armstrong's hand again, and watched as he and Ruffini strode back along the path. A minute or two later, the helicopter was airborne and thundering over the hills toward the sea.

Closing her eyes and tapping her lips, Daria pondered in silence. It must be a fluke, she said to herself. Millions of people wear New Balance trekking shoes and carry red-and-blue packs. Besides, she reasoned, Armstrong's weren't running shoes or athletic shoes as Clement had said, they were New Balance hiking, trekking shoes, more like boots than anything else. The pack was a daypack, not a cyclist's pack. And what could this Australian teenager possibly have to do with plastic garbage bags full of stolen body parts or an aged multimillionaire spook with possible Mob connections?

Clearly, Clement's testimony was not entirely reliable but was at least partly true. Had a desire to please, to spin a detailed yarn, led the illegal African migrant to embellish the facts? Or had he simply been unaware that Armstrong was also in the washrooms? Had it been Armstrong he'd seen jogging away or the driver of the van—or were they one and the same? And had it been Armstrong, not the driver of the van, who had emerged from the pedestrian underpass at the station in Rapallo, then climbed the stairs to take the early train to La Spezia?

Morbido raised a thick eyebrow and cleared his throat. "Anything I can do?" he asked. She shrugged in silence.

"It just gets more and more complicated," she remarked a moment later.

The helicopter had flown off. The silence of the cicadas had returned and so had the vultures. Daria and Morbido stood on the trail in the midst of tangled weeds and watched the vultures circle. She had seen millions of seagulls on the Riviera but had never noticed a vulture before.

It was Gino who found Joe Gary's handless, severed arm, and Leonardo who discovered the hand about ten feet away, caught in an arbutus shrub, its branches hung with spiky, bitter orange fruit the size of Ping-Pong balls.

"We need Bozzo," Daria muttered after wading through the underbrush and looking at the gore—the arm and hand crusted with dried blood, the flesh torn and mangled. "Now." Stopping to call the coroner, she made her case to him via the satellite link, prevailed upon him to get to the hospital's helipad in fifteen minutes, then rejoined the others. "Best not to move anything until Bozzo gets here," she said. "We need to find the rest of Signor Gary before any hikers or media show up. Gino, you stay here and guard the arm and hand."

The Alpino nodded, outwardly unmoved. The other three continued along the trail into a meadow dotted with the ivy-hung, weed-choked ruins of the farmhouses, barns, church, and manor house. Morbido swiped his fingers on the leaves of the shrubs and held them up for Daria to see. They were covered with a fine red powder.

"Not pollen?" she asked, "Or red sand from the sirocco?"

"Flame retardant," he said. Glancing around at the muddy ground, wet from the water bombers, Morbido grunted and added, "I bet more than one plane dumped water here. The wet area is too long and too wide for just one load from one plane."

"Unless it was one of those huge Chinese or Russian planes..."

Lieutenant Morbido croaked like a bullfrog, then began a dis-quisition on certain technical aspects of water bomber seaplanes. But Daria only half heard what he was saying. Her attention lay elsewhere.

Despite years of training, Commissioner Daria Vinci's imme-diate reaction when she spotted Joe Gary's cadaver was to hold her breath and stand stock still, speechless.

The body had clearly been hurtled from above, landing on top of the crumbling front wall of one of the roofless farmhouses. The man's back and neck were obviously broken. She had never seen such an unusual combination of rigor mortis and the after-math of crushed, snapped vertebrae. The fall and hard landing had caused the body to break backwards, like a chicken's back on the butcher block. As the muscles had relaxed in death, the body had sagged farther backwards before stiffening with rigor mortis. Now Joe Gary looked as if he were cast from plaster or rough fiberglass dipped in blood and mud. The left arm was miss-ing, the shoulder joint ripped out, and the surrounding flesh torn ragged, as if they had been chewed by metallic teeth. There were deep purple gashes on the lower legs, and what looked like the marks of sharp beaks and pecking by vultures or crows across the stomach and torso.

Joe Gary's swimsuit had also been torn open. His penis and testicles hung loose, shriveled and blackened, apparently by fire, and stained dark red by fire retardant and blood. The head seemed largely intact, though it too was blackened by fire and reddened by the chemical flame-retardant mixture. One eye had been pecked out, probably by a bird of prey, she guessed. A gold chain with a Saint Christopher medal glinted just below the jaw line. Gary's mouth was twisted by a nightmarish grimace of agony, as if he had not died immediately but in gruesome, agonizing stages.

Dante's *Inferno*, Daria said to herself, trying to remember what kind of crime would be punished by so horrible a death in the medieval poet's vision of Hell. Sniffing the air, Daria winced involuntarily at the stench. She checked her watch and calculated. The body had begun to decompose and outgas in the unseasonably hot sunshine. The caustic odor of festering flesh blended with the smells of doused charcoal, acrid chemicals, and candy-sweet spring flowers.

At the base of the wall were traces of fire, a real, sizable fire that had licked and marked Gary's lacerated body, like a sausage on a grill. Had it been burning when he landed, or had it been lit on purpose afterwards to roast him alive? Searching farther with her eyes, Daria recognized the mound of flares and smoke bombs lying in another corner of the room, the same kind of flares and smoke bombs she had seen in the bunker that morning. Was it only that morning?, she wondered.

"A perfect hit," she said at last, letting out her breath.

Osvaldo Morbido swallowed hard and wiped his brow. His eyes bulged. "An ace pilot," he murmured. "Amazing." He waited, the song of the cicadas ringing in his ears. "And then there were ten," he croaked. "Ten fires, not nine."

As Daria and Morbido crawled through the ruins taking photos and shooting video footage with running commentary, one of the Alpini came forward and reported he had found two mangled swim fins near the arm and hand. Moments later, they heard the thunder of the helicopter returning. Morbido looked up. He answered his phone, telling Ruffini in the copter to call off the search, the body had been found, and make way for the coroner's copter, which was about to arrive. They watched the first helicopter touch down, hesitate, then take off again like a dragonfly, making room for the next one that moments later would deliver Emilio Bozzo and the pathologist's photographer, Pino Brignole.

In less than two minutes, the shambling red-haired Lieutenant Ruffini reappeared on the trail, stepping into the meadow, breathless. He had spotted the severed arm and hand on the way, he said, and the mangled swim fins. Now he stood in silence, his mouth open, gazing at Joseph Gary's mangled body. "My God," Ruffini whispered, crossing himself. Then he turned. "Did you say Giuseppe Garibaldi was his real name?"

The growling beat of Bozzo's helicopter drowned out Daria's words. She said, "Hora fugit." Like God stretching a finger toward Adam in the Sistine Chapel fresco by Michelangelo, she raised an arm and pointed at the moldering back wall of the ruined farmhouse. Shading her eyes with her other hand from the blinding afternoon glare, Daria read out two short words, the letters scrawled a foot high in weeping, blurred black charcoal, written as if in answer to her own.

Jus Stat.

Seventeen

"You've made a miraculous recovery," Daria remarked, unable to disguise her surprise or the irony in her voice. With a practiced, measured stride that communicated self-possession, she crossed the dimly lit dining room of the Galleria Club, looking straight ahead to avoid eye contact with anyone she might know. Willem Bremach was standing erect, perilously gripping the edge of the dinner table, awaiting her arrival.

"Praise be!" he exclaimed with irreligious glee, "the mountain has come!"

When Daria reached him, he bowed, clicked his heels, and bent over her hand—then promptly fell forward into her arms. Daria helped him back onto his chair before the waiter could rush over or make a fuss.

"Thank your mother," he chuckled, gesturing at a handsome octogenarian with silvery hair seated at the table, smiling maliciously. Though less angular, the woman bore an uncanny resemblance to Daria. Barbara Vinci was a flattering future portrait of the commissioner in approximately forty years.

"Do behave, Willem," Priscilla chided, her Norwegian sense of propriety offended by the Dutchman's buffoonery. "No more silly remarks, please."

"But Pinky, Barbie is the proverbial faith healer," Willem continued in his theatrical mode, watching Daria and winking affectionately. "She gave me a knee brace and a walking stick she'd bought in Rome, got me out of the wheelchair, and commanded, 'Walk, Willem.' And I keeled over," he chortled, "just as I did now."

"You did no such thing," said Priscilla, rising and pecking Daria on the cheeks. "He is a pathological fibber."

"You mean a liar," Willem protested. "Flyers are liars, Pinky, how many times must I tell you? And once a flyer, always a flyer. We're like fly fishermen. A life of the ones that got away. Speaking of fish, the red herring is excellent tonight." He winked again at Daria.

"Willem, stop that," Priscilla groaned. "They are red snappers, dear, not herrings, and they are exquisite, simply grilled and brushed with olive oil, then scattered with fresh herbs, marjoram, I think, and perhaps some aniseed."

Barbara Vinci sat quietly at the table, a martyr waiting her turn for attention. Her bright, greenish-mauve eyes raked up and down her daughter's wrinkled blue uniform, disapproval admixed with something like grudging admiration for the lithe, athletic figure beneath it. Daria bent over her mother and kissed her on both cheeks. She took her mother's mottled hands and squeezed them. Then she apologized for being so late, and braced herself for an evening of emotional blackmail.

"It's only nine o'clock, dear," her mother murmured. The remark, delivered deadpan, was subtle. Dinner at nine was perfectly normal in Rome, after all, her tone insinuated. Being an hour and half late to dinner at a club in Genoa with your aged mother was not.

"Nonsense!" Willem Bremach objected gallantly. "We'll rouse the chef and have him slay another fatted calf or perhaps a lamb, if you prefer, unless you'd like the red herrings."

"Daria always *preferred* fish when she was growing up," Barbara Vinci said slowly in her deep, vibrating mid-Atlantic voice. It was a radio voice seasoned by nine decades of good drink and half a century of passive smoke inhalation. "We thought she would become a marine biologist," Barbara continued, fiddling with one of her many rings on her be-ringed fingers. "First it was giant squid. Then it was sharks and whales, then of course it was boys and boys and medical school, and then she turned into a secretive migratory bird like her father and flew away to DIGOS."

"Mother," Daria said softly, feeling disconnected, "I'm sure there are more riveting things to talk about." She accepted the menu proffered by the liveried waiter. Daria glanced at it and said, "Bring something light, please, whatever you like, I don't mind, and another bottle of sparkling water."

"And more champagne!" cried Willem, too late. The waiter had scampered away.

Glancing around at the familiar, stuffy old club, Daria squeezed her mother's extended hands again and added in a conspiratorial tone, "I'm glad to see you looking so well, Ma-Ma."

Barbara eyed her daughter, then turned to Priscilla and Willem. "Would that we could say the same of you, dear girl." She uttered the words ambiguously. They were a jest. Yet Daria knew her mother was secretly pleased to see her a wreck, relieved that she, Barbara Vinci, the original Barbie Doll, had been more beautiful, more alluring, sexier, and happier than her overwrought, earnest, incurably single, stripling, tired daughter ever would be. "A mature woman should not lose weight," Barbara added sententiously. "You are fading away, Da. Either you are overworked or in love."

"Both, perhaps?" said Priscilla in a bursting bubble of laughter. "I certainly hope so for Daria. This is the prime of her life."

"Here, here," said Willem, summoning the waiter with a snap of his long, bony fingers. "Do pour some champagne all around," he commanded smoothly, turning to Barbara. "The Black Widow all right by you? You are the guest of honor, *chère* Barbie."

Barbara nodded slowly and made what was meant to be a tragic face. "Veuve Cliquot black label was Roberto's favorite champagne," she remarked wistfully. "We shall drink to his honor."

"Here, here," Willem said again. "We shall and no one will stop us." He paused to raise an eyebrow at Priscilla. "An honorable man Roberto was indeed, a hero, I might say, and his daughter is lining up to rival and perhaps outdo him." He paused, eyeing Daria. "Developments to share?"

Daria drained her glass and refilled it with sparkling water, draining it again unquenchably, as if the chill distance separating her from her mother could be filled by liquid. "No, I cannot," she said, looking at Willem. "Ongoing, off limits, can't say a thing, very sorry."

"Good for you for telling him no," said Priscilla, clasping her hands and raising them in a gesture of victory. "We wanted to be liberated and got halfway there," she added. "Daria's generation has gone all the way. Had my family returned to Norway after the war and had I not met this dashing old English Dutchman I too might have lived free."

"Oh, poor Pinky," said Willem. "What a hideous life of enslavement you've lived with me." He chuckled and added, "Here's to liberation! Tomorrow is the seventy-something-th anniversary! We kicked the Krauts out for good—except they came back, mounted on deutschmarks, then euros."

Barbara raised an eyebrow and sniffed. "If liberation means not having a family, working twelve hours a day, six days a week, ignoring your relatives, and trying to look like a teenager when you're nearly fifty," she proclaimed, "I might want to revise my definition."

"What you mean," teased Willem, "is Daria isn't at your beck and call, and hasn't produced grandchildren for you. You disapprove simply because La Davinci hasn't added to your prodigious collection of descendants. Don't you agree, Pinky?"

Priscilla shrugged. "*I* only produced two, as you put it." She reached out and patted Daria's hand. "The conversation goes with the décor, *n'est-ce-pas*? They sound like stuffed animals."

"I think you mean embalmed animals," Willem quipped, "or prehistoric beasts, dinosaurs, tyrannosauruses, that sort of thing, in a natural history museum. They ought to rename the club Il Museo, though Galleria isn't bad, not as in tunnel or shopping mall or art gallery, but rather as in a rogue's portrait gallery." He chuckled and chortled and reached over to cover Priscilla's hand with his own, a gesture of peace and goodwill.

"Speak for yourself," she snapped, pulling her hand away. "That's no way to address ladies—or gentlemen either, for that matter."

Pivoting in her heavy mahogany chair, designed circa 1880 to accommodate the crinolines and bustle dresses of the Galleria's rare female visitors, Daria took in the unchanging look and atmosphere of this, the city's oldest, most exclusive club. It had opened its heavy double doors of oak and bronze to the gentle sex only in the 1990s, allowing women full membership when its prehistoric male members had begun to go extinct. *Exclusive* was no longer the right term. The thick damask curtains and padded carpets and polished, slippery marble floors, the heavy furniture, the wall sconces giving off dismal light, even the warped, purplish panes of glass in the Renaissance-style windows—everything evoked a yesteryear steeped in Genoese sepia. It was the ideal display case for her wizened, refrigerated mother.

The room suddenly reminded her of something else mothball-scented she had seen recently from the outside. Her mind scanned back and found it. Villa Migone. The revered name brought to mind a vision of the Questor. Why had Carlo Alberto Lomelli-Centauri III dined last night at Villa Migone, she wondered again, and why had he gone silent earlier that evening, when she'd phoned from the ruined hilltop farmhouse to say the body of Joseph Gary had been found? "Keep it under wraps," he had ordered in a choked voice, "until after the ceremony at Villa Migone, that's an order."

Why squelch it, she wondered? What was he up to?

"Well, well, well," Willem intoned, the diplomat again, trying to lighten the atmosphere. "We can safely say this," he suggested, raising a finger and searching thirstily for the waiter, "Daria and the authorities did *not* find Joseph Gary underwater today but they *did* find a marvelous shipwreck full of wine."

"Do you suppose it was Falernum?" asked Barbara, making an effort to be cheerful. "Nowadays they refer to it as Falernian wine."

"Or that muck with plaster in it?" suggested Priscilla. "The things the ancient Romans did to doctor and ruin good wine!"

As the three chatted in hollow tones about the shipwreck and ancient Roman beverages, segueing to the weather and the boat trip they would take the following day to Lerici and San Terenzo, near the Tuscan border, they waited impatiently for a bottle of champagne and for Daria to be served her dinner. The minutes ticked slowly, the pendulum of the century-old grandfather clock in the corner of the vast, echoing room seemingly stuck in aspic. Daria's eyelids were leaden. She wanted to be more attentive to her mother, but the accumulated fatigue reached up and began dragging her eyelids down. She was a pearl sinking into the depths of her cushioned seat. Her eyes closed. She nodded, then shook herself awake, smiling guiltily at her attention-starved parent. The words "no connectivity" kept popping up whenever she looked at her or thought of her. Squeezing her mother's hands, by an act of will she forced herself to stay awake, making her eyes rove around the half-empty dining room, praying they would not fall upon Lomelli-Centauri. The Questor was a regular, she knew, entertaining at the Galleria Club several times a week.

They alighted instead, with relief, on a table in a far corner. There sat the bespectacled, benign, beaming Simonetta Farina, the voluble director of the Palazzo Spinola house museum. She was flanked by an equally lively, elegant woman of extremely advanced age. A wealthy donor, no doubt, Daria said to herself, staring at the twinkling diamonds on the elderly woman's hair, or hairpiece, rather, and her gnarled fingers. Priceless sparkling antique cut stones also dangled from the woman's enormously long earlobes and encircled her lavishly wrinkled neck.

Catching Simonetta's eye, Daria waved, excused herself for a moment from her table partners, then padded across the carpeted room, eager to escape her mother's oppressive presence. She offered her hand to Simonetta and the distinguished, remarkably old woman with her.

"Please, do not get up," she insisted. "I just wanted to say hello to you, Simonetta, and how do you do, signora?" She nodded politely at the elderly woman before turning again to Simonetta. "Did you see Ambassador and Priscilla Bremach?" Daria asked. "There they are, across the room, with my mother."

Simonetta rose and gave Daria a gentle hug. "We've already spoken to them," she said, "at length, over cocktails. Your mother is charming and simply gorgeous. But they suffered mightily," she added with a trilling laugh, "waiting for you until after eight o'clock. Willem was clearly hangry."

"He gets *metabolistic*," Daria agreed, "if that can be said in any language I supposedly speak. I am feeling somewhat hangry myself right now." She turned back to the elderly matron. "I'm so sorry to have interrupted..."

"Not at all, how delightful to see you, Daria," crowed the woman, clasping her claw-like hands and straightening her question-mark back. She tilted her eyes upward, held out her sparkling fingers for Daria to take them, and chirped like a cicada. "You do not remember me, do you, my child?"

Daria felt confused. Simonetta laughed pleasantly. "We are all children to Giuliana," Simonetta explained. "Daria, you must know Giuliana, Madame la Marquise Augusti-Contini di Mandrella? Turn over a stone in Genoa and you will find a member of her distinguished family. She has been a friend of your godparents and mother since the beginning of time."

"Oh, long before the beginning of time," remarked the marquise gamely. "Willem Bremach almost crashed his silly little airplane into our house when he was the world's original beardless aviator, a mere boy in uniform during the war." She paused, laughing softly. "I also knew your father very slightly, many decades ago, a wonderful man, what happened to him was tragic, I give you my condolences albeit a quarter century late, I'm afraid, then again I have not seen you since you were a child." From under her shock of white hair, brushed up into a funnel-like hairpiece and held in place with a tiara, she studied Daria's rumpled police uniform. Hers were the black eyes of a crow, a venerable old bird. Daria suddenly felt naked. Though she had checked her sidearm with the manager in a safe in the cloakroom, her holster gaped open. The marquise glanced at it. "Not come to arrest anyone?" she asked in the warbling, jocular tone Willem Bremach favored. Then she laughed again.

Daria stared an extra beat before answering. She still could not place the marquise. She seemed the incarnation of a seventeenth-century portrait, a Genoese noblewoman lifted from the walls of Palazzo Spinola. Her animal magnetism and charisma were irresistible. "Why, of course we've met," Daria dissimulated, gaming for time. "What a pleasure, but it has been years, decades. I am so glad to see you."

"Still alive," the marquise quipped. "Your mother and Willem are whippersnappers compared to me," she added. "I have reached the age at which it is perfectly polite to boast," she continued, her voice warming. "Shall I give you a hint? In what year was the Treaty of Versailles signed?" From under drooping, wizened eyelids, the marquise observed Daria with her raven eyes.

Daria shook her head and feigned disbelief. "Impossible," she said, taking the marquise's hand. "What is the secret of eternal youth?"

"I do not possess it," she remarked. "I have eternal old age." Her laughter was full-throated now. The marquise smiled wickedly. "Egoism," she said, "and a desire to set the world straight or remake it in your image." She cackled now. "Passion, love, altruism, but also a sinful lust for revenge is very invigorating. And self-indulgence. You must drink quantities of champagne and fine liqueur. Do not let the quacks tell you differently."

"Good genes help," Simonetta put in.

"Good genes are essential, my dear," the marquise corrected. "I am one hundred percent Genoese."

Daria felt as if she had been slapped repeatedly by their words. Suddenly, she began paying attention. The smiling face of Zack Armstrong came back to her saying *good genes*, then the mangled corpse of Joseph Gary welled up, draped across the farmhouse wall. *Good genes?* Daria shook her head, feeling dizzy. She was faint from starvation but determined to learn what she could from the marquise.

"Giuliana is a phenomenon of nature," continued Simonetta Farina. "She still drives her own car!"

"Well," said the marquise, clearly delighted, "Ambassador Bremach still flies his silly little airplanes. What of it? If I weren't such a good Catholic, I would leave my body to science." She cackled loudly enough that several heads turned.

"Perhaps having many children is also part of the secret equation?" Simonetta teased. "The marquise had six, was it not? Like your mother, Daria."

The marquise assented, raised her glass of champagne, and smiled. "Yes, six, and all survived into adulthood, each had four, and the four had two each, all very boring and symmetrical, if you ask me, with even numbers, when I am a great believer in odd ones. In any case, the third generation is now ready to disgorge more of us into the world. So far, we are forty-eight by my count, scattered across the globe."

"I only know one of your children," Simonetta said, "Franco, a captain of industry."

"Long retired," said the marquise, batting away the flattery as if it were an imaginary insect. "Franco was the first, born during the bombardments, in 1942, in Genoa. We fled to a country property we owned at the time, like thousands of others. It was the house Willem Bremach nearly crashed his Spitfire into in 1945, silly boy. I called my son Franco for Franklin Delano Roosevelt, you know." She paused and openly studied Daria. "'Winston' was impossible to pronounce in Italian. Besides, I thought the Fascists might kill me if I tried to register that name. Everyone in my family was a zealous follower of Mussolini. I was the only dissenter. What times, what times!"

"Yes," Simonetta agreed, winking at Daria. "Thank goodness they are over."

"Are they?" the marquise retorted. "I am not so sure. You have read Nietzsche? The eternal return? I'm told that in Australia they hunt with boomerangs." She paused, raising an arm and perilously pretending to throw something. "You fling it out and the boomerang comes back. That is history, repeating itself. But it is your problem now, not mine. Over to you and the new generations!" She smiled again and sipped her champagne. "You must come visit," she added spontaneously, rising in her seat while shaking Daria's hand again with her gnarled fingers, her grip astonishingly firm. "Come to my summer house at Capo Augusti, near San Terenzo. Ambassador Bremach or Priscilla can give you my private telephone number." She pressed Daria's hand with insistence. "Why not come with them and your dear mother, tomorrow, now that I think of it? They're taking the ferry to Lerici and Portovenere in the morning and then coming to me. Bring swimsuits," she added with almost girlish enthusiasm, "I'm told the water is unseasonably warm."

Pleased to be asked, Daria made all the right noises, then slipped away, feeling she had already stayed away from her own table far too long. Crossing the dining room again, she was relieved to see a dish of salad and a basket of bread at her place. She was also alarmed to see her mother sulking. She knew what would follow.

"We haven't spent time together in months," Barbara complained in a mopey voice, the Dolce Vita radio broadcaster gone. "At the first opportunity, you get up and spend half an hour with that museum director and the enchantress marquise, whom you hardly know."

"It's all in a day's work," said Willem Bremach, running interference. He winked at Daria and patted Barbara's hand. "She must keep up her social connections, don't you think? How else will she become the Vice Questor?"

"That is true," said Priscilla decisively, "for once Willem is right."

"Pinky!"

Daria blinked. The screen in her brain had gone black from exhaustion and hunger. Now, as she ate and drank, the colors were coming back and she began to feel better. She was not sure where the salad and bread had disappeared to, or the second glass of champagne Willem had set before her. Rarely had she been so famished. She had devoured the food and drunk deep, despite the recurrent hologram image of Joseph Gary's ruined corpse and his agonizing grimace floating in the dining room, tormenting her mind on an encrypted channel invisible to the others.

Dessert arrived—they had *waited* for her, her mother explained, spiking the word with barbs. Daria dipped her spoon into the old-fashioned tiramisu and when it was finished, she could not remember what she had said or thought since sitting down to dinner. The words and talking heads of walrus-like Osvaldo Morbido, the smiling gap-toothed Clement, the morose Emilio Bozzo, the prerevolutionary marquise, young Zack Armstrong, and red-haired Ruffini yacked and yacked in her head as Gianni Giannini's strong hands pressed her to his naked torso.

What was it Ruffini had said, she asked herself suddenly, sitting up straight in her chair, the tiramisu spoon sticking out of her mouth? When they were leaving the Cinque Terre, Lieutenant Ruffini had remarked to her that everyone in La Spezia knew those farmhouses had been occupied by the Nazis and Fascists during the war, that they had been the headquarters of Mussolini's notorious Black Brigade, the ones in charge of reprisals and summary executions?

"And bad memories," Gino, the Alpino had added, unless it was the other one, she couldn't remember the second Alpino's name.

Crowding out all the other voices singing or shouting in her head was the fresh, velvety voice of the manager of the Galleria

Club, a rotund and affable gray-haired man. An hour or so ago, after welcoming her, he had locked her handgun in the club's safe and, when questioned, had confirmed smilingly and without hesitation that yes, it was the Questor, Carlo Alberto Lomelli-Centauri III, who had sponsored Joseph Gary's application to join the club, the Questor seconded by one of the club's longest-standing and most beloved members, Madame la Marquise Augusti-Contini di Mandrella.

"You really should speak to the marquise privately one of these days," Willem was saying, leaning over and staring intently into Daria's kaleidoscope eyes as if he were reading her thoughts. He lowered his voice so no one else would hear. "Ask Giuliana about Giuseppe Garibaldi, is what I mean. It is astonishing how much she remembers from those distant days. Giuliana was all grown up by then, you see. Garibaldi and I were still teenagers." Willem paused to gauge whether Daria was listening. Then he leaned closer and continued in a whisper, "Have you managed to see Andrew Striker yet? Homeland Security? Daria, are you all right?"

"No, I am not all right." Daria took a deep breath and shook her head, snapping out of it, flushed and almost angered by the mention of Andrew Striker, again. "If you only knew," she began to say. "I really have no desire to see Striker, but..."

"Oh, I can imagine," Bremach tried to reassure her, still speaking in a whisper. "Go tomorrow morning early, without fail, before you see the Questor. Striker is up at dawn to catch the early worms, so to speak. He won't mind. When you do see him, be sure to ask about Gary's connections in Libya, Morocco, and Russia, and his relationship with Centauri and certain individuals in Rome. While you're at it, ask Striker why he thinks Italy has been almost entirely spared a major terrorist attack, and why Centauri hasn't retired yet. There's not much time left, my dear. When you join the dots, you might be surprised, not to say alarmed."

"Surprised?" Daria stared at her godfather incredulously, wanting to tell him that it was *he* who constantly surprised and alarmed her. "I'm too tired to speak, Willem," she said. "I really must get home to bed." She stood and glanced around, feeling giddy.

"Surely you're not going to work tomorrow?" Barbara warbled, watching her daughter rise from the table and prepare to leave. "It's a national holiday, dear. Why not come with us to San Terenzo, so you can continue your discussion with the marquise, whom you clearly find irresistible? All this can wait, can't it?"

"All this?" Daria smiled wryly as she shook her head and spread her arms in a gesture of exasperation. "A man has died, Mother. Bodies have been desecrated, there are people being held in jail pending the outcome of my investigation—some of them no doubt innocent, others possibly guilty. I can say no more. But I will try to drop by the villa tomorrow night. If I can. Promise."

"Yes, do come to Villa Pinky if you can," said Willem, struggling to his feet.

"Don't call it by that dreadful name, Willem," Priscilla grumbled, blowing Daria a kiss. "Come if you can, but above all, rest. You will wear yourself out at this pace."

Barbara put on her best wounded, long-suffering look. She stood shakily and reached for a cane that had been leaning unseen against the wall behind the table. "I would come visit you at your apartment," she warbled, "if I were invited, and if I could climb all those steps. Perhaps when you grow out of your eternal adolescence, you will take a flat with an elevator?"

Daria kissed her mother on the cheeks, held her free hand for a moment, and left the dining room swiftly and silently, headed for the cloakroom, where the manager awaited with her revolver. As Daria walked past Simonetta Farina's table, the marquise raised her champagne glass with one hand and with the other waved like the Queen of England.

Eighteen

ew things were as pleasing to Daria as the wordless dawn walk from her apartment atop the medieval city walls of Genoa to the fortress-like headquarters of the Divisione Investigazioni Generali e Operazioni Speciali a mile west. The DIGOS headquarters faced another, even more imposing, city wall. It dated to the 1500s, the heyday of Admiral Andrea Doria, the cunning pirate who helped make Genoa the richest, most powerful city in the western world for half a century.

The way took her down dusky zigzagging alleys, between hewn-stone houses nine stories high and nine hundred years old. She passed bustling market stalls and scores of cafés, trattorias, hole-in-the-wall houseware shops, grocery stores, and bakeries thriving in the labyrinthine, permanent semidarkness. Surfacing into the bright morning light when she reached Piazza di Sarzano, she crossed the handsome square, then veered left onto the arches of the Carignano Bridge.

As unexpected as it was harmonious, the span of Carignano had been built and paid for some three hundred years earlier by the colossally rich and ostentiously pious Sauli clan, so they might drive smoothly and with decorum in luxurious carriages and alight at their freshly erected Basilica di Carignano, long the largest and most ornate place of worship on the Riviera.

From the Saulis' cupola-topped basilica crowning the hill, Daria threaded around blocks of faux-Renaissance and Baroque palazzi until she reached Andrea Doria's breathtakingly tall six-teenth-century bastions. The views from them hovered over slate rooftops to the glassy modern skyscrapers near Brignole Station. Farther out, they embraced the forbidding, steep, dry, saw-tooth mountains cupping the city, Genoa's natural, impregnable bulwark.

It was said the harsh landscape and stony cityscape had shaped the character of the Genoese. To these two influences, Daria decided she must add a third: the sea—for its unpredict-able, stinging violence, and rare beauty.

Daria had fallen into the habit of stopping each morning at an anonymous neighborhood café along the bastions, where she sipped a cup of hot, black caffè americano and devoured a slice of oil-daubed, sea salty, spongy focaccia flatbread. Why she had not gained weight over the years, and why the Genoese were rarely fat and almost never obese, baffled her, given the quantities of focaccia she and everyone else ingested. Was the olive oil the secret to long life? Or was it the stairs and hills and gusty iodide-laced winds—or the Ligurians' genes?

As she chewed and sipped, standing at the polished steel-topped counter of Bar Zena, she thought of the marquise and her remarkable physical and mental condition. If Giuliana Augusti-Contini di Mandrella had really been born in 1919, the year the Treaty of Versailles was signed, she was a centenarian and then some. Yet she indulged herself like a young woman, went out on her own legs to the Galleria Club and enjoyed her seaside summer villa, and, if Simonetta Farina was right, still drove a car. That seemed an accident waiting to happen, Daria reflected, reaching for a second slice of focaccia and pondering the eventuality with a shudder. Surely there was an upper limit to a driver's permissible age? She could not remember and would have to check the current Italian driving code.

The thought of disasters and accidents waiting to happen brought her mind back to the challenges at hand. Today, perhaps in only a few minutes, she might have to face the Questor, Carlo Alberto Lomelli-Centauri III. His family wasn't quite as rich or pious as the Sauli clan of Carignano but nearly so, and the Lomelli-Centauri had certainly always been at least as devout and reactionary.

She and the Questor had only one thing in common, as far as Daria knew. Like her he was routinely up long before daylight. He always arrived before his subordinates and could be seen pacing back and forth in his top-floor office, making a nuisance of himself the moment anyone else arrived and could be seized upon and put in motion. The highest-ranking police official in the province, his thumbs were in every investigative pie, truly a recipe for disaster. The long hours Centauri put in justified the long lunches that he took, his long-suffering assistant and secretary would routinely explain. Likewise, the Questor's frequent absences were to be forgiven. They were taken, it went without saying, at government expense and in the line of duty.

Daria comforted herself with the knowledge that the Genoa office would soon be free of him. Having crossed the statutory threshold for retirement years ago, the notoriously venal Centauri was holding on for another stint of six months, reportedly expecting yet another symbolic promotion, followed by a ministerial appointment in Rome which, though of necessity brief, given his age, would increase his pension manyfold. To say that he did not need the extra money was gross understatement.

Daria had long thought that what the Questor wanted most of all was an uneventful finale—a seamless transition to administrative apotheosis in Rome, the Eternal City, the cradle of Fascism and mother of all bureaucracy.

But then the populist-nationalist administration had won the elections and Centauri's mood, expectations, and priorities appeared to have changed, revivifying him and making him more ambitious and obnoxious than ever. In any case, for now, the farewell party he was getting looked the opposite of uneventful: garbage bags stuffed with dismembered cadavers discovered near war memorials, and the death of an aged Italian-American spook, a personal friend of Centauri's—not to mention a brewing diplomatic row with the new government's preferred authoritarian regimes, Russia and China, and, she had just learned via text message, a protest march from City Hall to Villa Migone set to begin at high noon. Would violent rioters take part? Possibly. Why? Only they knew—unless you were a conspiracy theorist. In that case, the range of possibilities became infinite.

She paused on the overlook at the western edge of the city walls, above the lavishly landscaped parterres and the arcaded Fascist-era rationalist white marble expanse of Piazza della Vittoria. Victory Square? Hardly. Unless you counted as victory the reality that Fascist-era legislation still made up much of Italian law, and the children and grandchildren of former Fascist capos— few of them punished—still ran everything.

From the panoramic point, Daria looked directly across into the upper-story windows of the DIGOS headquarters one hundred yards away. Most of the offices in the building were still dark. Not those of Carlo Alberto Lomelli-Centauri and Lieutenant Osvaldo Morbido. Clearly, they had punched in before her, holidays be damned.

She watched now as Centauri's silhouette marched back and forth, arms shooting out and flailing in all directions as he snarled down the telephone at someone, somewhere, probably in a different time zone. How easy it would be for a sharpshooter to pick him off from here, then jump in a getaway car. So much for high security.

Outside the massive faux-Renaissance police headquarters, the usual line of immigrants requesting visas, political asylum, and war refugee status snaked along the sidewalk for hundreds of yards. Many had camped overnight. Europe needed them, but

Europe, the greatest single engine of war and overpopulation in human history, did not want them. Daria supposed no one had told them that the admin offices were closed on April 25, that it was a national holiday. They might as well attend the protest rally or go home and come back another day.

The word "home" stuck in her throat. The problem was, most of these war-weary people of color were homeless. Many were without a country. There was nowhere for them to go. They would be too scared to take part in a protest march—and they were right to be scared.

Striding through the security barriers and metal detectors, Daria was surprised to see few armed officers on duty. Taking the stairs instead of the elevator, she climbed five stories and ducked left into a florescent-lit hallway running like a mouse maze toward the middle of the building.

Osvaldo Morbido, arms crossed over his paunch, was leaning on Italo Gambero's desk. The desk was small and cluttered and had been wedged years ago into a windowless corner carved out of the corridor. That was why Daria hadn't seen Gambero's lights on from the viewpoint on the bastions. Lieutenant Gambero pocketed his smartphone and looked up, anxious, gaunt, and pale. Both men appeared to have shaved hastily. Their cheeks and necks were marked by red razor cuts.

"Fresh as roses," Morbido croaked before she could speak. "And you?"

Daria nodded. "Champagne always gives me nice dreams."

"Of romantic hikes to panoramic bunkers," Morbido chortled, "holding Adonis's hand?"

"The capo awaits you," Gambero said, attempting humor. "He's thrilled we put the Russian and Chinese commercial attachés in the pen. No, I was not aware of their diplomatic status. We had a slight language and attitude problem."

Morbido chimed in. "Centauri is already wearing his generalissimo outfit and Pizza Margherita red, green, and white sash. He's rearing to get to Villa Migone to show off his stripes to the protestors this afternoon—the way American presidents hold the Bible for a photo op."

"Good," Daria said, "if he's in a rush, that will speed things up."

The pair of lieutenants glanced at each other skeptically.

"Want company?" Morbido asked. He stood straight, pulling up the pants of his undersized plainclothes outfit.

Daria shook her head. "Let's brief and debrief each other and get you on your way. Then I'll go in to Centauri. Later we can reconnect by phone."

Gambero and Morbido glanced at each other again as if they knew something she didn't. Neither spoke.

"Where to start?" Daria muttered. "How about, the body?"

The coroner's initial analysis before autopsying Gary was that he had been severely injured but had not died when the seaplane scooped him up. Gary had not died by drowning in the airplane's water bay either—according to Emilio Bozzo, there was no water in the lungs. Rather he died from having his neck and back broken, or from loss of blood resulting from having his arm sheared off, presumably by the release mechanism of the seaplane. A coronary collapse would have followed, probably when he was being roasted alive by the fire at the base of the farmhouse wall.

Now that they had a body, and the death was clearly not an accident, unless extraterrestrials were involved, they had every right to hold the air show organizers until they cooperated, whether they were diplomats or not. "A murderer's accomplice is a murderer's accomplice, no matter what his status," she said.

"Unless he's the democratically elected president or prime minister of a major industrial power," Morbido remarked, "or the head of the provincial offices of a police department."

Daria did not rise to the subversive bait. She continued, a mounting sense of dread enveloping her as she heard her own words. The bags of body parts per se were no longer a priority, she explained, telling them what she had learned from the coroner. They were bits and pieces left over from the medical school, slated to be incinerated. No murder had been committed and no threats issued by the perpetrators of the crime, unless the promise of final justice—*jus stat*—could be interpreted as a threat. It was, in a way, given what had happened to Joe Gary.

Either way, presumably the same gang was responsible for the bags and the lethal seaplane. The message in the delivery van and the scrawled slogan on the farmhouse wall confirmed that much.

The men grunted their assent.

The seaplanes and pilots had to be tracked down. That was the priority. Who was the best water bomber pilot in Italy? In the world? How many could be skilled enough to scoop up a moving swimmer and deliver a bull's-eye hit? Did the pilot know what he or she was doing? Were they told it was part of the air show exercise, for instance, and led to believe the swimmer was a dummy? Was that incredible? Absolutely! It was nonsensical. But so many things about both cases seemed like nonsense.

It also seemed incredible, she added, that social media and the usual search engines had not yet produced an image of the water bomber or bombers that overflew the Cinque Terre a few minutes after ten on the 23rd of April, with a million swimmers, sunbathers, and hikers taking selfies and videos and panoramic shots. They needed to make sure Rome was on the case—had they all left on vacation down in the research department or gone on strike? Or was it a conspiracy, a cover-up?

And while she was on the topic of research, had anyone checked the land registry in La Spezia as she'd requested by text message last night, to find out who owned those ruined farmhouses? Had anyone read up on local history to find out what went on in the houses and barns during the war? If Lieutenant Ruffini was right, the torturers and hunters of Communist partisans, and the extrajudicial killers of lost foreign aviators and other wartime "spies," had been based in those haunted, blasted, burned-out farmhouses. Who were the torturers and murderers? Had any survived the war on either side, and were any still alive today? If so, they were very, very old.

She paused, thinking back to the farmhouse, the body, the Rolex, the one-coincidence-too-many breaking the camel's back. "Is there any easy way to find the name of the Italian great-great-grandmother or great-great-great-aunt of that Australian boy, Zack Armstrong?" Gambero and Morbido glanced at each other and each shrugged and said *bo*. "She's still alive," Daria added. "That's what the boy says."

"Why not ask him?" said Gambero.

"Because then he'll know we've figured it out," said Morbido.

"Figured what out?" Gambero was confused.

"The old woman driving the getaway car," Morbido said, winking at Daria. "Right?"

Daria glanced away. Morbido had done it again, outwitted and out-reasoned her, or at least kept pace.

What else was there, she asked? Someone, probably Gambero, given how well he had gotten along with them at the last encounter, needed to swallow an antihistamine and get back to Villa Glicine and Joe Gary's people. They needed to get Maurizio Capurro or Morgana Stella to come in and positively identify the corpse and help contact the nearest living relative—one of the sons who was not estranged from Gary, presumably. They needed to provide the authorities with detailed lists of dinner guests and others invited by Gary to the villa in recent months.

Who knew Gary's habits intimately and knew he'd be swimming in that spot at that time? Had Gary ever mentioned fears or threats, had he received letters, messages, emails that might have tipped him off to an attempted murder or kidnapping? Did anyone at the villa have any idea who might have done this, who had a motive?

"A motive?" Morbido guffawed. "Probably only ten or twelve thousand people worldwide had a motive, by the sound of it."

Daria nodded grimly. "Yes, if not twice that. So, we'll have to talk to a few hundred thousand people and try to get some answers." She tapped her lips. "Whoever did it must have known from someone—the air show organizers or someone somewhere in the bureaucracy—about the fires in the bunkers, and the flares and the smoke bombs. They applied for permits for nine artificial fires?"

"Correct," Gambero confirmed.

"There were ten," she said. "The tenth was the real target, but only for one of the planes, unless two or more were involved."

"Right," Gambero said, "bearing in mind that the pilots did not know how many fires there were or where they were or that they were not real fires."

"The tenth one was real," Morbido chipped in, "the smoke bombs and flares were there, but they had also built a hell of a bonfire in the ruins. The water bomber didn't fully extinguish it, unless someone went back and lit it again to roast Gary's cadaver."

"I thought you said he wasn't dead yet?" asked Gambero. "So technically he wasn't a cadaver yet."

"Okay, okay," Morbido grumbled. "Whoever did this, deserves a medal," he added with a bleak, basso croak.

"In other words," Daria said, "the pilot really may not have known what he or she was doing? It may have been unintentional manslaughter? A freak accident?"

"Maybe," Gambero agreed. "In that case, the real killers are the people who dreamed it up."

"Isn't that always the case?" Morbido remarked. "It's the minds, not the hands, that are guiltiest."

"So, we need everyone in DIGOS to drop what they're doing, come back from vacation, and drag in every person in the prefectures of Imperia, Savona, Genoa, and La Spezia, plus all the municipal offices of the villages, towns, and cities involved, the people in the parks departments, and the paper pushers in Rome who knew about the air show organizers' plans, and interrogate them and do background checks until we find the connection."

"Right," Gambero said, "plus the people who might have overheard conversations or read emails or talked to boyfriends and girlfriends or just seen the permit requests as they passed through the bureaucracy either in paper format or by interagency email."

Daria shook her head and held up her hands. "There's no time for that," she said. "Tempus fugit and we're standing still. As soon as I get out of here, I'm going to try to find a guy named Striker, Andrew Striker, with Homeland Security. They seem to know everything. He must have the dirt on Gary or my godfather wouldn't have suggested I see him. Then I'm going to grab Bozzo and drag him to the Albenga airport, but only if at least some of the water bombers are still there, so he can look for evidence—blood, genetic material, torn clothing, dents on the fuselage, whatever it might be. We're in a process of elimination. A seaplane out there somewhere is involved."

Morbido croaked, "Okay, I'll get onto it."

"Has our discovery of the body been leaked?" she asked. "Is there anything in the media yet?"

Morbido shook his jowls. "Amazingly enough, it's still under wraps." He paused. "What I want to know is, why does Centauri want it kept secret?"

"Why not ask him?" Daria suggested, raising an eyebrow.

"The official explanation," said Gambero, "is they don't want to fuel a fire—the so-called anarchists and anti-Fascists are back. The peaceful protest march might not be so peaceful."

"But that's precisely what Centauri and his friends want," Morbido blurted.

No one rebutted him. They fell silent, their eyes jumping from face to face, then seeking refuge in studying the worn flooring.

"What about the air show people in the lockup?" It was Gambero asking, breaking the silence.

"Let them stew," Daria said grimly. "One might cave in and hand over the video footage or make a confession. Until we know who did this, all are potential confederates and suspects."

"The capo isn't going to like it," Gambero said. "He and the Russians are pretty tight."

As if the capo had overheard them, Daria's phone rang. Simultaneously Gambero's desk phone and Morbido's smartphone also rang. "It's him," she said, glancing at the caller ID and paling.

"Spartacus on the warpath," Gambero whispered.

"Break a leg," croaked Morbido. "I'm leaving the building before anyone can stop me. If you need me, I'm in Albenga eating fried artichokes at that stand near the airport."

"We're gone," said Gambero, locking the drawers of his desk. "I'll be in La Spezia. Friends in City Hall will know how to get me into the land registry when it's closed."

Nineteen

espite her best efforts, Daria could not help seeing the Questor as the splitting image of Augusto Pinochet circa 1990, dressed in his best generalissimo uniform. Everything about Carlo Alberto Lomelli-Centauri III evoked the Chilean strongman of her increasingly distant youth. He had the dictator's same small sleepy gray-blue eyes and the same salt-and-pepper caterpillar mustache. He wore a similar blue single-breasted uniform with brass buttons and gold-encrusted epaulets clustered with gold stars, not to mention the gold filigree band around the collar of his jacket.

Daria had never heard Pinochet's voice, nor had she been there in person to see him strut and strike poses, so she could not confidently ascribe the Questor's cock-in-a-farmyard performance that morning to South American influences. Still, had he been carrying a riding crop, the autocrat outfit and performance would have been complete.

Back in her office after their catastrophic meeting, she stared out of the window, watching pairs of tennis players hitting balls back and forth at the tennis club across the way. The club had been built on a long, wide terrace against the old city walls. She idly wondered if Willem Bremach had injured his knee there or at another tennis club. Like Centauri, her godfather was a member of all the clubs worth belonging to, starting with the Galleria Club. Therein must lie one of the keys to the enigma of Joseph Gary.

Tempus fugit? The words came back to her. Time was still flying. Like her lieutenants, she too needed to fly from the office. But another Latin adage sprang to mind: *Festina lente*. Make haste slowly. It was the great oxymoron, the paradox that explained the essence of martial arts, modern military strategy, and successful lovemaking.

Daria hastened to order her thoughts, to plan the radical, life-transforming steps she knew she must now take—slowly. She drew a long, deep breath through her nostrils and silently recited her personal mantra. *Calm, quiet, methodical.* The three-word formula had gotten her out of more than one corner in the last twenty-five years.

Do the background first, she told herself. It was common knowledge at DIGOS that the Questor's blue-blood grandfather and father had been *fascistoni*—super-Fascists. They had backed the Fascist regime from the get-go in the early 1920s, becoming eager personal friends not only of Benito Mussolini but, later, of Adolph Hitler and Francisco Franco. You could not condemn a son for his father's or grandfather's sins. But Centauri's case seemed special. Carlo Alberto III had apparently inherited the jackboot gene. How else could he have ordered the brutal beatings and killings of peaceful protesters during the summertime 2001 G8 Summit in Genoa, a massacre quickly overshadowed by the fall of the Twin Towers on 9/11?

Overshadow was the word. Another was *sneeze*. America sneezes and the world gets a cold, wasn't that the expression? America gets hit by Al Qaida, passes the Patriot Act, and heads toward authoritarianism, and Italy follows suit fifteen years later. America, still sneezing, elects an autocratic narcissist with help from Russia, and, in an imperfect revival of the 1920s and '30s,

Italy and the rest of the world votes heavily for and sometimes elects populists and neo-Fascists, and no one in America notices. Italy, Hungary, the Czech lands, Austria, Poland, Sweden, the UK, and how many others?

After this latest and possibly final Hobbesian meeting with Centauri—it had been ugly, brutish, and short—Daria was more convinced than ever that the pseudo-American Joe Gary had been a crony of the Questor. Clearly, the two had sympathized, as Willem Bremach might put it. They had dined together regularly at the Galleria Club. That may have been purely for professional reasons. But maybe there was more to the friendship. The Questor had told her during their heated exchange that Gary was an inexhaustible if not always reliable source of information and inspiration. *Inspiration?*

Daria still couldn't help wondering how well connected the former spook really had been, and how active he had been in recent years. His name had never come up in any investigation or incident she knew of, except when Steve Bannon's crowd had blown through town, feted by the Italian far right in the spring of 2018.

In the middle of the meeting with the Questor, Willem Bremach's silly ditty had popped back into Daria's mind. "Once a flyer always a flyer, and flyers are liars."

Once a spook always a spook, and spooks are of necessity liars or actors in a murky clandestine world closed to public scrutiny. The image of Andrew Striker came to mind. She chased it away, but not before she remembered his sinister silhouette and striking widow's peak, his boyish charm and boiling, repressed rage.

With a sigh, she watched now as a middle-aged man in tennis whites had a temper tantrum and smashed his racket to the asphalt surface of the court, then kicked it once, twice, three times. Below the club stretched the lines of immigrants on the sidewalk. Several looked up, pointing and laughing.

When she had asked Centauri skeptically whether DIGOS had really lost such a valuable asset with Joe Gary's death, the Questor had snorted at her ignorance, striking his right fist into the palm of his left hand as he marched back and forth across his office, its windows blazing with early sunlight. The light had caused the photosensitive lenses of Centauri's glasses to darken first on one side, then the other, emphasizing his demonic qualities.

Joseph Gary, he had barked, had been "a master of discord, of dissonance and disruption," pitting colleagues, employees, associates, and lovers against each other. He had never been a strategist and was not a thinker. He was a man of action, with his feet on the ground, ready to fight wherever Communists or terrorists appeared, a short-tempered, violent man whose gut reactions had somehow gotten him through rough patches in a unique if checkered career spanning nearly seven decades. Gary had not been *useful*, Centauri had growled, Gary had been *essential*.

Wiping the steam off his sun-sensor lenses, checking his watch, then pounding his desk with his fist, Carlo Alberto Lomelli-Centauri III had asked Daria if she had seen the latest images taken off social media and sent to DIGOS Genoa by operatives in Rome just minutes before. No, she had not, she had said, she had been briefing Morbido and Gambero before stepping into his office and had not seen her feeds yet.

"Well, look for yourself, captain," he had mocked, turning the screen of his desktop computer so she could see it. "This is the plane that flew from the gulf fronting Portofino to the Cinque Terre at 10:07 a.m. on April 23rd." He opened a second window on the desktop screen and clicked. "This is the graphic study Rome worked up of the fuselages of all known makes of seaplanes built in the last fifty years, including those designed for search and rescue and convertible to water bombing. There are surprisingly few, no more than a dozen." Approaching the desk, Daria had leaned forward, glancing back and forth from the blurry amateur social media photo to the airplane silhouettes. "Well?" Centauri had barked.

"My opinion, sir," she had said, "as a non-expert eyeballing this comparative study in haste, is that the plane in this out-of-focus photograph was probably not one of the newer, larger, dedicated water bomber models or the convertible water bomber/search and rescue models shown in the workup."

"Oh, how very perceptive of you, captain," Centauri had scoffed. "What you mean is the plane that scooped up Joe Gary was not of recent French, Belgian, Russian, or Chinese design and manufacture, but rather a classic, out-of-date Canadian-built Canadair, the garden variety of water bomber, in service for nearly forty years?"

"That would seem to be the case, but only if that photo on your screen shows the plane that actually scooped up Signor Gary." She had leaned forward and studied the images, zooming on the photograph, aware that Centauri was bristling. "There is no proof as yet that only one of the seaplanes flew over the fire near La Spezia and dumped water on it. There may have been two or more planes involved."

"No proof?" he had snarled. "Nothing else has come up. This is it. How many planes flying along the coast between Chiavari and Imperia, miles north of the drop site, could have known about or spotted a fire deliberately set near La Spezia? I'll tell you how many—one! And this is it."

She had shaken her head in disagreement, recalling the width and length of the water-soaked area near the farmhouse. It had seemed to suggest multiple deliveries of water. She had restated this observation to him and then rolled on before he could interrupt her. "And if you look closely," she had said, undaunted, tapping the computer screen, "you will note that there are no registration numbers visible on this seaplane. They appear to have been painted over."

Centauri had glowered at her, torn off his glasses, stepped up, and squinted at the screen. "Well, that would make perfect sense, would it not? You have subverted your own logic. If you were about to murder someone you would black out the registration, wouldn't you? Rather, you would *white* it out, as they've done here, with water-based white paint, we can safely assume, paint that can easily be removed afterwards to cover your tracks." He had stroked his mustache with grim satisfaction and stared at her. "Unless the reason we cannot see the registration numbers is the angle of the fuselage and the reflection of the sun, which is more likely. Look again, captain, with your excellent uncorrected vision."

Daria had stared at the screen and shrugged. "That also might be the case," she had admitted.

"But this is missing my point," Centauri had roared. "My point is, the diplomats from our essential, strategic trade partners China and Russia could have nothing to do with this case of what is clearly left-wing subversion and agitation, because *their* planes did not carry out the attack. The Canadair plane did. That is why, when I received that image and the analysis from headquarters in Rome not ten minutes ago, I immediately ordered that the Chinese and Russian attachés be released and their planes be allowed to fly. I personally made an official apology to them, promising that those responsible for this breach of diplomatic immunity would be duly reprimanded and punished."

Daria had hung her head, knowing what was coming next. Turning away from Centauri to look out of his windows at the once-proud bastions of the city, she had said, "Sir, there was no way to know what kind of seaplane was involved. The air show organizers refused to cooperate with us. We were obliged to keep them in custody pending developments. What are they trying to hide?"

"Well," he had said, savoring the words, "I am obliged to remove you from the case, Captain Vinci. You, Gambero, and Morbido are suspended from duty. You will be reassigned, and your individual cases reviewed in due course." He had paused for effect, his wrath reaching a climax. "Be good enough to hand over your research and any contact information you have to my assistant. I will pass it on to the Vice Questor and brief him thoroughly when he arrives. Having heard reports about the events of the past days, on his own initiative, your immediate superior Colonel Ruggieri has cut short his well-earned vacation in Morocco and is flying back as we speak." Centauri had paused. "That is all, Vinci. You may go."

Saluting, she had said, "You realize I will contest this decision, sir."

"That is your right," he had snapped, raising his hand in a wavering dismissive salute. She had turned to leave, but his words had stopped her in her tracks. "Be prepared to explain to the review board why you cut out the Carabinieri from your investigation, why you have been conspiring with your godfather Ambassador Bremach to this end, why you and the coroner of Genoa failed to fully disclose details of the theft of human and monkey bodies from the medical school, why you bullied and threatened Joseph Gary's fiancée, why you grounded fire-prevention and emergency aircraft in Albenga, thereby imperiling innocent lives and making it impossible to battle the blazes destroying the region, why you allowed a municipal policeman from Rapallo with whom you are reportedly having an affair to drive a DIGOS vehicle, and why you flew the said coroner of Genoa by helicopter to the province of La Spezia to inspect Gary's corpse, instead of relying upon the local authorities and the province's own coroner with whom we have an excellent working relationship.

"And there is more," he had snarled. "How did social media know almost before we knew of Gary's background in operational intelligence? And what of that Signor Striker of Homeland Security? Another of your conquests! He will not be operating in this country much longer, rest assured. I am confident other irregularities will be revealed at your hearing, unless your behavior turns out to be the result of hysteria, female hormones, or the menopause. Now go! And not another word to the media or you will face immediate disciplinary action. I will place you and your fellow conspirators under house arrest pending court martial."

Trembling with rage, Daria had opened the door to Centauri's office and stepped out without answering.

Now, as she watched the tennis balls bouncing and the rackets swinging at the club across the way, she found the words she had been searching for, starting with "sandbag." Centauri was trying to sandbag, bury, and derail the investigation. Why?

In that moment, she also knew what she had to do. In haste. Slowly.

The Vice Questor would not be back until late afternoon at the earliest—Ruggieri could not possibly arrive from Morocco before then. Morbido and Gambero had already left and, knowing them, would have disabled the Bluetooth and GPS tracking devices embedded in their DIGOS cars, ignoring calls from Centauri to return to headquarters. Centauri would be distracted, busy preparing for his speech at Villa Migone that afternoon for the commemorative celebrations. It was the perfect bully pulpit for this Fascistic sorcerer's apprentice, with a national television audience in the millions.

This was their last best chance to make sense of the case.

She swiveled the screen of her desktop computer away from the glare of the windows, entered two passwords, and opened the reserved-access area of the DIGOS website, then called up the image of the Canadair plane Centauri had shown her. She had just finished taking a picture of it with her smartphone and grabbing a screenshot to email herself, when the screen went black and the computer rebooted automatically. Trying to reenter the website, her passwords were refused. ACCESS DENIED appeared. She tried entering with her smartphone, but got the same message and another—NO SERVICE. Switching to her personal SIM card, she saved the screenshot photo in a subfolder tagged "mamma." Prying eyes in this society where mother worship was the norm were unlikely to open it.

Using her safe, encrypted land line, she called Emilio Bozzo and was relieved to find the coroner at the morgue. "Meet me at the Orange Nightmare in an hour," she said quietly. "I'll explain later." She hung up, then took the stairs to the street.

Twenty

Daria knew they were on her tail from the moment she stepped onto the sidewalk fronting the DIGOS headquarters. Striding swiftly up the pseudo-Aztec-Incan staircase on the southern end of Piazza della Vittoria, the same way she had come to work an hour earlier, she watched, amused, as the unmarked police tail tore up the ramp to the coast highway. The regulation anthracite-gray Alfa would have to travel a mile then double back to reach the bastions where Daria emerged from the staircase in the fortifications and began trotting west.

Taking refuge in Bar Zena, she gulped a glass of sparkling water, then shot down a bitter espresso, observing with professional detachment as the Alfa cruised slowly by. It was pointless playing cat-and-mouse on main streets. They knew her habits and had guessed where she was headed. That suited her fine.

Letting herself into her apartment building by the main door outside the city walls, she quickly changed into blue jogging shorts, a light blue-and-white top, and a pair of all-terrain Nikes. Then she wrapped herself in a bathrobe and grabbed her cordless land line telephone. Throwing open the French windows,

Daria stepped onto the balcony, gesturing and gesticulating as she spoke at the automated voice answering machine of the telephone company's client relations service. It assured her the call would be answered within *ten* minutes. That meant she had ten minutes to put a mile between herself and the tail.

Peering down, she spotted the unmarked Alfa below, idling in the alleyway beyond the walls. A pair of bored-looking operatives sat inside, their arms out and cigarettes twitching, their eyes glancing up every ten or twelve seconds, waiting for her to reappear. Mario and Celestino. The Questor's attack dogs.

Leaving the French windows open, she stepped in, pulled the diaphanous drapes, and retreated to her bedroom. There she took off the dressing gown and hung it in the closet.

Calm, quiet, methodical, she said to herself.

Rolling up a bright yellow wind shell and a pair of ultralight running pants, she pressed them into a fanny pack, afterwards adding her wallet, badge, and ID, and then her service revolver. Hesitating, she reached into her night stand, slipping a tube of red lipstick into the pack's zippered compartment. With her smartphone strapped to her upper arm and a bud in her ear, she completed the outfit by twisting up, then stuffing, her long, chestnut hair into a billed cap. Her alpine sunglasses dangled around her neck on a strap.

Daria knew headquarters was listening through the land line, sending updates to the tail. So, she turned on the sound system and left the handset by one of the speakers. The phone company voice assured her she had only *seven* minutes left on queue.

Swiftly and silently, Daria let herself onto the landing, then dashed down the stairs two at a time, taking the back door to a cramped, malodorous courtyard, and from it into the hulking old building next door. Passing through another courtyard lined by double columns of carved marble, she exited one floor below into another alley and wended her way north, jogging slowly and glancing around calmly, until she reached the bottom of the hill and emerged near the medieval city gate, Porta Soprana, and the house of Christopher Columbus.

Picking up her pace, she wriggled forward, a fish swimming through schools of tourists around the Columbus house. Then she darted between cars stopped at a red light, crossing the main thoroughfare marking the frontier of the rebuilt post-medieval city. Choosing a one way and heading for the hills and the leafy lanes of the Acquasola Park, she galloped under the soaring arcades of the Mussolini-era palazzi. Anyone following her would have to detour many blocks to pick up her trail.

Genoa was just possibly the hardest city in Europe to successfully follow anyone. Built over a span of two thousand years atop a dozen hills and hillocks, over dips and river valleys and promontories jutting into the sea, it was infinitely more labyrinthine and confusing than Venice or Rome. With its hundreds of light-less, crevice-like alleyways and sudden dead-ends, countless connecting courtyards, and endlessly long, steep staircases surrounded by a tangled roller-coaster of one-way streets, Genoa was the proverbial maze inside a labyrinth. If you knew your way around, even a top-notch pursuit team on motor-scooters would be hard pressed to stick to you. Not even a drone could do it.

In less than three minutes, she had slalomed around shoppers and commuters on Via Venti Settembre and picked her way up the staircase flanking the tiger-striped Santo Stefano, an abbey nearly a thousand years old standing alone in a sun-washed piazza. Putting on her sunglasses, she sprinted as far as the serpentine upper ring road, then headed east at a gentle jog. There was little traffic here, but glancing down at the area around Brignole Station, Daria was surprised to see a massive tailback. Jogging in place, she peered down and, with increasing alarm, counted two dozen swat and riot squad vehicles, and a dozen or more armored trucks of the Polizia di Stato and Carabinieri lining the teeming streets behind the train station and in front of Villa Migone and Villa Imperiale.

Sucking her lower lip, Daria recalled how, two days earlier, she had recommended DIGOS dispatch a mere handful of men and sharpshooters to guard Villa Migone during the commemorative ceremonies. A small team was all anyone needed. What was this full-blown crowd-control circus? As far as she knew, there had never been big, dangerous, violent protests on April 25th before, not in Genoa. Centauri must have been warned of potential rioting. She had been cut out of the loop. Unless... unless what?

Running again, confident no one was following her, she slackened her pace and breathed freer as she neared the San Martino hospital facility from the hills above, planning to walk the final stretch to Corso Europa and the Orange Nightmare. Then her phone vibrated with a message. She checked the screen. It was Emilio Bozzo.

Someone followed me to the café. Meet me in the tunnel from the hospital to the morgue, level −2.

What about the security cameras? she texted back, jogging in place. His answer came seconds later.

The system is down—again!

That final word, *again*, and the exclamation point, spoke volumes.

No one attempted to stop Daria or asked for ID as she pushed through the desperate crowds in the airless, stinking-hot emergency room, found the staff elevators marked OFF LIMITS TO PATIENTS AND PUBLIC, and rode down two floors. She could feel the perspiration prickling on her forehead, back, and thighs, and she tugged uncomfortably at her sweat-soaked jersey molded to her torso. The subterranean cool of the tunnel gave her a welcome chill. Then the scent of sickness and death hit her. She began shivering, goose bumps rising on her tanned, tendril arms.

Emilio Bozzo's hand was as sweaty as hers, but his was a cold, clammy sweat. She could not help thinking it was cadaverous, the pale hand of a corpse fished from water. He mumbled a greeting, and looking behind to make sure they were not being followed, ducked through a double door that he locked behind them, shushing her and catching his breath. Standing silently in the dark in the underground chamber, Daria saw in a blinding flash in her mind's eye an epiphanic inkling of eternity. She saw a tunnel of perpetual darkness and the finality of the grave. Then insects, rot, mulching, dissolving flesh. Cremation would be better, she shivered. It was perhaps un-ecological but a swift shortcut to elemental being. The reduction of wet fleshy matter to ash and gas had to be less awful. She would need to spell out her wishes clearly so her mother, siblings, and colleagues knew.

Silently repeating her soothing mantra, *calm, quiet, methodical*, she could hear Bozzo's irregular breathing and wondered if he were hyperventilating. His acrid halitosis filled the air with the stench of bile. Several minutes went by. He turned on the light. She followed him silently across the echoing, empty room, through another set of double doors, into a florescent-lit tunnel, and from there into the familiar cold storage area of the morgue.

"You've come to see the body?" he asked, gulping and wiping his face with a handkerchief. He was as pale as the sheet covering the mutilated corpse of Giuseppe Garibaldi.

Daria shook her head without looking down. "No," she whispered. "I've come to see you, because I need your help."

He blanched a paler shade of white. Giving Bozzo a quick, redacted version of her meeting with Centauri, she added, "Someone has been ratting on us, someone has been listening and watching, someone wants the murder of Garibaldi hushed up, at least temporarily, and I need to know why."

"Have you seen the TV news?" he asked. "It looks like the G8 Summit all over again or the riots in America. I haven't seen so many swat teams and police trucks in Italy in nearly twenty years."

Daria emitted an affirmative growl and told him she had just observed the scene from above and wondered if it might turn ugly. She dared not say it, but the footage she had viewed in the police academy years earlier of coups d'état in countries from Argentina to Greece, Brazil to Zimbabwe, had looked exactly like that.

Bozzo nodded gravely. "So, what is it I can do?" His voice quavered. "I'm not a policeman, I'm actually a coward, and I've seen so much death and dying that I'm not in a hurry to join the cadavers."

Daria explained that what she needed was a ride to the container port facility in Voltri, and then the airport in Albenga, or perhaps the other way around. "I want you to inspect the seaplanes that are still there, if any are," she said. "An hour ago, the Questor gave permission for them to fly. But Lieutenant Morbido should be there by now, so it might not be too late, he might find some pretext to hold them."

"You realize Albenga is in the province of Savona?" he asked. "That's not my territory."

"Those farmhouses were in the province of La Spezia," she said, "but you flew down because this is your case."

"My case? The bags of body parts were my case."

"You saw the words on the wall of the farmhouse," she said. "You realize Garibaldi's death and those plastic bags are related. When you agreed to come to Prati di Bovecchia you agreed tacitly that Garibaldi was your man."

Bozzo gulped, nodded reluctantly, and began packing a tool bag with his equipment. He held up the swiveling police light he always suction-cupped to the roof of the morgue's car, staring at it portentously. His shoulders slumped. "Should I call Pino Brignole?" he asked, gloom overtaking him.

Daria shook her head and said, no, the two of them could take photos and videos with their smartphones. It was too risky to get anyone else involved, even Pino Brignole. Who could say who had betrayed them to the Questor?

"Not Pino," Bozzo said, stiffening. Daria shrugged. Bozzo cleared his throat and stood straight. "You're too tall for me to hide you in the Fiat," he mumbled, shyly sizing her up and appraising her seemingly for the first time as a human being, a body, a woman, a future corpse.

They could not very well go to the container port or airport in a hearse, he added. Besides, it was a national holiday and no hearse would be available. "We could call a taxi, an SUV or van, and smuggle you into it," he suggested. "We'll bring it right up to the exit of the morgue and open the car doors this way." He motioned inward. "No one out there will be able to see who is getting in."

Daria pondered for several seconds, then pursed her lips and squinted. "We'll get the taxi for you, and you'll get into it without being seen," she said. "Put on a hat and a lab coat or whatever you have here that will work as a disguise and bend double when you walk." Bozzo listened and began tapping the screen of his phone, ordering the taxi. "For me," she added, "call an ambulance from the hospital rank. There must be a clinic in Voltri." Bozzo looked up, his cheeks twitching, then he nodded. "When the ambulance arrives, tell them to take the corpse to the clinic," she continued, "and tell them you'll follow them there with the taxi. Put that swirling light on the taxi's roof and make sure the driver glues his car to the ambulance's bumper."

Bozzo shook his head uncomprehendingly. "What corpse? Garibaldi?"

"Me," Daria smiled. "You'll wrap me in a shroud and I'll lie on a gurney. The ambulance crew will never know."

Bozzo's cheeks flushed, but he could not help smiling. "What if someone follows the taxi?"

"Then we go into the clinic in Voltri and figure out how to get out and lose the tail. Maybe we call another ambulance or taxi and both hide in it. But I doubt they'll follow you or the ambulance. They're concerned about me and won't imagine I'm posing as a corpse."

"Okay," said Bozzo skeptically, his fumbling, sweaty fingers missing keys as he used the morgue's land line to call the ambulance rank out front. "Twelve minutes for the ambulance," he said, cradling the phone. "The taxi will be here in eight minutes. It will have to wait." He swallowed hard. "How do we pay for this? I mean, how do I justify it with the accounting office?"

Daria drummed her lips. "Put the ambulance on the morgue's tab," she suggested. "You had to take Joseph Gary to be ID'd by a very busy man named Andrew Striker, a U.S. agent who knew the deceased but could not come to the morgue. I'll pay for the taxi with cash." She handed him two fifty-euro bills.

While Bozzo readied the shroud and gurney, and ferreted out a driving cap and beige raincoat for a disguise, Daria drifted over to the open refrigerated drawer where the body of Joseph Gary lay, covered with a sheet. She reached out, started to lift the sheet, glimpsed one stiff, bloodless arm, halted, and let the sheet fall back.

When Bozzo reappeared, she asked if he had found a signet ring on the cadaver's remaining hand. "A large, gold ring," she said, remembering what Lieutenant Morbido had told her. Bozzo shook his head and said no, there was no ring. "It must have fallen off when he was ejected from the plane," she reasoned. "Unless someone stole it from the body."

"You'd better lie down on the gurney now and let me cover you and strap you down, as we always do," he said. "I assume your phone is on silent mode?" Daria nodded. Glancing down, Bozzo pointed to her shoes. "Dead bodies leaving the morgue don't usually wear running shoes," he added, waiting and watching her slip them off, "or socks."

Taking off her socks and stuffing them into the shoes, she saw him staring with something like rapture at her perfectly pedicured, tanned, slender feet, the toenails freshly painted with glossy red polish, her one, secret concession to femininity. Twinkling them self-consciously, she wondered if Emilio Bozzo had a foot fetish, if he were married or had a fiancée or perhaps a boyfriend. She knew nothing about him, his sexuality, beliefs, or background. The extreme impersonality of their vocations struck her. How different were they really from nurses, doctors, monks, or nuns?

Daria had been brought up a nominal Christian, by a Catholic father and Protestant mother, but she had never found faith and rarely thought of religion. Duty was her creed, the law her golden rule. Resisting the temptations of superstition, she relied on reason to get her through each day. But as she climbed onto the gurney and allowed Bozzo to wrap her in a white linen shroud, feeling him tightening the straps uncomfortably over her, then attaching a label to her right big toe, she found her fingers irresistibly making the sign of the upside-down horseshoe, the horns of the bull, pointing down for good luck and protection from evil.

The last thing she saw before Bozzo pulled the shroud over her head was a pair of stubbly cheeked ambulance drivers smoking cigarettes as they slouched across the parking lot toward the morgue. Moments later, the gurney was lifted unceremoniously and slammed into the vehicle, the doors banging loudly behind. Jerking away and roaring out of the parking lot toward Corso Europa, the young drivers in the front passenger compartment began laughing and joking, then turned up the thumping teeny-bopper music on the car stereo, the siren suddenly screaming into life and the ambulance's deafening air horn blowing as they tore across town toward the autostrada, heading west. She breathed intentionally, reciting her mantra. The interior was air conditioned and cool, almost cold.

Unable to move or see through the shroud, she repressed a burning cough and sneeze. They were smoking inside the vehicle, she realized, flouting every health regulation in the book with insouciant disregard for the dignity of a dead body which just happened to be very much alive. The cigarette smoke drifting into the back where she lay was nauseating and acrid. Suddenly seized by panic, she hoped Emilio Bozzo had remembered to take her shoes and her fanny pack with him, and that his taxi was managing to keep up. If it could, it would be a minor miracle.

Twenty-One

As Daria lay immobile on the gurney, jostled by the reckless, bouncing ride, she thought of many things—of shoes and ships and sealing wax, of cabbages and kings. She thought of novels and romance, and the men she had loved, men life had separated from her, walruses weeping as they swallowed oysters and carried on with their careers, wives, and families. Andrew Striker was one of the walruses. She had loved him, briefly, but her survival instincts had forced her to break away before he swallowed her alive.

Reciting as many lines of Lewis Carroll's surreal masterpiece as she could call to mind, she remained calm beneath the shroud for the first half hour of the journey. But current events kept circling and swooping in, crowding out Alice and the looking glass, the walrus and the carpenter—and the idealized, reassuring image of Gianni Giannini, the first man to stir her emotions in many a year, since the departure of Striker.

With a sudden pang, Daria wondered what would happen if she were separated from her fanny pack containing her wallet, badge, and gun, and they wound up in the wrong hands? Centauri would throw the book at her.

Shoes and ships? How could she run, let alone walk, from the clinic in Voltri to the wharf and container port if Emilio Bozzo had forgotten her shoes? With a stab of discomfort, she felt the bareness of her feet. The twine attaching the tag to her big toe was cutting off her circulation. The toe was beginning to throb.

Shoes and ships and sealing wax, she said to herself again, thinking of Clement and Zack, the misery of migration, the inanity of tourism to the "sink-we terry," and the draconian heartlessness of anti-terrorism legislation. When was it not only all right but necessary to put the shoe on the other foot, break the sealing wax, bend the rules, break the law, kick off your shoes, and step barefoot through the looking glass or dive into the rabbit hole in pursuit of the unknown? Break or bend to preserve? Could a state of emergency or martial law, for instance, potentially save a democracy, the way an artificial coma could save certain patients? Is that what Centauri and his friends were up to? Or were they bent on the opposite?

Shoes, shoes, shoes, she thought, trying to puzzle through the tale of Clement and Zack. Was Clement wearing shoes Zack had discarded in flight? Or were they the shoes of the driver of the red bread delivery van? Was Zack that driver?

But the most frequent recurring chain of thoughts tormenting her brain ran something like this. Centauri knew Joe Gary and must have dug up dirt on him, so he could run him. Or the opposite. Did Joe Gary know Centauri and have dirt on him? Why, otherwise, would the Questor stick his neck out, befriend Gary publicly, attend his parties, get him into society? They were propping each up, aiding and abetting, conspiring. To do what?

Willem Bremach said Andrew Striker had dots to join. Bremach knew Striker. Striker must have known Joe Gary—or at least known everything there was to know about Gary, thanks to the American secret services he worked for. Bremach knew Gary and Centauri and must have had dirt on them both. Bremach,

Centauri, and the marquise had allowed Gary to join the old-money clubs of Old Genoa. Why? Bremach loathed Centauri and seemed glad Gary was dead, and the marquise surely could not have known Joseph Gary in the past, a peasant turned spy, or enjoyed his company? But Bremach had hinted she did know him. Had she sponsored Gary at the Galleria Club to please Centauri or Bremach? And who devised Gary's punishment, who stole the body parts, and who piloted the plane?

Morbido's words about the rioting came back to her. *That's precisely what Centauri and his friends want.* A state of emergency? Martial law? Trump had toyed with the idea. France had done it for a full year and had come out as free as before, still the flawed, partial democracy it had always been, at least since the days of General de Gaulle. Clumsily, the Italian political right had tried but failed more than once to impose martial law: in the 1960s, during the failed coup d'état, and the 1970s, during the Years of Lead, when the Red Brigades and right-wing extremists were each running amok, kidnapping, killing, setting off bombs, and then blaming the other side to sow confusion.

Confusion was the deep state in Italy. After World War Two, the Allies had helped write the Italian Constitution, devised to make the country ungovernable and keep another Mussolini from taking power. The real "historic compromise" wasn't about Communism and Christian Democracy. So far, the compromise had been about avoiding military rule by maintaining a mostly benign police state with draconian anti-terror legislation, a pseudo-democracy clothed as a representative republic and watched over by the victorious allies of old, America foremost among them. But America under Donald Trump had changed, morphing into a strange new hybrid authoritarian police state aligned not with Britain and the historic allies but with Russia.

Daria's head and stomach were beginning to ache from the combined effects of the cold, the cigarette smoke, and motion sickness.

When the siren of the ambulance finally fell silent and the

bucking stopped, she sighed out loud—too loud. Taking a deep, anxious breath she braced herself. She must not move. She must not make noise. They must not see she was alive, or this caper would get back to Centauri and then the game was up.

She heard and sensed car doors opening and slamming, heard the adolescent banter of the drivers, then felt the gurney being yanked out and lowered, and pushed jerkily through hot sunlight across asphalt and up a concrete ramp, banging through swinging doors, and coming to a halt in a cool corridor. New voices joined the scrum, someone of authority snarled and commanded and said he knew nothing about it—the "it" being her arrival. The shroud jerked up from her feet and the label was tugged, a name read aloud, then the label and shroud dropped. The gurney lunged forward again, rumbling down the corridor, through more doors and into a chill, quiet place that smelled of tainted meat and antiseptics. The doors flapped and banged. The voices retreated. Daria took a deep breath. She heard the whirring of the air conditioning, then realized that no, it was not air conditioning. It was a refrigerator. The gurney was in a cold room, a room for dead bodies. From experience, she knew that in such facilities the stinging temperature hovered a few degrees above freezing. She was cold already. And scared. All she had on were a pair of jogging shorts and a jersey. They were damp. Her body was still daubed with sweat. Her bare feet were now protruding from the bottom end of the shroud. Where was Emilio Bozzo? How long would it take for him to arrive?

Shoes and ships and sealing wax, she whispered to herself, feeling light-headed, her big toe burning and aching from lack of blood.

Several more minutes went by. Her teeth began to chatter. Her lips, toes, and fingers began to go numb. She calmly, slowly, methodically tilted her head back, so her jaw was held shut by the taut shroud, stopping the chatter that might give her away. She could barely move. She was not an escape artist, she had no knife up her sleeve. She had no sleeves. Tears of anguish, fear, and terrible, killing cold welled up in her eyes. Taking slow, deep breaths through her flaring nostrils, her lips clamped shut, she repeated her mantra. But the mantra only worked when you were in control of your environment.

After what seemed an hour but may have been only five or ten minutes, fearing she might die from hypothermia, Daria began wriggling and shouting, gasping for air through the shroud, her face, hands, and feet now entirely numb.

"Shhhh," shushed a familiar voice, the mouth and bad breath close to her ear. "We're moving you out of here now."

Quaking and gasping, Daria forced her eyes shut and felt herself sinking. Once again, the gurney bucked forward, then rumbled and bounced, and finally rolled to a halt. She felt the straps being loosened and she smelled Emilio Bozzo's nauseating halitosis as he panted, his face hovering over her, wrestling off the shroud and forcing her to her feet. "You've got to get up and out," he whispered hoarsely, "before anyone comes in."

Daria opened her eyes and saw Bozzo standing before her, her shoes and pack in his outstretched hands. Dazed, her hands transformed into frozen lobster claws, she worked the tag off her toe and wrestled on the shoes. Leaning on Bozzo's arm, she hobbled out of what was clearly an examining room and down a short hallway to another empty room. "Sit here and get warm," he whispered, leaning close. "Can you hear me?" He shook her. She nodded back. "I called another taxi," he said. "It will be here in a few minutes. Can you put on your windbreaker and running pants?" She nodded again, watching him unzip the fanny pack and pull them out for her. "I have to find some way to get that gurney back to the ambulance without being seen and explain what happened to the corpse," he added, his voice choked, fluty, and panicked. "This is crazy," he added. Then he disappeared, reappearing moments later just as Daria felt the numbness at last leaving her lips.

In the taxi, with her billed cap pulled low on her forehead and the sunglasses covering her exhausted, bloodshot eyes, she shivered violently despite her nylon windbreaker and running pants. Asking the driver to turn off the air conditioning, she opened her window to let in the day's staggering, humid heat. Bozzo listened with dismay.

"Where to?" asked the cabbie, eyeing her with resigned annoyance.

Daria concentrated for half a minute before speaking. "The airport in Albenga," she said, as she clawed and fumbled in her fanny pack. "Step on it," she added, flashing her badge. Then she leaned over and took the swirling roof light from Bozzo's limp hands. Switching it on, she reached up and out of the window, suction-cupping it to the roof. "Five minutes," she said, turning to Bozzo, "just give me five minutes of silence to thaw and think."

When the taxi pulled up at the off-limits staff entrance of the Albenga airport half an hour later, Osvaldo Morbido emerged from the shade of an open hangar where he had been waiting, a paper cone of fried artichokes in his hands. He tossed the greasy cone into a garbage can and strode over. Beckoning, he led Daria and Bozzo inside the hangar, toward an office. "No point wasting time talking to the administrators," he croaked, looking with a gimlet eye at Daria's jogging getup and haggard face. "No one knows anything about anything, and the important people are off today, except one, and he's a mechanic." Morbido paused and raised a thick eyebrow, expecting a reaction. "Cat got your tongues? What happened? You look half-dead."

Bozzo muttered something incomprehensible about hypothermia and studied his feet while Daria said, deadpan, "You are correct, Osvaldo, I'm half dead but very happily back from the underworld."

Shrugging, used to her enigmatic utterances, the lieutenant said he thought they were wasting their time with the seaplanes, and they would see why shortly.

Morbido's vigorous knocks on the glass-fronted door to the office of the airplane maintenance department summoned a stocky man of medium height and middle years. He appeared wearing a pristine, starched and ironed mechanic's outfit. It consisted of dark blue, short-sleeved coveralls cloaking an ironed short-sleeved white cotton shirt. His hair was black, graying around the temples, and his fingernails, Daria noticed, were immaculate. The man's name was stitched on the left breast of the coveralls. She raised her sunglasses, peered at it, and read *Vincenzo Bianchi—Capo Reparto Tecnico*. As head of the airplane maintenance department, Bianchi clearly no longer got his hands dirty.

"My pleasure," he said in an affable tenor, stepping out and closing the door behind him. They shook hands. Unabashedly astonished by the way Daria looked and the cadaverous temperature of her hand, he glanced down and asked, "Do you travel holding an ice bucket, captain?" When Daria did not answer, Bianchi added, "I already showed your lieutenant why it could not have been any of these planes…"

"Please be kind enough to show me and the coroner," Daria said, politely but firmly. "We are trying to solve a peculiar case and cannot reveal the details. Thank you for your forbearance."

They walked out of the hangar and across the tarmac, following the head mechanic. The airport was eerily empty. No planes appeared to be landing or taking off, presumably because of the long holiday weekend. They heard the tinkling sound of wrenches and the whirring of power tools in the distance, coming from another hangar. A solitary forklift trundled by, loaded with what looked like sections of bleacher seats, the driver waving at Bianchi. Otherwise it was a ghost town airport, a few short runways surrounded by endless fields of artichokes.

"It's mostly charters and private planes we deal with here," Bianchi volunteered, as if sensing her thoughts, "plus the Civil Defense and Fire Prevention Corps, as you know. Now that the air show is over, and we've cleaned up, things will go back to being nice and calm—except for fighting fires and rescuing folks."

She nodded. The scorching sun felt wonderful, heating her back through the windbreaker and jersey. She walked at an unnaturally slow pace, savoring the heat, feeling life and energy returning. Daria now realized that what she craved was a bottle of water, a double espresso, and a slice of focaccia. Later, she told herself.

A row of four Canadair water bombers stood in line, their yellow-and-red detailing and fuselages spotless and glinting. They were remarkably small, squat, stubby machines, Daria could not help thinking, from nose to tail no longer than a standard city passenger bus and not particularly tall, either, perhaps three or four meters from the ground to the top of the wings, she judged.

Beyond them were two much larger seaplanes, one clearly Chinese, from the red ideograms on the side. The other was Russian, she assumed, vaguely recognizing their outlines from the hasty research she had done over the last thirty-six hours—and from Centauri's silhouettes, burned into her visual cortex earlier that morning. She pointed.

"These first, please," she said to Bozzo and Bianchi, indicating the big Chinese and Russian airplanes.

"Be my guest," the mechanic replied. "The pilots won't be here for another hour," he added, glancing at his watch. It was nearly 11:00 a.m. "They went to the beach for a swim. It's not every day people like that find themselves on the Italian Riviera."

Morbido laughed sardonically. "Well, the Russians have their own Rivieras now, don't they, on the Crimean Peninsula? Better than those old Black Sea resorts. And there's always Syria, nice and sunny there, as long as the chlorine gas and barrel bombs don't get you."

No one laughed. As usual, Bozzo stared at his feet, blinking in the glare.

Raising a finger, Daria pointed to the forward section of the underbelly of the Russian plane, where, presumably, the water was taken in. She asked if Bianchi could open it, but he shook his head. "I have no idea how to do that," he said, "and I would never go on board without permission." He smiled knowingly. "The thing is, on both these planes a protective screen mechanism fronts the intake bays. I have seen it. If you look at the manuals online, you'll understand. There's no way you could scoop up a human being with either of them, unless that protective screen was removed, and it wasn't, not while they were here in Albenga, anyway."

Morbido smiled wryly. "So, the capo was right," he said, "for once."

"And the Canadair planes?" Daria asked.

Bianchi dipped his head and smiled affably again. "As I explained earlier to your lieutenant, it's more or less the same story—come over and I'll show you."

They trooped back to the Canadair water bombers. They were identical and of recent manufacture by the look of them. Bozzo scratched his hollow, pale cheeks and scrutinized the front end of the first plane while Bianchi climbed inside, threw a series of hydraulic switches, and called out of the open cockpit door for them to stand clear. The belly of the plane sank slowly, the scoop stopping a foot or so above the tarmac. Bianchi reappeared as Bozzo and Morbido stepped up and studied the intake mechanism.

"See," said Bianchi, "you might pick up some small fish, and maybe a dog or even a small child, but it would be virtually impossible to scoop up a grown man." He paused and watched the disappointed expression on Daria's face. "I'm guessing that's what this is all about?"

"Nothing is simple," Morbido muttered.

Bianchi splayed his arms wide and laughed good-naturedly. "This is Italy," he said, "but it's not just Italy, it's the world, it's all the same now, all very complicated."

Bozzo grimaced at the banter, continuing to study the mechanism of the plane's jaws and bay. He took several photos with his smartphone, zooming in for a series of close-ups. "In any case," Bozzo remarked glumly, glancing back at the others, "the likelihood that any genetic material would be left in this kind of mechanism is low. How fast does this plane fly when it's taking in water?" he queried Bianchi.

"Between thirty and fifty kilometers per hour," Bianchi said. "Any slower and it falls to the surface and wallows. Any faster and it trips and flips."

"And how many liters does it take in?"

"About six thousand."

"And how far does the plane travel with the bay open while filling up?"

"Approximately one kilometer."

"Well," Bozzo replied, shaking his head, "imagine the scouring power of seawater running over stainless steel at forty kph for a kilometer." He rapped the mechanism with his knuckles. "I will say this, however. The wounds on the subject's body, and the lesions and tearing of the shoulder, as well as the shearing of the hand, might well have been brought about by a mechanism of this kind during the uptake or else as it released its payload." He stuck his head through the cowcatcher into the bay. "If this screen mechanism had been removed," Bozzo mused aloud, "There would be ample room for a man the size of the subject to travel undamaged or at least in one piece in it and breathe, if he were conscious and could raise his head above the water, assuming the bay is never filled to the top."

"Correct," said Bianchi. "It is never fully filled, and I have stood up inside these scoops many times in the old days."

Taking off her sunglasses, Daria stared at the jaws and complex mechanism and turned to the mechanic. "From what you say, the Russian and Chinese planes could not have scooped up the victim—the cowcatcher device or whatever technical term you have for this screen would prevent that." Bianchi nodded. "These new Canadair planes are also designed to avoid that danger, possibly because of accidents that occurred in the past, in Canada?"

Again, Bianchi nodded. "And elsewhere," he added, "it's rare but not unknown."

"What about older models? These planes have been around for nearly forty years."

Bianchi cautiously said yes, it was conceivable with the early models of Canadair, though most of them had been updated, retrofitted, and equipped with safety devices.

"Could a plane be modified to make it easier to scoop up more water, for instance, with no protection?"

"Affirmative, captain," Bianchi said. "I have seen it done. The old Canadair planes that are sold on Third World markets, for instance," he added, "where safety is not a consideration, and they want maximum water intake over the shortest stretch, where they're dealing usually with rivers or lakes."

"Any of those old models around? Any of them used in the last few days, during the competition, or otherwise?"

Bianchi shook his head. "Not here," he said, "not in Albenga."

"But elsewhere, nearby, perhaps?"

"Possibly," he said, grimacing and crossing his arms as if a realization had struck him.

Daria drummed her lips. "Might we step into your office?" she asked, walking toward the hangar. She stopped and turned. "Osvaldo, I think we can let Emilio get back to work now. If you run him to the train station, he can be in Genoa in an hour, whereas a taxi will take twice that, with the traffic from the protest march near Villa Migone." She glanced at Emilio Bozzo and smiled wryly. "I cannot thank you enough," she said with a friendly, quiet laugh. "Cremation is definitely the way to go."

Bozzo raised an eyebrow, his cheeks coloring. "Keep me posted," he said, picking up his tool bag and following Lieutenant Morbido, who was already clomping toward his unmarked car, one hand raised to shade his eyes from the glare.

Twenty-Two

Inside Bianchi's orderly, nondescript office, Daria took a seat and accepted his offer of a cup of coffee.

"American, please," she found herself saying. "With lots of hot water."

He studied her, a quizzical smile on his round, affable face. "No focaccia delivered this morning, I'm afraid," he apologized, "but I do have some of those toxic, packaged breakfast rolls, if you'd care for one." He paused and frowned. "Are you all right, captain?"

"Absolutely," she lied. "I caught a chill this morning, that's all."

"A chill, in this heat?" He seemed incredulous. "Well, the coffee and chemical brioche will fix you."

Picking up the thread of their conversation begun as they had crossed the hangar, Bianchi confirmed that the Civil Defense Department had retired two veteran Canadair planes recently, one of them approximately two years ago, the other six months ago. "The last one was my favorite," he said with a sigh. He had nicknamed her Gilda, for a tortoise he'd had when a boy. "She was slow and persnickety and might even try to bite you, but she was tough and indestructible, and I loved her," he remarked, shaking his head.

"The tortoise or the plane?"

"Both," said the mechanic.

It was normal that, after a given number of years, the Civil Defense Department would auction off older planes, he added. When they were too old, metal fatigue set in. Also, the early models of Canadair were equipped with piston engines. They could be temperamental and were sluggish. Now they came equipped with turbo props. The retired ones, like old buses and trains and hospital equipment and everything else that's out of date or worn and unwanted and sometimes dangerous, goes from Italy to Eastern Europe or Africa.

Because he had been so fond of the plane, Bianchi kept tabs on it and knew Gilda had been sold at auction to a company named Aviation Repair Systems Italia. It had bought most of the Civil Defense Department's obsolete planes over the years and was going to rebuild and refit her, then deliver her to foreign clients. "I happen to know she was on the way to Morocco two days ago," he added wistfully.

Aviation Repair Systems Italia had its own airstrip and worked out of facilities that once belonged to Camp Darby, the U.S. military base near Pisa. Daria knew that parts of the sprawling camp were still being used by the U.S. Army for unspecified activities. Most of the compound and its many runways had been leased out to private companies and the Italian government. The increasingly busy Pisa airport, a hub for low-cost airlines, occasionally redirected overflow charters to Camp Darby and farmed out maintenance to several companies there. "They rebuild old planes, convert passenger planes to freight, and decommission military planes," the mechanic clarified.

Holding up her smartphone so Bianchi could see the screen, Daria showed him the image from social media of the seaplane that had been spotted shortly after 10:00 a.m. on April 23rd flying toward the Cinque Terre. "Might this be Gilda?"

Bianchi peered curiously at the screen, tilted it this way and that, trying to see through the reflection from the overhead lights, then tapped the screen accidentally, causing the image to disappear. Daria brought it back. "It could be," he said. "That's a blurry photo, but, let me see, let me blow up this part of the fuselage... Yes, I do recognize her." He pointed at the screen again, careful not to touch it. "See the ding there, by the cockpit door? That was Mario, with the forklift, eight years ago. They obviously tried to straighten and flatten it, but I can still see it. And the oddity of the black and red stains on the tail? In other models, the tail was modified so the chemicals and exhaust would not blow back and stain the metal."

Daria glanced at the screen, could not actually see what he was referring to, and concentrated instead on studying Bianchi's expressions and manner. He seemed to be a straight shooter.

Finishing her watery coffee and wondering out loud if Bianchi could now make her an espresso, she asked with feigned distraction if it was normal that registration numbers be whited out on decommissioned planes. Yes, said the mechanic, it was not unusual. A temporary permit would be issued by the aviation authorities to allow the plane to get to its destination, then it would be up to any new owner to re-register it according to local laws.

"Old amphibious planes never die," the mechanic said cheerfully, "I've seen some from the '50s or even the 1930s, still flying." He paused. "You can use seaplanes for all kinds of things. I heard there's a millionaire in Sardinia using one of our old Canadair planes for sea skydiving." Bianchi shook his head for emphasis. "Ever heard of it? He and his friends parachute at sea and the plane picks them up."

"Picks them up?" she asked. "How? Surely it does not scoop them up?"

"No, no. It's been modified for search and rescue. There's a big sliding door and a ramp." Before Daria could speak, he began again. "There are dozens of vintage seaplanes in Africa and Asia. Like I say, they're used for all kinds of activities."

"And in Canada, too, presumably," Daria ventured, holding onto the vision of the millionaire skydiver in Sardinia. "I assume such planes are not habitually used for drugs and smuggling in Canada," she added, fishing for a reaction, "or for search and destroy missions when the object is to find and kill migrants, not save them?"

The mechanic glanced at her warily but said nothing. He listened now as she asked him if he might know who the best water bomber pilot anywhere might be, perhaps the millionaire's pilot, in Sardinia?

Pacing back and forth across his office, Vincenzo Bianchi shook his head and said that he could not say who the best water bomber pilot *in the world* was, but he thought he knew the best one in Italy, and it wasn't the young pilot out in Sardinia, who was competent but nothing more. "Umberto Ansaldo," the mechanic declared with admiration. "He retired about fifteen years ago."

Ansaldo, the cadet scion of one cadet branch of one of Genoa's oldest families, had flown for the Italian Air Force, then Alitalia, in the good old days, Bianchi added, then, for a lark, flew Canadair water bombers for the Civil Defense Department. "He was getting ready to retire again when I was hired," Bianchi noted, "and that was about twenty years ago."

What distinguished Ansaldo was his daring. He had been trained on prop planes in the 1950s and been a stunt pilot in the 1970s for Italy's Hollywood—Cinecittà—before special effects.

Daria interrupted, asking how old this Umberto Ansaldo was and if he were still alive and flying—and, coincidentally, if he might know the Sardinian millionaire skydiver.

"Oh, he's probably in his seventies or early eighties, but he's still flying all right," the mechanic said, pointing to a twin-engine Cessna in a hangar visible from his windows. "That's his. He comes in once or twice a week. Whether he knows the Sardinian I have no idea."

"And he did not fly in the competition?"

Bianchi shook his head, as if the question were ludicrous. "The best pilot in Italy could not have participated in that air show or scooped up the subject of your inquiry," he said, "for any number of reasons, I suppose, but primarily because he was flying that plane over there with his son, Sandro, who is also a pretty good pilot. Ansaldo was gone most of the day. I could tell you exactly when he flew out and when he flew in," the mechanic added, reaching out and pecking at the keyboard of a desktop computer.

Noting that Umberto Ansaldo enjoyed flying to Corsica, Sardinia and the Tuscan archipelago in particular, Bianchi confirmed that the Cessna had taken off at 7:45 a.m. and returned to Albenga at 4:47 p.m.

"Could that type of plane have flown as far as Olbia or Pisa?" she asked quietly.

"Of course," the mechanic said, "it could fly to Moscow or Oslo!"

"And could one man fly it, without a copilot?"

Bianchi nodded.

"How long would it take to get to Pisa?"

"From here, about forty-five minutes, an hour," he answered.

"Any record of where he might have flown that day?"

Bianchi explained that private planes don't have to file detailed flight plans—they are used for tourism, entertainment, excursions. Improvisation and freedom are essential to the experience. "You want lunch in Olbia?" he asked rhetorically. "Sure! How about dinner in Florence? Plus, it's the long holiday weekend, so he may have landed at a private airstrip somewhere to visit friends, go swimming, see his mistress, who knows? Why not ask him?"

Daria said she would be glad to and wondered if Bianchi might supply the contact information for Ansaldo and the Sardinian millionaire. The mechanic consulted the computer again and wrote two names and mobile numbers on a sticky note, handing it silently to Daria.

"So, this Signor Ansaldo could have flown to Pisa," she summed up, "parked his plane, and then flown Gilda? It is conceivable?"

Bianchi smiled wryly and shook his head, seeing where she had been heading. "Anything is conceivable," he admitted, "but that is highly unlikely. As I mentioned, I know Gilda was on her way to Morocco by the time the air show was under way."

"Then perhaps her pilot, for the hell of it, flew slightly north to see the air show before heading south? Or the millionaire's modified Canadair from Olbia flew over, piloted, perhaps, by the son of Signor Ansaldo, or by Ansaldo Senior, the father, why not, with the son taking over the Cessna and flying to Pisa? Perhaps both independently flew over from Olbia and Pisa to the Ligurian coast to see what was going on and give a hand to put out a fire near La Spezia?"

Bianchi continued to shake his head. "You would need to ask them. But I doubt anyone in Sardinia will speak freely with you, they're a strange bunch, and I don't think you will find anyone at Aviation Repair Systems Italia now. It's a national holiday."

Daria nodded amiably but, finding the number with Google, she called the company in Pisa nonetheless and was gratified when someone answered after the third ring. She identified herself and explained that she was trying to track a Canadair plane the company had just rebuilt and presumably sent to Morocco. Yes, said the male voice on the other end of the line, he knew the plane and knew it had been scheduled to fly out. No, he answered again, he wasn't on duty yesterday or the day before. He did not know who was flying the plane to Morocco. He had been on vacation and had just returned and was holding down the fort while everyone else took their turn on vacation. Tapping at the keys of a computer, he came back on and told Daria the company registry showed the seaplane had flown out, heading for Morocco, at 11:15 a.m. on April 23rd.

"Was it also flown earlier that same morning?"

"It might have been," said the voice, hesitating, then rattling the keyboard, "to make sure all systems were go before such a long flight, that would be normal practice."

"Exactly," Daria said. "Might I speak to the pilot?" she asked.

The man laughed heartily. "He's not back yet," he said at length. "He had three refueling stops and an overnight in Malta on the way." It was a slow plane, not designed for long hauls. The pilot would be returning to Pisa in two days, on a commercial flight. She could talk to him then, if she wanted. Daria noted the man's name, Stefano Molfino, thanked the helpful employee, and disconnected.

"You're barking up the wrong tree," Bianchi said, scratching his head and frowning. "That's my opinion, for what it's worth. Stefano Molfino would never do what you think has been done and he wouldn't be capable of doing it, either."

"Obviously there is no odometer in an airplane," she said, her voice flat. "But there must be some way to know how far Signor Ansaldo's Cessna flew on April 23rd?"

Reluctantly, Bianchi checked his computer file and told her the number of hours the Cessna had logged that day. "We check it every time a plane comes in," he explained, "for maintenance."

"And?"

"It could have flown to Sardinia or Pisa or both," he said warily.

Daria drummed her lips, fully restored now. "Any other candidates for our mystery pilot? Someone capable, as you put it, of scooping up a moving swimmer and dropping him alive on a bull's-eye thirty kilometers away?"

The mechanic whistled quietly and almost whispered, "I figured as much." Buying time, he glanced at his watch and wondered out loud what had become of Daria's lieutenant, Morbido. The train station was only fifteen minutes away. Then he said, "I can think of a few candidates, but none of them could have done it. Either they're dead or out of commission right now." He typed a name into his computer, then swiveled the screen around as a series of photos appeared on Google Images. Daria peered at them and smiled despite herself, recognizing the grinning, horsey face of Willem Bremach. "Now, this gentleman was an authentically great pilot," said Bianchi, "good friend of Umberto's too, kept a private plane with us for about thirty years. But I happen to know he's injured himself and isn't flying these days. He's also over ninety."

"He's ninety-three, to be precise," Daria remarked. "Ambassador Bremach could not have flown that plane, he was watching the incident unfold from his villa."

"Ah, so you know l'ambasciatore! What a marvelous character, what an inspiration!"

Then Bianchi told her how Willem had flown Spitfires, an astonishingly overpowered fighter aircraft for its day, and could dive them like the Nazis' Stukas, then slow them until they almost hovered above a target. "Then he would slide open the cockpit, pull the pin, count, and toss out a hand grenade, dropping it right into a foxhole or the turret of a tank, for instance, and then pull up the Spitfire before anyone knew what had happened." The mechanic's admiration appeared to be boundless. "You see, he was born in Genoa, but he's half Dutch and half English, so, when the war was over, he left the RAF and the Dutch drafted him and sent him to fly in some horrible colonial war in a godforsaken place..." Bianchi paused and shook his head, crossing his arms and smiling. "I saw him flying Gilda more than once," he whispered conspiratorially, "but we were sworn to silence. Everyone was. He didn't want his wife, la signora Bremach, to know. She is a very severe Nordic lady and does not want him to fly anymore. But Willem—I mean, his Excellency the Ambassador—would always say, 'Look at the Queen! If the Queen of England wanted to fly, who would stop her, and she is two years older than I am!'" The mechanic chuckled, beaming.

Daria signaled her agreement, the pennies dropping one after another. She stood up when Lieutenant Morbido knocked on the office door. Through the large single-glass pane, she could see he was dusty and grimy, and was panting and sweating profusely. Did he suddenly have high blood pressure, she wondered? Diabetes? He looked like a heart attack about to happen.

"I guess you're both under the weather," joked Bianchi, glancing at Morbido. "A storm is coming," he added, nodding at the horizon, "and it's going to be a big one, a red-sand sirocco full of thunderheads."

Twenty-Three

"**T**here you are, Daria. I was beginning to wonder."

Andrew Striker had a soft but persuasive voice. His smile shone bright with polished white teeth each the size and shape of a small, perfect white corn kernel. The voice and smile matched his tall, lean, good looks and his expensive, understated casual sportswear in shades of khaki, tan, and olive green.

The only visible flaws in this apparently ideal specimen of manhood, Daria thought as he took her outstretched hand and shook it, were his ghostly complexion, slightly jutting jaw, and remarkable widow's peak. She had not seen Striker in several years—their separation had not been amicable. It had been acrimonious. His thick, salt-and-pepper hair was brushed back vampire-style as it always had been. But in the intervening years, it had receded so far on either side of his untanned forehead that what remained looked like a tongue of fur thrown on a Carrara marble floor. The effect was bizarre, almost demonic.

"Your man Morbido looks like he's seen a ghost," Striker observed, watching the lieutenant pull away from the parking lot.

"He's feeling under the weather," Daria remarked, wishing Morbido had stayed with her. "I mean that literally." Freeing her hand from Striker's grasp, she stepped back to what she thought was a safe distance. But he was clearly unsatisfied with a simple handshake. Leaning down from his six-foot-something height, Striker gently pulled Daria back into his arms and kissed her on both cheeks. Before she could wriggle away, his lips were squarely on hers. She opened her mouth to protest and felt his thick, muscular tongue dart in. Daria was suddenly glad she had been sucking on breath mints all morning. Realizing simultaneously how appalled, angry, hungry, and thirsty she was, she hoped Striker would stop trying to molest her and offer her some coffee and focaccia instead of sexual passion. Otherwise, violence would ensue and she knew who would lose.

"Honestly, Andrew, that's not why I've come to see you," she said, pushing him away and stepping back a full yard this time, prepared to aim simultaneous blows at his throat and genitals. "What is it with you middle-aged men? It must be the weather."

"Yes," he laughed, a strange, strangulated laugh. "Storms make men horny."

She had forgotten how forceful and crude Andrew Striker could be, despite his suave exterior. He was that perfect ripe nectarine at the supermarket, a cleverly displayed piece of luscious fruit that when bitten into had no flavor and gave you a stomachache from greenness and chemical pesticides.

The stomach ache had also come from the physics of their intimate relationship, she now recalled. Striker made love like so many American men, brutally, as if he were a cowboy and she a bucking bronco. The style, rhythm, and timing were very different from the suckling, gluttonous, worshipful, slow lovemaking of the Italians she had known.

The fact that he had been shamelessly two-timing her when the split occurred did not help matters now. She remembered how she had lectured him when he had accused her of being old-fashioned and uptight. "Women are different," she had said.

"When you allow someone to penetrate you, you think twice about sleeping around unless you belong to the fractional minority of uninhibited, sexually voracious females who have more in common with men than other women. People think I'm one but I am not. I am an intensely private person."

Striker looked her up and down now with a wry smile, clearly amused by her colorful jogging outfit and running shoes. "Gosh, and here I thought you were pining away all these months and years." He cut short her silent reflections. "I love your fanny pack and baseball cap, by the way. Very sexy."

"Don't be sarcastic or offensive, please, it doesn't flatter you, Andrew."

"That's weird," he remarked, laughing a percussive, sardonic laugh this time. "Carla always said that."

"*Said.* Past tense?"

Striker fashioned an exaggerated, artificial grimace. "It was short and sweet, like our little romance, though you and I never married. Carla insisted. They say third time lucky. They're wrong."

Daria raised an eyebrow but stayed quiet, eager to change the subject.

Beyond the plate-glass window of Striker's high-tech, air-conditioned office spread the endless wharves and storage facilities of what was Italy's biggest container port. Looking like Lego constructions, the bright red, yellow, green, blue, or pink shipping containers—almost all of them marked with Chinese brand names—were stacked sometimes four or five, sometimes seven, high. The port area had been built on landfill and was shaped like the deck of a giant aircraft carrier. Dozens of cranes the height of skyscrapers edged the wharves, each rising steeply above four widespread fretwork legs and appearing to Daria like a herd of monstrous metallic horses.

"Did you know," he said, raising a finger to point, "that when there are more than five of them stacked up the containers are empty?"

Daria did know—it was one of the first things Striker had told her years ago. "I had heard rumors," she said.

Striker grinned. "They are a silent commentary on the state of the European economy," he continued, offering Daria a leather-upholstered swivel chair at a long, gunmetal work table. It was covered almost end to end with computers, scanners, telephones, modems, routers, and other electronic equipment she could not identify. "They arrive full of cargo from China, are unloaded, and sit empty for months or years because Italy in particular and Europe in general have nothing China wants—except money and real estate, and those don't travel in containers. A few years ago, some bright young man in Genoa finally decided to collect all the recycled packaging from the Chinese goods, fill the empty containers with it, and send them back to China. It's a lucrative business, I'm given to understand."

Daria nodded again. She had heard that one before as well. His repertoire had not expanded. "Find anything interesting lately?" she asked, searching for a diplomatic way to back into the topic that had brought her to Striker. "Still x-raying those containers with that giant machine of yours?"

Striker watched her and smiled brightly. "You know we are," he said, "and you know I can't tell you what we've found lately, unless it falls under your purview. So far, in the last five years, you've made sure Lieutenant Morbido was my interlocutor, not you."

"I'm sure it was the capo who made that arrangement," she remarked, "not I."

Striker shrugged and thrust out his lips. "Whatever. The scanner works away, Daria, but it's the algorithm that finds the stuff we want to keep out of the country. Same as before, except the new algorithms are much more powerful, much more efficient, than a few years back, when you and I were, well, friendly." He paused again. "But that's not what you've come to see me about."

Daria shook her head and studied her fingernails, deciding they needed care. "Greetings from Willem Bremach by the way," she said. "My godfather seems to think you're the Wizard of Oz and knows everything there is to know about Joseph Gary and my boss, and Libya and terrorism and human trafficking, and so on."

"Your *boss's* boss, you mean? Il Generale Centauri? Your immediate boss is Ruggieri, isn't he, and he's a good guy, he wears a white hat." Striker smiled his bright smile again. Walking to an espresso machine in the corner of the office he prepared a caffè americano for her. "This is how you like it," he said, "if memory serves. Long, black, no sugar. Very tough. Very alpha."

"Correct," she said, taking the Styrofoam cup with thanks and glancing around, hoping to spot cold sparkling water and focaccia hidden amid the array of computers.

"Local staff is off today," he remarked, watching her eyes. "We can speak freely. There are no bugs in my office." Striker winked. Daria raised her eyebrow again, this time in obvious, profound disbelief. "He must be handing in his resignation right about now," Striker continued in a mild, neutral tone, glancing at his watch.

"Who would that be?" she asked.

"Well, you haven't changed an iota," he laughed. "Doubting da Vinci, that's what I used to call you, wasn't it? You know who." Pausing to gauge her reaction, he went on. "Centauri is ancient history. Seen the news lately? I mean, in the last five minutes?"

She shook her head. "I've been on the move. What's up?"

Striker seemed sincerely delighted. "Well, this is breaking stuff, Daria, fresh news. You need to keep up. The latest development five minutes ago is Centauri has had some kind of health issue and has resigned. Heat stroke, the doctors say. I think it must be that heavy old military uniform of his, with all the stars and epaulets. Naturally he is eager to defend the honor of his family, dragged in the mud by being associated with Gary Garibaldi and the Mussolini Brigade, so he's stepping back and hiring lawyers. Ruggieri has taken over and will give the speech shortly at the commemorative ceremony, in another two hours, I think it is."

Before the thunderstruck Daria could ask for an explanation, Striker flicked a remote control, and a screen lit up on another long desk. A local 24/7 news channel came on. Images streamed across the screen. Joseph Gary was shown alive at his villa wearing a tuxedo, with Steve Bannon's entourage in the spring of 2018, then in a swimsuit on the deck of the vintage Riva speedboat, then dead—very dead. Aerial views showed the sites where he had been scooped up and dumped.

"Wait, our photographer, Pino Brignole, took those shots from the helicopter," Daria said. "I reviewed them on site. And I took those," she blurted again, pointing at the screen. "How did they get them?"

"Shhh," Striker shushed her, as the newscaster spoke. He raised the volume.

The American undercover agent known as Joseph Gary, accidentally or deliberately lifted from the sea off Portofino by a Canadair water bomber on April 23rd, as we reported earlier today, was found dead yesterday evening by police authorities from Genoa and La Spezia. The discovery was kept secret until now to allow the investigation to proceed unimpeded, it has been claimed.

The mangled body of the victim was dropped from the air on a fire burning in an abandoned farmhouse near the Cinque Terre on the morning of April 23rd, a date and time coinciding with the start of the Insurrection of Genoa in 1945. Signor Gary and the farmhouses played a role in the insurrection—an evil, unpardonable role in one of the region's darkest hours.

Channel 5M can now confirm that Joseph Gary Baldi was none other than Giuseppe Garibaldi, formerly an Italian citizen, born in Prati di Bovecchia, Province of La Spezia, on March 24, 1927, in the same farmhouse where his body was found hideously disfigured and nearly broken in two, draped over a wall, having fallen from the seaplane...

Who was this mysterious individual, and why was he targeted on such a symbolic date?

Now a series of black-and-white historic archive shots came on screen. They showed Giuseppe Garibaldi young, a teenager, holding a rifle, among a group of other Fascist youths. A white circle appeared around his head, then underneath ran the subtitle *Giuseppe Garibaldi, Mussolini Brigade, spring 1945.*

Standing behind the group was a tall, older man, an officer. The frame zoomed to him. Now a circle appeared around this man's head, followed by the subtitle *Colonel Carlo Alberto Lomelli-Centauri II, Coordinator of the Genoa and La Spezia Committees of the Mussolini Brigade in 1945.* A final image showed the words *Jus Stat* scrawled on the farmhouse wall and the translation, *Justice Abides.*

The newscaster's voice was somber. *Justice bides its time— that might be a better rendering of the ancient Latin motto. After the war, Colonel Carlo Alberto Lomelli-Centauri II was court-martialed, tried in civil court, jailed for war crimes, then inexplicably exonerated in 1948, later joining the Polizia di Stato. He was decorated numerous times for his courage and zeal combating organized crime and terrorism in the 1960s and '70s during the Years of Lead. He rose to the rank of three-star general during his long and distinguished career and died in 1998 of natural causes.*

His son, General Carlo Alberto Lomelli-Centauri III, is the current Questor of the Province of Genoa and, like his father those many years ago, was a personal friend of the victim, Giuseppe Garibaldi.

The Questor has declined to comment on these startling revelations, and Channel 5M has so far been unable to reach spokespeople for the Questura, the Provence of Genoa, or the Ministry of the Interior in Rome. All are closed for the public holidays.

Striker cut the sound and turned to look down at her, grinning. "This is Italy," he chortled. "I will believe anything. How about you?"

"This is how you stop a coup before it starts," Daria said grimly, "by pulling back the curtains and revealing the plotters before they can strike."

Striker chuckled as he thanked her with sardonic irony for the elucidation. "We still don't know who did it, who killed Gary, I mean," he said.

Daria laughed darkly. "Don't we, Andrew?" She glanced at the TV again. The Centauri report had ended. The local weather report had come on. Daria could not help staring at the orange thunderbolts and storm warnings in red-and-black lettering that stood out starkly on the big-screen TV. "So, you said Vice Questor Ruggieri is already back from Morocco?" she asked, trying to hide her surprise.

Striker laughed. "Ruggieri never went to Morocco. I guess you really were out of the loop. You should have kept in closer touch, Daria. You should have come to see me earlier, as certain parties suggested. No matter, everything has worked out for the best."

"In this, the best of all possible worlds?"

"Precisely," he laughed again. "Voltaire, *Candide*, I wrote a paper about that once."

"As did I," she remarked, "and every high school student I know."

Striker thrust his lantern jaw out, rubbing it pensively, clearly stung, then glanced through the window. "My guess is there will be a cabinet reshuffle in coming days, with the interior and defense portfolios reassigned, and some jockeying for the vice premiership. The Questor will 'retire' with full honors and a fat pension, voices will be raised and fists clenched in the air, then everything will go back to normal. Coup aborted. End of story. This has happened half a dozen times in the last, what, fifty or sixty years? Most Italians aren't even aware of it. A banana republic by any other name wouldn't be the same."

"And how many times has it happened in America?" she asked, coloring with pique. "The difference is, when it happens in Washington, no one can stop it and you wind up with a mob egged on by a president, storming the Capitol and..." She left the sentence to hang.

"No comment," he replied blandly. He turned back to the TV set. Seeing the same images of storm warnings and sirocco sands, he flicked it off. "Want a ride to La Spezia?" Striker's teeth sparkled as he smiled suavely again. "I'm guessing that's where you want to go. Can't go back to your office yet, not until things simmer down. Morbido has gone home to bed taking your car with him. Come on, we can talk about it on the way to La Spezia. Ambassador and Mrs. Bremach and your mom are down there, at San Terenzo, right? Playing bridge with the remarkable Madame la Marquise Augusti-Contini di Mandrella. And Gambero is still in downtown La Spezia, about to snack on some of that excellent local chickpea tart. He's waiting to hear from you. Very loyal, Lieutenant Italo Gambero, I must say. I wish he worked for us. In fact, I keep wishing *you* would work for us. That offer of an all-expense-paid vacation in Langley still holds, Da."

"How do you know..." Daria began to ask, rising up in the swivel chair. But Striker put his fingers to his lips, then smiled his patented plastic Ken doll smile.

"You don't want to know how I know what I know," he said, winking. With both his hands, he made elephant ears and formed the word "big." "So, boat or copter, you choose, Daria. As I recall, you get seasick pretty easily. Not sure we ever flew together. We've got a big Egyptian freighter detained in La Spezia with some very interesting cargo on board and I need to be there soonest."

"Copter," Daria said, motioning vaguely at the blank TV screen. "What about the storm?"

"We'll beat it," Striker replied, glancing again at his watch. "But we better get going. You can watch the news while we fly. There are TV monitors in front of every seat. It's a great little egg-beater, a reconverted military OH-58D Kiowa, not very different from the things my dad flew in 'Nam but a lot faster."

"Well," she said dryly, "I hope your dad did not use this one to spray Agent Orange. The contamination lingers."

"Gee, maybe that's what's happened to my hair," he joked. But there was anger in his eyes. "My dad sprayed Agent Orange and your dad escorted war criminals to freedom. So, I guess we're even-steven. It was all in a day's work back then, and you know what? The more things change, the more they stay the same."

Twenty-Four

The blue-and-white Kiowa awaited behind the building in the otherwise empty parking lot. It apparently doubled as a heliport.

Uneasy, Daria glanced at the bank of boiling, black clouds on the southern horizon. The temperature and humidity had increased to tropical levels. How strange that a desert rainstorm full of red sirocco sand could feel so muggy, she thought.

The distance from downtown Genoa to La Spezia was exactly 122 kilometers east by southeast on the autostrada, Daria knew, meaning less than one hour in the Kiowa, unless they encountered headwinds or the engine sucked in the fine red sand of Morocco, seized up, and froze. Then it would be a very short flight.

"Where's the pilot?" she asked.

"Here's the pilot," he said, pointing at his breast.

Dismayed, she remembered Willem Bremach's description of Striker as a *damn fine pilot, though reckless*. She was even more dismayed to think he would fly without a copilot with a sirocco approaching.

Hesitating at each step but unwilling to show fear, Daria

climbed on board and pulled a helmet over her head. It cut the noise of the engine and rotor and acted as a headset.

"Like being my copilot?" Striker asked in his velvet voice, speaking softly into his mike.

Daria did not have time to answer. The copter roared and hopped into the air, then spun on its axis, rising swiftly and heading east over the wharves along the Gulf of Genoa. She glanced down at the port facility with its teetering toy containers and giant fretwork cranes, then turned in her seat looking south at the approaching storm front.

"Can you hear me?" she asked.

"Loud and clear," he said, accelerating toward downtown Genoa and its touristy, Fisherman's Wharf–style old port. "No need to shout. The mike is very sensitive." He raised his hand and pointed. "See that homely little church over there?" Daria recognized the church, perched on the edge of the medieval walls of the city. Directly below it was the notorious elevated freeway that had blighted the center of the city since the 1960s. Immediately beyond the freeway were the defunct refrigeration facilities for what used to be Genoa's active but now dying local fishing industry. "You ever been in the tunnel that leads from under that church into the old port area?"

Daria waited, then shook her head and, in a soft, defensive voice said, "No." She sensed what was coming. Everyone in Genoa knew about the "Ratline" escape routes set up by the Allies along with the Italian postwar administration, the Vatican, and the Red Cross, routes to whisk "strategic human assets" to safety abroad after the war. But it was still a taboo subject in Italy, seventy-plus years later.

"That's where we smuggled them out," Striker said gleefully. "*They*, the Nazis and Fascists *we* wanted on *our* side." A triumphant, vindictive look came over his face. He pulled the helicopter up to a higher altitude and hovered long enough to finish what he was saying. "Ever talk to your dad or your godfather about that? Probably not," he continued before she could shake her head again. He nudged the copter forward, pointing down. "From there, to there, underground, then onto a freighter bound for Brazil, or maybe New York or Montreal. Yep, Montreal, Canada."

She knew of the tunnel and the ex-filtration activities but had never broached the subject with her father. He had never spoken about his job and, if she had asked, would have denied being a spy. He was a diplomat, a functionary, a little gray man laboring away for the Ministry of Foreign Affairs. Maybe now was the time, she realized, to ask Willem Bremach what he knew, before it was too late. She swallowed hard.

"Are you trying to tell me Joe Gary was ex-filtrated through that tunnel on the Genoa Ratline and my father and godfather may have been involved?"

"I'm not *trying* to tell you, Daria, I *am* telling you. I'm not sure about Willem, he was awfully young, and the Dutch sent him to Borneo or Java or some such place to quell the restless natives after the war. But I know your dad was a low-level agent as of 1946 based in Genoa, and I know he helped get Eichmann out. Nice guy, Adolf Eichmann.

"So, God knows, Roberto Vinci may have taken Joe Gary's hand and led him through that tunnel, then given him a one-way ticket to Montreal not to mention a Canadian passport. Gary had people there, you see. Big old Italian community in Montreal. The cathedral or whatever it is has this great mosaic of Mussolini on horseback way up under the dome. You ought to see it, Daria, it gives you pause for thought. Then from Canada we eventually moved him into the U.S. as a Navy Intel officer. It was cleaner that way, like laundering rubles. It's fascinating stuff, Daria. I've got your dad's file if you want to see it one day. You're all grown up now. Drop by. I'll take you to lunch."

"I'll find out," she said stiffly. "Willem will know."

"Oh yes, Willem will know. Willem knows everything," Striker laughed, but seemed to be growing angry again.

"Willem says *you* know everything."

"Well, then we're even again," he snapped.

Accelerating away from the old port area toward the Portofino Peninsula, Striker pushed the Kiowa to top speed. She wondered if he were purposely trying to scare her. From this unusual angle, the fearsome promontory looked like an immense Gothic cathedral studded with pinnacle spires of conglomerate stone. On the saddle leading to it from the mainland stood the local answer to the Eiffel Tower—a microwave broadcast tower hundreds of feet high, covered with dozens of parabolic antennas ranged in clusters at various levels. The dishes halfway up were used by DIGOS and the Polizia di Stato, she knew. Those below them belonged to the Carabinieri. Each law enforcement agency spied on the other, intercepting communications and keeping watch. She wondered how many of the other dishes were leased out to Homeland Security and the various other espionage agencies feeding into the NSA's Big Ears network.

"Let me give you a little history lesson, Da..." Striker said in his velvet voice. "Skipping blithely over the country's Fascist heritage, the foundation myth of modern Italy begins with the end of the monarchy by referendum and the creation of the Italian Republic in 1946, right? Skip again to the elections of 1948, when the Italian Communist Party looked like it might win outright and create a bridgehead for the Soviets. That's where the Allies' benign interference comes in."

"Benign interference?" Daria interrupted, incredulous. "More like unabashed vote rigging, vote buying, and political violence by about ten thousand U.S.-paid agitators and thugs," she scoffed. "America invented the Christian Democrats to fight the Commies off. Who cared how many Christian Democrats were undemocratic and un-Christian and had been Fascists or were corrupt and in cahoots with organized crime?"

Striker laughed dismissively. "Why the righteous wrath? We had happily worked with the Mafia during the Italian campaign in 1943 and '44. So why feign surprise we would again after the war? Our policy goal at the time was to coopt the war criminals and Mafiosi and keep the Commies from taking power, and at the

same time avoid the reemergence of a Mussolini-style authoritarian. And our writ has not changed much over the last seventy-odd
years, despite the disappearance of Communism and the coming
and going of seventy governments in as many years. Seventy,
Daria. Think about it. Less is more, weakness is strength. This is
what we want."

Daria felt her cheeks flush. She knew from her political science
courses at the police academy that the Italian Constitution had
been drawn up by Allied fiat. The victors worked in concert to make
the country ungovernable. Institutions were pitted against each
other. The Polizia di Stato belonged to the Ministry of the Interior,
for example. The rival Carabinieri were under the Ministry of
Defense. Other police and secret service corps were controlled by
yet other branches of government. A Byzantine balance of powers
had resulted. Onetime fanatical Fascists like the Lomelli-Centauri
family were exemplars of the reinvented post-Mussolini political
landscape. They were ductile, virulently anti-Communist, and con-
veniently if falsely pro-American—and often in bed with the Mafia.

In his own way, Joseph Gary Baldi was also an exemplary
postwar Italian, she knew, but he'd been drawn from the lowest
caste—the peasantry. He had a dirty past and a bright future,
because he had morphed into a dedicated anti-Soviet friend of
America. He was the perfect recruit for the CIA.

"The country is still on training wheels," Striker continued,
seemingly pleased by the sound of his own purring voice so
clear in his helmet and Daria's. "It's a strange country unofficially
administered in many places by the Mob. You know that better
than I do."

Daria pondered before speaking again. "So, has your algorithm determined that it was the Mob that did it?"

"Did what?"

"You know what. Snatched Joseph Gary! Extraordinary rendi-
tion, kidnap, murder, you choose."

"If they did, then I don't know about it and don't want to know
about it," Striker said.

"So," Daria countered, "correct me if I'm wrong. Joe Gary switched from being a true-blue Fascist to an American operative and therefore in recent years was by default pro-Russian and pro-Mafia. He and Centauri may have been plotting something, a palace coup, possibly with the backing of seditious groups in my ministry, plus the Carabinieri and God knows who else around the country."

"God knows? Naturally you mean us, me, we, the Americans?" he laughed. "Ridiculous!"

Daria shrugged. "No, not you. That seems unlikely." She slipped another mint between her lips. She sucked. "A coup d'état is messy. Why support one when a soft touch has already done the job? Washington has the kind of government they have long wanted in Italy, a new Christian Democrat Party without Christian charity or democracy. My guess is the Oval Office is queasy about Centauri and his ilk."

"Queasy is a wonderful word," Striker said, "but I want to go on the record as saying I have no idea what you're talking about. What happens in the Oval Office is a mystery to everyone, starting with the people in that office."

"Well," Daria continued, undaunted. "I'm guessing some in American officialdom would probably like to see a coup over here, but the smart people, the top advisers, are against it, and if the Russians are trying to engineer the coup with a madman like Centauri, the Americans will subvert it to maintain the balance of power with a subservient, moderately reactionary, moderately authoritarian regime friendly to Russia and the Mob, and it's already in place."

Striker laughed and snorted again. "Are you really expecting me to confirm your outlandish theories, Daria?" he asked. But she could see he was doing precisely that. He even nodded his head and winked.

"They don't want Putin to be entirely in control of the world's eighth largest economy," she pursued. "Italy may be a strange, ridiculous little country, but it's still dotted with NATO bases and bristling with Euromissiles. They are watching, nudging, pushing, and thwarting, as usual. But they—you—aren't actually doing the heavy lifting or dirty work yourselves. Therefore, they or you did not kill Gary."

"They or we certainly did not," Striker said with another sardonic laugh. As if sensing what Daria was thinking, he picked up the thread he had let drop in his office. "Other than releasing useful information at strategic points, we actually had nothing to do with it and have no idea who accidentally or willingly killed Gary, and frankly we don't care. You might want to seek closer to home for that. It might turn out to have been a freak accident no one wants to dig too deep into." He winked exaggeratedly, so she could see he was being ironic, then paused long enough to make his studied Hollywood grimace from under the helmet, his teeth gleaming. "Gary's convenient departure has flushed out Centauri and his pals in Rome, and that's all we care about. Gary and Centauri were useful to us in the past, but they were always loose cannons, and this time they stepped too far out of line. By the way, do you really think the Questor is senile or merely has delusions of grandeur?"

Daria glanced nervously down through the wraparound Plexiglas section of the cockpit and nodded her head. "Senile, yes, probably," she said. "If not senile," she added a moment later, "delusional. Ever since the League got in after the elections of 2018, he has not been himself."

"You mean," said Striker, laughing, "he *has* been himself, his *real* self, like so many people in this beautiful country. Haven't you noticed how the mood has changed? The sweet-tempered, sunny, happy-go-lucky Italians of *La Dolce Vita* are reverting to their true, dark default as nationalistic racists, lovers of authoritarianism, brutality, thugs, Mafiosi. Even the meretricious mercenary restaurateurs and salespeople of the Riviera who are usually so solicitous of tourists with fat wallets have begun to show their hand. It's a black hand, Daria, black as in the Black Shirts."

Daria swallowed hard. What Striker said was true—but it galled her. She shifted uncomfortably in the bucket seat and bit her lower lip. She did not enjoy flying in the best of circumstances, not even in fixed-wing aircraft. To be racing across a sultry sky full of thunderheads with a hothead jilted lover at the controls was a bridge too far. She felt the helicopter accelerate again dramatically, veer north, and dive low over the crags and spires of the promontory.

"Gorgeous, isn't it?" Striker asked. "A natural fortress. When the Fascists and Nazis were hunkered down in those bunkers waiting to kill us, at least they had a nice view, eh?"

Daria nodded, feeling sweat break out and prickle her brow. She heard the echo of her own words to Gianni Giannini in the bunker above Rapallo, and wondered if Striker had heard them. How? "I'm concentrating on my composure," she said after a minute of leaden silence, watching fascinated as a group of hikers clinging to guide chains on a sheer cliff turned to glance, then wave, at them.

"They'll have fun in half an hour, when the storm hits," Striker chortled, shaking his head. "You'd think they'd have the wits to check the weather report before going out hiking on those trails. That's a great place to die, isn't it?"

"You're being sardonic again," she snapped. "Why not call the Civil Defense people instead and warn them that climbers are on those cliff faces and might need to be rescued?"

"Not my table," he scoffed. "This way they'll learn. That's the only way. The hard way."

"Andrew, that's cruel and just wrong. By the same token we should not be flying here."

"Wrong? You're wrong. Hiking with a storm on the way is foolhardy and foolish. We are taking a calculated risk, fully aware of the dangers."

Daria pulled out her smartphone instead of answering him, but he shook his head. "No go," he barked. "Won't work. Relax and enjoy the ride. Isn't it breathtaking?" He pointed at the landscape. "That's the Cala degli Inglesi, the Englishmen's Cove, where the ladies and gentlemen of old used to bathe," he added, mimicking a hoity-toity British accent. "Now some fancy duchess has torn up the protected parklands and has planted her vineyards." He pronounced it vine-yards. "Everyone says she's a royal pain in the Portofino Peninsula, a real alpha female of the regal variety." Striker chuckled and chortled, shaking his head.

Daria was too agitated and too angry to enjoy the view or anything else, especially Striker's strange, juvenile sense of humor. But, she had to admit to herself, this was some of the more spectacular scenery she had ever seen. Pine trees leaned from crazy escarpments hundreds of feet high. Vineyards and orchards spread behind villas and gaily painted houses above the famous horseshoe-shaped bay of Portofino. But her head was beginning to spin, and she could tell she was blanching.

"Speaking of alpha," he said. "I heard Centauri describe you once as an alpha female." Striker laughed savagely, as he had earlier. "He said you ought to drive an Alfa Heifer," he added, "not an Alfa Romeo." He guffawed, louder, provocatively. "If only he could see you now. You're whiter than a sheet. Relax. Enjoy."

"Andrew," she warned, "this is no time for displays of machismo. Centauri is senile and went around saying things like that. But you're not senile, are you? Maybe you are!"

Instead of answering, Striker accelerated again, then veered back out to sea, straightening their flight path moments later, aiming for the Island of Palmaria facing Portovenere and the Gulf of La Spezia. "This happens to be the fastest way to get there, Daria, so hold on tight. The lightning and wind and sand are only a couple of miles behind us now and it's no time to dither." When she didn't answer, he added, "You want me to drop you at the villa or at the heliport in La Spezia?"

Daria hesitated, wondering what affect her dramatic entry by helicopter onto the scene at the marquise's villa would have, and if it might not be better to call Italo Gambero and arrive with him at the villa by car after resting and eating something. "Let me phone Italo," she said a moment later, brandishing her smartphone again.

"I'm telling you, your phone won't work," Striker said. "There's too much interference from the equipment, and we're flying too fast and too low, and most of all we jam anything not recognized by our system. I'll call Gambero for you. Just talk into your mike when he comes on."

"I want to call his private number, not the DIGOS number."

"No worries," he chortled.

"You have his private number?"

"I have his private number," he chortled again. "I have everyone's private number."

A moment later Italo Gambero was shouting into his smartphone, asking who was calling. Daria identified herself, instructing him as quickly and soberly as she could to drive to the marquise's villa at Capo Augusti and wait outside the gates if he arrived before her. "And Italo," she added, hastily. "Call the Civil Defense outpost in Portofino or Rapallo or Santa Margherita and tell them to send out a helicopter or a rescue team, there are hikers on the seaside trail near San Fruttuoso, hanging from chains on the cliffs."

"Anything else?" Gambero asked.

"Yes, pick up some of that *farinata* chickpea tart for me, I'm starving." She nodded to Striker and he disconnected.

"Great electrical conductors, those chains," he laughed. "Daria saves the day."

"How do you know you can land at the villa?" she asked calmly, cognizant of the approaching danger. "I've seen photos of it. That promontory is covered with trees, and there is no helipad on the property. I checked the other day after I met the marquise at the club."

"Trust me," he grinned. "I've been there before."

Daria nodded grimly, unable to repress a smirk, then said, "With my godfather?"

"You bet," Striker confirmed. "Willem's quite a guy. Too bad he hurt his knee, that kind of spoiled the fun for him." Before Daria could ask him what he meant, she saw the island of Palmaria welling up below them, separated by a few hundred yards of sea from the rocky peninsula of Portovenere. "Didn't Lord Byron die here?" Striker asked suddenly, glancing down. "Swimming across the Gulf of La Spezia?"

"That was Shelley, I think," she answered, eager not to distract him.

"Oh yes, how stupid of me, it was Percy Bysshe Shelley, in 1822. How could I forget? I guess you didn't read much poetry in medical school, but maybe you got plenty of highbrow reads at those fancy private prep schools in Rome and London? It's a funny thing, I was a product of blue-collar America and a mere scholarship boy, but I read all of Byron and Shelley in college and graduated first in my class in English lit. Here I am, flying a helicopter and playing 007 with a girl who no longer loves me and probably doesn't even like me anymore."

"I'm not a girl," Daria started to say.

"It's a manner of speaking," he interrupted. "Poetic license. Never mind. I'm sure it's my fault. One of the drawbacks of the profession. It's hard not to become an asshole." Striker laughed his savage laugh again. "Just watch out for that Gianni character," he added in an apparent non sequitur. "Gianni Giannini is no average traffic cop. I did a little checking and guess what, he's got a PhD, in philosophy. Talk about a worthless, useless degree! No wonder he wound up issuing parking tickets in Rapallo. But I'll bet he reads lots of poetry and is dying to recite some for you. He's got a pair of kids in tow. I'll bet you didn't know that."

Nonplussed, Daria nodded, then shook her head, confused, offended, angry, unsure how to reply and increasingly concerned by Striker's erratic behavior. "I barely know the man," she began.

"That's how you 'Begin the Beguine,'" he snorted, singing a snatch from the old Cole Porter tune from the 1930s. Then he changed registers and quoted Jane Austen from memory. "A man who has once been refused!" he declared like a ham actor, taking one hand off the controls to wave it. "Is there one among the sex, who would not protest against such a weakness as a second proposal to the same woman?"

Daria was momentarily speechless. "Are you really quoting *Pride and Prejudice* to me in a helicopter with Armageddon on the way?"

"I am," he said.

"And you imagine you're playing Mr. Darcy to my Elizabeth? That's absurd."

"You know it's my favorite book. I've been rereading it for the fourth time."

"Please concentrate on flying this helicopter, or we'll both get killed."

"That might not be so bad," he said in a melancholy tone. "United again, forever, with Shelley and Byron too, why not?" Striker was strangely silent for an interminable minute. Then he sighed and spoke again, this time calmly. "I'm sorry, Daria, I don't usually make such a fool of myself. But it is hard to be rejected twice by the same woman, especially if she's a woman you have never stopped lusting after, God knows why. And by the way, love and lust go hand in hand in my book. I still lust you."

Daria bit her lower lip until it hurt, then took a deep breath, her nostrils flaring. "Andrew," she started to say, then faltered, then began again, "we'll have to continue this very disconcerting conversation another time. I appeal to your professionalism."

"Right you are," he cut her off, his voice cold and hard now. "Look ahead of you. There's the Castle of Lerici, and there's that perfect half-moon beach at San Terenzo. We went there once, remember? And there, on that crooked point of land, is the marquise's villa at Capo Augusti, and now we're going to sneak in between those trees and try to land on the lawn, *try* being the operative concept."

The helicopter slammed on its air brakes. It felt to Daria like an express elevator in a New York skyscraper—the old Twin Towers, she now realized she was thinking. The rushing whirlygig rose, slowed, then fell all at once in a dizzying, sick-making movement. She stared down longingly at the solid ground—but what she saw was a dangerously beautiful, rocky, wave-lashed promontory with nowhere to land. It was cloaked in dense vegetation, bristling with flame cypresses, bay laurels, and parasol pines. A long, low Renaissance villa at the end of a gated, looping driveway nested in its center. She spotted two cars in a parking lot, one an SUV of some kind, the other a white four-door passenger car she vaguely recognized as belonging to Priscilla Bremach. Italo Gambero was neither outside nor inside the gates with the DIGOS BMW.

Before Daria could turn her head and speak to Striker, with breathtaking speed, the black cloud of thundering rain and red sand had wheeled around and was upon them. Lightning struck simultaneously on three sides, and the wind lifted and tilted the helicopter, shaking it like a child's toy. Through the horizontal, red rain she saw one of the towering pine trees below them burst into flames, then snap in half. Scorched, the trunk blackened and burning, the orange flames from the tree hissed in the rain. Hovering precariously in the gusting winds, Striker attempted to lower the copter to land on a wide expanse of lawn ringed by a greenbelt.

"Damn it," he shouted, the explosion of words nearly blowing out Daria's eardrums. "The top of that burning tree is on the lawn," he growled. "I can't touch down." Striker expertly held the Kiowa about ten feet above the lawn and took one hand off the controls to flip a switch. Daria heard a whirring sound and saw a hatch pop open. A ladder uncoiled beneath her on her side of the helicopter. "Out you go," Striker said, waiting for her to make a move.

She stared down in horror and realized she was shaking her head. "I can't," she started to say.

"Better a twisted ankle than death by crashing and burning," he roared, his sardonic laughter scaring her more than the prospect of the ladder or falling to the lawn. "Go on, Daria, or we'll crash for sure, I can't hold her much longer."

"I won't," she said, unzipping her fanny pack and clutching her service revolver. "I order you—"

Striker cut her off with a snarl. "You can't order me for chris-sakes, you're on U.S. territory in this fucking helicopter, so put your pathetic peashooter away and climb down that ladder, goddammit."

The copter jerked and swung like a swing seat on a roller-coaster. Daria felt her gorge rising but choked it back. She tore off the helmet, flung open the Plexiglas passenger door, and somehow found a way to turn sideways and get her feet on the top rung of the slippery, swinging aluminum chain-link ladder. "Be careful," she shouted at him, her words lost in the wind and rain.

"It's been great," Striker shouted back, taking one of her outstretched hands and pressing it for a split second. "Give my best to Willem."

As if on a trapeze, Daria clutched the rungs of the whipping, swinging lifeline, clambered crazily down, and dropped to the lawn five or six feet below. Skipping away in a crouch, her ankles and knees intact, she turned and watched the helicopter tipping to one side then the other, quaking, rising, and spinning into the gale, then zipping like a giant dragonfly back out to sea, headed for the port of La Spezia. Within seconds, it had disappeared into the quivering curtain of bruised, reddish-black clouds that wrapped the cape and villa, thundering and flashing, the lightning striking the white-capped sea.

Clutching her billed cap and fanny pack, Daria crouched for a moment longer under the flailing branches of the pine trees, trying to regain composure and make sense of what Striker had said. *Spoiled the fun?*

"Calm, quiet, methodical," she recited to herself out loud, running across the lawn toward the pale ocher silhouette of the villa's terrace. It was long, narrow, and paved with slippery stones. The darkness was intense. She stumbled and almost fell while climbing the lichen-etched staircase, her shoes making a sloshing sound.

Leaning on the inside of a set of tall French windows thrown open for Daria, four familiar figures stood waiting. Two of them were propped on canes. In the darkness, they looked like weather-worn caryatids holding up the ancient sculpted marble threshold.

Twenty-Five

The cumulative age of the caryatids, Daria calculated, identifying first the marquise, then her own mother, then Willem and Pinky, must be around three hundred and fifty years. They were soaked to the skin, but smiling, beaming, at her approach.

"Magnifico!" shouted the marquise, her hands clutched together.

"Deus ex machina," Bremach chuckled mischievously, taking Daria by the arm and pulling her behind as they retreated indoors and shook themselves like wet dogs. "Hail!" he added, bursting into mirthful laughter, "Da Vinci has descended!"

She could not help noticing that Willem looked even more dashing and sporty than usual. He was wearing a summer-weight seersucker suit and a dark blue cravat loosely knotted around his wrinkled neck. The neck was that of a venerable tortoise. The tortoise brought to mind Gilda, the tortoise-seaplane, but also Andrew Striker's words about spoiling the ambassador's fun.

Standing upright unaided, Willem began clapping. "I'm so glad the mercurial Mr. Striker chose not to prune the pine trees just now with his rotors. It *was* an impressive landing."

"But he did not land," corrected Priscilla, coming up from behind. "Daria jumped, she was magnificent, as the marquise said!"

"Yes, magnificent," repeated Willem. He paused to chortle. "And to think, we merely drove down in Pinky's ancient jalopy while you arrived like a demigod, nay, like Zephyr himself, riding the winds, with lightning, rain, and Saharan sands. Brava, Daria!"

Daria glanced at her glowering, silent mother and saluted the voluble marquise, but was so disoriented she did not know what to say. Leaning forward, she pecked Pinky on the cheeks, then her mother, then Willem.

"You are very welcome at my villa, commissario," crowed the marquise, extending an avian hand, and drawing Daria further into the salon. As they stood under a vast crystal chandelier that was swaying in the wind, a flash of lightning struck another tree in the garden and thunder clapped violently, blinding and deafening everyone for several seconds. The lights flickered, then went out. When Daria's eyes adjusted to the gloom, she saw the exquisite pearls around the marquise's neck shining as bright as Andrew Striker's teeth, reflecting the gleam of a lantern someone had lit on the other side of the room.

"Come, give me a kiss too," admonished the marquise. "We are all so very glad you have come at last, right in time for the denouement."

A butler and maid in formal, antediluvian black-and-white uniforms stood clutching a candlestick and lantern, waiting at attention in one corner of the long, wide frescoed salon. Imperturbable, they appeared to be almost as old as the marquise, though that seemed impossible. Surely, they would retire before reaching eighty, ninety, or one hundred? Adding their prospective ages to those of the rest of the company, she estimated the total would top five hundred.

Game as ever despite the storm and her wet clothing, the marquise commanded her servants to remain where they were, holding the only lights. Daria's mother beckoned, but before Barbara could speak, Madame La Marquise insisted on leading the commissioner by the hand down a long, dark hallway to the bathrooms, where il commissario capitano might wash her hands and powder her nose.

"My nose is very long," quipped the marquise.

"And mine is remarkably prominent," said Daria.

"Then we are both like Pinocchio," the marquise replied, "and must stop telling lies."

The facilities were at the far end of the many-windowed hallway. A dusky gray light seeped in from outside, the storm still raging. Like the salon, the hall was frescoed floor to ceiling with mythological scenes. Daria stared at them as she and the marquise crept along, the elderly aristocrat leaning on Daria's forearm. Had these works of art been executed, Daria wondered wryly, by one of the Republic of Genoa's celebrated geniuses, those great masters of mannerism or the baroque unjustly, tragically unknown to anyone outside the region?

"Luca Cambiaso," crowed the marquise, reading Daria's mind and glancing from her to the dark walls as she shuffled forward, bent like a bishop's crook by age and osteoporosis. "They say it is his best work. I'm sure in Rome you would not give it a second glance, but by our provincial standards it is quite good. Hercules wrestling the Centaur," she continued, pausing to wave with her free hand at something Daria could barely make out. "Highly original. Found in every property in Liguria. Oh well. There is an extra helping of centaurs on the walls of this particular villa. If you are wondering, the answer is yes, my child, General Carlo Alberto Lomelli-Centauri and I are distant cousins, very distant cousins. This house belonged to the Centauri clan during the time of the maritime republic's greatest admiral, Andrea Doria, in the sixteenth century."

"I'm sure the artwork is priceless," Daria said, clearing her throat. "But might we speak alone for a moment, confidentially and undisturbed?" she asked.

"Oh yes, my child, that is why I have led you here, away from distractions, including your charming mother. But first, wash your hands and powder your elegant nose. I shall await you down there, in the vestibule, by the front door. Your mother and the others have been instructed to stay in the salon. Your mother is most anxious not to have her rubber of bridge interrupted, but that is life, is it not? I'm afraid Willem scolded her a moment ago, when we heard the helicopter flying over the garden. He told her to stop pouting and complaining and stay quiet for as long as you were here, because you had very serious affairs of state to discuss with me. What a handsome boy Willem was back then," she mused. "He nearly crashed his plane into our house," she added. "Not this one. The house in Prati di Bovecchia, I mean. But surely I've already told you that?"

Daria bowed politely, then stepped into the bathroom and took a deep breath, more pieces falling into place. The bathroom was the size of a cupboard. It appeared to have been retrofitted a century or more ago into a niche in the hallway. Opening the twin antique silver spigots above a marble basin, she splashed water on her dusty, grimy face, arranged her tousled hair as best she could, pulled her wet windbreaker to the left then the right until it appeared less bulging and baggy, and reappeared a few minutes later in the corridor. Cocking her head to listen, she felt confident the salon was too far away for anyone there to hear what she was about to say to the marquise.

Joining her in the vestibule, she found the antique noblewoman sitting up straight on a wooden bench upholstered in red velvet. The legs were gilded, ornately carved, and made to look like the stylized limbs and paws of antelopes and lions. It and the marquise made a perfect match. Daria guessed the unusual piece of furniture was four or five hundred years old, like the frescoes and everything else she had seen in the villa.

A tall glass of sparkling water sat on an end table. The marquise motioned toward it. "Drink, Daria," she said. "You must be thirsty. I know you like your water sparkling. Willem says so. Flying always dries one out. I believe it's the air conditioning." She smiled and peered up. Then, before Daria could speak, she added, "Say the word, my dear, I am ready to leave when you are, storm conditions permitting." She indicated a small overnight case packed and waiting in a dark corner by the front door.

"Leave?" Daria asked. "With me?"

The marquise laughed. "I thought we were going to stop telling lies," she commented. "I will, you shall see." She paused and with a nod indicated the suitcase again. "We got used to being prepared, you see, during the bombardments. It's not the kind of thing you forget easily. Willem will explain to your mother and Priscilla. You are only doing your duty. No hard feelings. I am ready."

"May I sit down?" Daria asked, not waiting for the marquise to answer. The many moving parts of the case that had been a blur of separate motion began to slide together, a synchromesh transmission slipping smoothly into gear. She hovered next to the centenarian, careful to test the strength of the bench before putting her full weight on it. Then she settled down and glanced out of the tall windows on the other side of the vestibule. With rain streaming down the outsides, the panes rattled but held and did not leak. The gale had already begun to blow itself out.

"They certainly knew how to build back then," the marquise remarked, raising her dry, raptor voice over the wind and rain. "This property was finished in the 1560s. So, you see, it is not that very old by the standards of Genoa but still, it has weathered many storms."

"I hope you don't mind if I ask," Daria began, shifting from first to second gear. "Did one of your siblings by chance marry an Ansaldo?"

"Why yes," the marquise said brightly, perking up, a foxy smile stretching her lips.

"So, you are related to Umberto Ansaldo?"

The smile spread. "He is my favorite nephew," she said, joining her hands as if to applaud. "Such a dear boy, and so clever with machines."

"Flying machines?"

"Why yes," she paused. "How clever of you to know."

"A famous stunt pilot, he was, I believe?"

"Oh, above all an excellent fighter pilot, flying for the Air Force."

"A patriot?"

"Of course! Everyone in my family is, like you and your father, dear girl."

Daria nodded silently, her greenish eyes locking with the marquise's shiny black raven stare.

"Do you happen to know or be related to a young man named Zack Armstrong?"

The marquise clapped her hands again quietly. "Oh, you are even cleverer than I thought, how wonderful. Isn't Zack delightful? A pity he speaks no Italian, but one day he will learn. Such a dear, helpful boy. He is my elder sister's great-great grandson," she said. "That branch of the family emigrated to Australia between the wars. The Australians were not very friendly to Italians at the time, but all that has changed. So many things have changed, my dear girl."

Daria waited, listening to the storm.

"Now," said the marquise, "I want you to have this. From Zack. He so enjoyed meeting you and getting to know Priscilla's niece and nephew, the Norwegians. I know he greatly admired their sangfroid and skill. No one was injured, you will have noted. No one lost his life, even the bakery van had already been stolen, and they did not damage it when they borrowed it." She opened a tiny purse dangling from her wrist and drew out something. "I understand you found the watch and the Saint Christopher medal, but you did not have this, the third element of the demonic trinity." She opened her claw and held up a ring. It half-filled the palm of her hand.

Daria took the heavy gold signet ring and studied it. "Joseph Gary's?" she asked. The marquise nodded and folded Daria's fingers over it.

"Listen to me now, I want you to know how and why," the marquise whispered, "but also to *understand*." She paused. "What you can't possibly have discovered from your methodical research is the following. I am old enough not to blush over such things, let my dearly departed husband Eduardo rest in peace. You see, Daria, my elder brother Alvaro Spinola di Voltaggio was a, how should I put it, an enthusiastic follower of Benito Mussolini from the earliest days. Il Duce started out as a muckraker and agitator, calling himself a socialist at first. Alvaro's best friend from childhood, a lovely, gentle young scholar named Giulio Cesare De Ferrari, was also a socialist, but of a different kind." She paused to make sure Daria was following her.

"Yes," she said, "I understand."

"You see, I am not ashamed now to tell you that I adored Giulio, I loved him, he was my only true love in life, though naturally it was never consummated in any way, you can imagine, in those days..." She paused, colored, then gathered strength. "Though young, I was already married and a mother during the war. Giulio had also married, appropriately for his station in life. He was fifteen years my senior and had no idea I worshipped him. Our entire family fled our palazzo in Genoa and took refuge at our summer manor house in Prati di Bovecchia. We were all refugees from the bombardments, like tens of thousands of others in Genoa." She paused again. "I witnessed the scene from the windows of our country house. You saw the ruins of the house, I believe, when you visited Prati and found the body of Giuseppe Garibaldi the other day. It was where we spent summers to get away from the heat of downtown. Across from the main house were the farmhouses, where the sharecroppers lived year-round."

"I understand," said Daria, glancing over her shoulder to make sure no one was approaching. "Giuseppe Garibaldi and his family were the sharecroppers. Go on. What did you see from the window?"

"Why, I saw Giulio shot dead by the Mussolini Brigade, of course. Why else would I have done this?" She smiled a sad smile and made a soft, clucking sound. "They did not bother us, naturally. We were considered untouchable, friends of Il Duce himself, thanks to my brother, who was also a very good friend of Carlo

Alberto Lomelli-Centauri, the Questor's grandfather. But, you see, they took Giulio Cesare away, he was hiding with us. He was a partisan, yes, a Resistenza fighter hidden by Fascists, hidden because we loved him. And they shot him in front of the farmhouse where the Garibaldis lived. I saw it, standing there with my infant son in my arms. Naturally I did not know what was happening until it was all over."

"And Giuseppe Garibaldi was in the firing squad?"

"Yes, he and his father. They had been our sharecroppers for generations. They were brutal, beastly men, but they had always respected and obeyed us. How could we imagine..." She did not finish her sentence. "You see, the Allies were only a few miles south of La Spezia by then. It was nearly the end of the war. The Insurrection had begun in Genoa. It was April 23, 1945, a happy day for millions of Italians, and the saddest day of my life."

The marquise slumped momentarily but soon righted herself and, clutching Daria's arm, got carefully down from the bench.

As if he had been listening in secret from a room nearby, the aged butler appeared, holding the lantern. The marquise nodded at the overnight case by the front door. "Please be good enough to carry that," she instructed.

Daria stood abruptly. "Wait," she said to the butler, "you may take that to the marquise's bedroom so she can unpack it later." Handing the signet ring back to her, Daria leaned forward and took the marquise gently by the elbow. "Thank you for elucidating some of the background information regarding this bizarre, one-in-a-million accident," Daria said. "As you may know, I have been taken off the case. I'm afraid it is destined to remain a mystery." She pivoted and asked the butler whether Lieutenant Gambero had arrived yet.

"Yes, signora," he said deferentially with a slight bow. "The gentleman came in a few minutes ago and is with the others, in the salon. I believe they have prevailed upon him to join them and finish the rubber. I tried to dissuade them, but Ambassador Bremach insisted and said Inspector Gambero would do honor to the marquise's hand."

"Good," Daria remarked with a wry smile, "please accompany the marquise back to the salon and ask the ambassador to join me here, if you will. And tell the lieutenant to finish his hand of bridge, then bring the car around."

"Very good, signora," the butler said, bowing and setting down the overnight case.

"One other thing," Daria added. "Tell the ladies that, sadly, I have no time to pay my respects to them today but will look forward to seeing and speaking to them soon."

"Yes, signora," said the butler. With the lantern still held in his right hand, he waited until the marquise had laid her hand on his left forearm. She turned to smile at Darla, her knowing, beady raptor eyes sparkling. Together the pair left the vestibule, moving slowly down the long, dark hallway, the frescoes quivering in the lamp light.

Daria stood by a window and stared out at the storm, wondering what had happened to Andrew Striker and the helicopter. He was a mercurial madman, but fundamentally a decent human being. She hoped he was safely in La Spezia by now.

Eager to check her messages and voicemail, Daria fingered her smartphone impatiently. The last time she had glanced at the screen in the helicopter she had seen among the urgent messages a text from the traffic cop, as Striker had dismissively called Gianni Giannini.

"Exeunt noblewoman and butler," said Willem, hobbling up to where Daria stood and clearing his throat. "Enter Ambassador of Holland, having made a remarkable recovery in time for the denouement, also known as the final scene." Bowing, he laughed, then whispered conspiratorially. "Now listen, Daria, Pinky has no idea about any of this. I do hope she never hears of Gilda."

Daria waited several beats before answering. "I won't pretend to condone your behavior, Willem, but your extramarital affairs are your own business."

He arched a bushy eyebrow, then smiled toothily. "And the niece and nephew? What will befall them?"

Daria thrust out her lips and waited, watching his expression. "Aren't they in Poland by now, with Zack Armstrong? If not, they should be."

"Gone for a last swim off Portofino, I think," he said brightly.

Daria frowned. "In this storm? It might well be their last swim."

"Nonsense, they're Norwegian, they're used to cold, stormy seas. The Mediterranean is like a wading pool to them."

She drummed her lips, relieved the rain was abating.

"There now, you see," Bremach said soothingly, nodding at the windows, "it was a mere squall. Everyone is so terrified these days of the weather. It is not merely a question of climate change but of cynical, concerted meteorological terrorism."

"Speaking of terrorism," she interrupted. "There were no riots in Genoa?"

Willem grinned and shook his head. "No Questor, therefore no agents provocateurs, no rioters, many valiant law enforcement officers suddenly retired, suspended, or on leave, very mysterious. You will be cleared and exonerated, eventually, but it will take time, Daria. All is chaos for now, a political maelstrom." He waved at the rain and chuckled. "You will have to return to Rome for a time, but not forever."

Daria shook her head incredulously. "Down the road you'll have to tell me about Genoa in the good old days," she said. "You, my father, and Eichmann, that kind of thing."

Bremach nodded pensively. "Before it's too late and I kick the bucket, you mean? Better not wait too long. Plenty of memories will go to the grave with me, including a few you'd rather not hear."

"One more thing, Willem," Daria said, turning to go. "Priscilla's old white Saab, the one with the outsize plates? There's an APB on the driver and it. So, park it somewhere, under those trees, for instance, down a garden path, or in a greenhouse, and lose the Norwegian plates for the time being."

"How extraordinary," he said, genuinely impressed. "How did you work that one out?"

Daria volleyed back one of Bremach's mischievous smiles. "A

kid from Congo with no front teeth. Admittedly, we thought it was a Volvo."

"Excellent sleuthing," Willem commented. "Pinky really had no idea she was the getaway driver." Then he sighed. "She will not be amused. She loves that bloody old car for some unfathomable reason. I shall have to invent something."

"You're pretty good at that," Daria remarked. "Why not ask Gambero to try to start it—and fail. Then tell Pinky it has broken down. From the rain and red sand. That sand is very hard on engines. Take a taxi to the train station and have someone pick you up."

"Diabolical," he said, grinning. "You are your father's daughter after all. Now, in exchange, I promise you that your darling mother will be on the Rome express tomorrow at dawn. Not a peep out of her before then. No doubt you will see her in the Eternal City shortly, when they summon you to the ministry for a formal dressing-down or perhaps an unexpected promotion and transfer, which is much more likely."

Daria shrugged, eyeing her godfather skeptically. With relief she saw Gambero outside, dashing across the parking area through the raindrops toward the BMW. "Why me?" she asked, catching Bremach by surprise.

He shifted and shuffled forward, uncomfortable. In his wheedling, ancient-child voice he said, "We needed a pair of safe hands, my dear. It is all very incestuous and abject, I admit, but it had to be done, you must agree, and I knew in the end you would see the wisdom of our ways." He paused and nodded toward Gambero and the car now idling outside the vestibule. "Tempus fugit," he said softly. "Time flies and so does Daria."

Pecking him goodbye, she let herself out of the front door and strode to the waiting car.

Pale and nervous, Lieutenant Gambero looked more dead than alive, just as Osvaldo Morbido had earlier. But he smiled and waited patiently until she had buckled up. Then he pulled away and drove slowly out of the gates.

"Any reports of a downed helicopter?"

"No," Gambero said, shaking his head and stifling a yawn. "But it might be too early to know whether Striker crashed or not."

Daria nodded and stared straight ahead. She closed her eyes and felt the world whirl.

"So, it wasn't a Volvo after all," Gambero remarked. "And it wasn't the marquise driving it."

"No," Daria replied, opening her eyes and touching her smartphone screen. It twinkled to life.

"It was Signora Bremach?" Gambero asked.

"Who knows, Italo. Think of it as another strange coincidence. I for one am not filing a report." She scrolled through her messages, emitting a series of sighs, grunts, and scoffs until she came to the one from Gianni Giannini. Reading it twice in silence, she closed her eyes again, the words imprinted on her retinas.

There's a double room reserved in my name at the Hotel Panoramico, that place on the beach, in the cove, at Zoagli. Will you come?

Driving in silence until they reached the outskirts of La Spezia and the first signs pointing to the autostrada for Genoa, Daria turned to Lieutenant Gambero and in a strange, self-conscious voice he had never heard before said, "Italo, I'm so tired and so hot and so perplexed by all this that I can't bear to go home. I've just reserved a room for myself at a place I know in Zoagli, on the beach, the Panoramico. I'm taking a few days off. Can you drop me there?"

Gambero yawned and nodded, rubbing his eyes. "Good idea," he said, "I'm going to sleep for a week. Not even the children will be able to keep me awake."

Turning back to her smartphone, Daria typed a one-letter reply to her traffic cop, hit send, and smiled, blushing. "Where's that chickpea tart?" she asked, glancing around the passenger compartment. "I'm starving."

FINIS

IF YOU LIKED *RED RIVIERA*, STAY TUNED FOR *ROMAN ROULETTE*!

COMING IN JULY 2022 FROM ALAN SQUIRE PUBLISHING

It was supposed to be a night off for Commissioner Daria Vinci, attending an elegant concert and fundraiser hosted by her maestro brother in Rome. But when she hears the unmistakable sound of gunfire, Daria is called into action again. Now she must solve the riddle of a mysterious ritual suicide—or was it murder?

The second Daria Vinci Investigation is set amid the catacombs and ruins of Rome, where secrets run deep, and revenge can be served both hot and cold. Daria must confront obstacles personal and professional as she struggles to uncover what really happened the night of the fateful concert.